I0683221

VOICES

By A.J. Brown

Voices

Published 2018 by Stitched Smile Publishing
Copyright ©2018 A.J. Brown
Front cover design by Lisa Vasquez
Edited by Donelle Whiting

All rights reserved. No part of this publication may be reproduced in any form, electronically or mechanically. No part of this publication may be photocopied or recorded without written consent by the author, except where permissible by law.

This book is for your enjoyment and entertainment.
This book may not be resold.

Disclaimer: The works in *Voices* are works of fiction. Names and events are creations from the author's imagination, except where noted.

Dedicated to Lisa Vasquez. You know why.

Table of Contents

In the Shadows, They Hide   1
Chet and Kay's Not So Marvelous Adventure   15
The Scarring   47
Claire, the Movie   53
Black Storms   65
Anymore   81
Crisp Sounds   91
Numbers   117
To Bleed   129
Not Like You   135
The Sad Woes of the Trash Man   147
The White   189
Apartment 306 and Poor Jenny Harris   201
A Memory Best Left Alone   215
Letter to the Readers   233
Author Notes   237
Great Big Page of Appreciation   247
Author Bio   249
Other Works by A.J. Brown   251

In the Shadows They Hide

"Why are you so afraid of the dark?" Sarah asked. She stood across the room, near the door that separated us from the rest of the world. Beyond the door was the hallway that led to the stairs that went down to where the foyer and hall split off into several rooms. Right then, it was just her and I in the house, me, the fourteen-year-old boy who had never been in a room alone with a girl who wasn't my mother or sister, and she, the girl two years my senior, her low cut shirt showing more breasts than I had ever seen, even in my dreams.

"I'm not afraid of the dark," I said, nervously glancing down at my dirty sneakers. When I looked back up, a smile had spread across her face, showing hints of teeth and signs of mischief. To her right was a light brown dresser. Two stuffed teddy bears side-by-side sharing an ice cream cone, sat in its center. Directly behind her was the door. To her left … to her left was what had me fixated. The light switch was the color of sand and less than a foot from her left elbow.

"Come on, Spencer," she said, and gave a giggle. "Every-one knows you're afraid of the dark."

She was going to test that theory. I could see it in her green eyes, hear it in her drippingly sweet voice, feel it in the sweat beading along my forehead. My stomach groaned, rolled and knotted up. It tugged on the muscles of my groin, shriveled my nuts to raisins and sent electric pulses throughout my body like tiny shockwaves dancing along my nerves.

"It's not the dark I'm afraid of," I said, my voice a weak whisper. I cleared my throat and repeated, "It's not the dark I'm afraid of."

Sarah raised her eyebrows. "Really? Then what are you afraid of?"

How do I explain my fears without sounding like a nutcase who should be in an asylum? I didn't know, so I shrugged and

1

looked back down at my dirty shoes.

"Are you afraid of me?" she asked. She took several steps, stopped in front of me, and leaned forward. I looked into her eyes, passing over the open portion of her shirt that showed her breasts in all their glory, nipples included. My face grew hot. I'm sure she leaned down intentionally to frustrate me. She succeeded.

I stammered through my answer, barely getting it out without dripping a glob of slobber out the side of my mouth. "No, Sarah. I'm not scared of you." That was a partial lie. I wasn't afraid of her. That much was true. But, I was terrified of Bobby Jenkins, the typical football stud who was the size and shape of a brick wall and Sarah's boyfriend.

She gave a smile, one which said she knew I liked what I saw and she would use it against me if she could. Sarah stood straight. I exhaled, glanced around her room at all the things teenage girls have: posters of rock stars or movie stars missing their shirts, make-up cases, cute little outfits hanging on a hook on her closet door, which was slightly open. I could see a swath of darkness peeking out at me. If I looked hard enough I could have probably seen it wink at me, a smile on its gray face. Fear made my head swoon and I turned back to Sarah. She stood at the light switch again.

"It's hard to explain," I said, and glanced out the window. The purple curtains were pulled to the side. When did it grow dark out? My skin crawled as if a thousand hands ran their fingers along it. Outside, in the dark … I could feel them waiting, hisses on their tongues, clawed fingers longing to sink themselves into my ivory skin.

"Try," Sarah said.

Why do girls do these things? Why do they hold boys captive with their sweet eyes and pouty lips; their curvy bodies? I didn't want to look at her, but I couldn't help it. She was fifteen feet from me. I could smell her cinnamon perfume, or maybe it was the unlit candle on the night stand by her bed. I don't know, but the scent was intoxicating, much like I imagine getting a little drunk would be.

I stood and went to the window, putting a few extra feet between us. It was cruel what she was doing, playing with my fear. But, she was a girl—and not just any girl, but Sarah Poe, a blonde, a junior in high school, one of the more popular girls. And we were alone in her bedroom.

How was this so? We were nothing alike. I was chunky—not fat, just a little overweight—with dark hair that sported constant cowlicks, even when I used gel or hairspray to hold it down. Brown eyes and hauntingly white skin made me stand out, even in the dark. I think that's why they like me so much—not people, but *them*, those things that hide in the shadows.

How did I end up a few feet away from every wet dream I had ever had, with her parents gone for the better part of the evening? And why wasn't Bobby Jenkins here instead? The books on the bed reminded me: the guise of studying. Certainly, her parents trusted the geeky kid who had no chance of getting into their daughter's panties. Would they have trusted Bobby so easily?

"Why am I here?" I asked, and glanced out the window. A streetlamp on the corner came alive, casting a yellow glow in a circle a few feet in every direction. I saw the first of them flee the glare, its black tendrils pulling away as quickly as the light flooded the new night. In the dark, gray objects moved toward the house. Hairs stood on the nape of my neck. My eyes watered. I closed them and forced back tears.

"You know why you're here, Spencer," Sarah said, and walked over to me. She put one of her arms around me and pressed her breasts to my back. My breath caught and my jeans grew tighter around the crotch. She kissed the back of my neck. I shivered and moved away from her. My hands shook and my breath came in short bursts. I tried to slow my breathing, to keep from hyperventilating, which would have been very bad in front of Sarah.

Just outside her window, the motion sensor lights came on. Most people would glance out, see nothing and switch them off. I knew better. I wanted to look, to see how many of them were there pacing the shadows, waiting for someone to flip

3

the light off. Instead, I moved further away, focused on shoving my books in my bag. I would call my mom and wait for her in the living room with all the lights on.

"Don't you like me, Spencer?"

A false hurt spread across her face. It had to be fake, with her eyebrows lifted and her bottom lip poked out.

"Y-y-yes, I like you … a lot." I hated the tremor in my voice.

"Then why won't you talk to me?"

"I have been," I replied.

I could almost feel her eyes roll. When I looked at her, that expression of hurt was still there. Maybe … No, it had to be a lie—a girl like Sarah wouldn't dig a guy like me. She liked them hunkier, better looking. That's why she and Bobby had been an item for the last few years.

"Spencer, what are you afraid of? If not the dark and not me, what is it?"

Why did the question sound so wrong in my ears? If she wanted to talk, why not ask me what my favorite color is or what I like to do on weekends when I'm alone, or why not ask me about the weather? Why ask about my fears?

"Is it being touched by a girl? If so, I can help you—"

"No, that's not it." Another lie. I was afraid of being touched, more because of how I looked with clothes off, not the actual physical contact. But, that wasn't what she was getting at. I knew it, and I should have asked for the phone. I should have finished packing my bag and called Mom and … "You won't understand," I said. "No one understands."

She turned me around, and we stared eye to eye. She was inches from me. My face grew warm again. "Try me," she said. Her breath smelled of spearmint.

I licked my lips and took a step away. The backs of my legs hit her bed, and I sat. I looked at my shaking hands, then up at her. "It's called Sciophobia."

"What?" Her face scrunched up and one side of her mouth lifted in a confused grin.

"Sciophobia—the fear of shadows."

"You're afraid of shadows?" she asked. I could hear the

laughter in her question. "Like that?" Sarah pointed to just beneath the clothes hanging from her closet door, at the gray, boxed-out portion beneath them.

"No, not quite. Those are normal shadows. This room is bright—the shadows that bother me are not like that at all."

"Then what do you mean?"

I looked over her left shoulder to the window. Did I see lightning? Was it supposed to storm? I listened for a few seconds until I heard the faint rumble of far off thunder. Tears tickled the corners of my eyes. They liked storms, the way the lightning flickered for less than a second, casting the room in white or yellow with hundreds and thousands of black shadows dancing along the walls and floors. In those moments they were free to roam, only hampered by the electric bolts and then only for a mere second or two.

She put her hand on my chin and lifted my face to meet hers. "Help me understand."

The closet still sat slightly open. The blackness within dripped with malice. They were in there, biding their time. "Your closet," I said. "Do you leave it open all the time?"

"No," she said with a shrug. "I keep it closed at night."

I went over, put one hand to the side of the knob and shut it. "There are shadows in the darkness," I said. "You can't see them when the lights are on. You can only see them when it's dark, when there is just enough light to give them life."

"You're not making any sense."

Outside, lightning flickered across the sky. Thunder followed a few seconds later.

"I need to get home. There's a storm coming."

"Don't worry about the storm, Spencer. Mom will take you home when they get back."

There was no comfort in her words.

"You don't understand, they like storms. They—"

"Who does? Who are they?"

"The shadow people."

"Shadow people?" Sarah let out a long breath. This time she did laugh. It was the sound of disbelief; the sound of a girl wondering why she had a geeky, fat kid in her room and not the hunky jock. It was the sound of a girl who just realized she has wasted her time on something or someone she thought would be worthwhile. It was the sound of a lie.

"Sarah, there are things in the shadows, kind of like the boogeyman, but so many more of them than just the one monster under your bed."

"You believe in the boogeyman?" This time she rolled her eyes. "Seriously?"

I looked at the tops of my shoes. One of the laces had become untied somehow. I pulled my feet onto the edge of her bed, lifting them away from the darkness beneath it, where small hands could swipe at my ankles or tie my laces in knots.

"I told you, you wouldn't understand. No one does." I stood, shoved the last of my books into my backpack and slung it over my shoulder. "Can I use your phone?"

"Wait," she said and grabbed my arm. "Don't get all panicky on me, Spencer. Just relax and tell me about this … about this boogeyman."

"They're shadow people," I corrected.

"Okay, whatever," she said and shook her head. "Who are these *shadow* people?" Another roll of the eyes and sarcasm filled her voice.

Lightning flashed. Thunder rumbled. I groaned.

My muscles quivered, stomach knotted, released, knotted again. Those short breaths were back, this time worse. My head grew light, and for a moment I thought I would pass out. I pinched my right cheek, forcing the world to even out.

Concern filled Sarah's face—for me or not, I don't know, but when I regained myself, she looked worried.

"Are you okay?"

"No," I said. "I need to get home. Can I please use your phone?"

"Sure," she said and grabbed her purse from the floor by the bed. She rummaged through it until she pulled out a pink cell phone. Sarah extended her arm, but pulled it back when I reached for it. "Tell me about the shadow people first."

6

I wanted to scream. I wanted to cry. I wanted to run from the room and down the stairs, find one of the house phones and call my mom—anything but sit there and wait for them to come get me.

"Sarah, don't do this. Please, just let me use the phone."

"Tell me about the shadow people, and you can have the phone."

Another streak of lightning was followed by a louder boom of thunder. I pushed by Sarah and practically ran to the window. Outside, they gathered. With each flicker of lightning they drew closer, their lithe bodies bleeding into the darkness.

"Who are they?" she asked again.

I turned to her. Tears fell down my cheeks, and I felt like the wimp she was sure to tell everyone I was. But she didn't look as if she were enjoying my shame. Maybe she *did* like me. Maybe she *did* want me instead of Bobby Jenkins. And maybe a boy's heart can lie to him when his fear is heightened.

"They're not really people," I said quickly. "They're not really anything. They're shadows that live within shadows. They wait for the lights to go out at night and come crawling from the darkness. You see them as clothes hanging from your closet door or the teddy bears on your dresser, just average things ... but they aren't so average after all. They want you to believe they aren't real so they cling to the stuff that is, and if they want you they just wait until you're asleep and tear you to shreds. They're not like any other creature out there."

"That's crazy, Spencer."

"Is it?" I asked, as lightning flashed beyond the window. The rumble of thunder shook the glass.

"Yes, it is," Sarah said. "There's no such thing as shadow people. Or the boogeyman."

"Then why do you close your closet door at night?"

She shrugged, that confused expression spreading across her face again. "I don't know. I just do."

"You don't just do something without a reason," I said. "Someone either told you to keep it closed, or you figured it out on your own. You've seen the shadows in your closet, haven't you? You've felt the pit in your stomach as you stared at the open door, trying to get up enough courage to jump out of bed and close it."

Her mouth—such a beautiful mouth—hung open. This was no lie. She had seen them, she just never realized it.

Rain pelted the window, a *rat-a-tat-tat* that resembled mobster movie gunfire.

"You're crazy, Spencer, just like everyone said you were."

"What?" I asked. The lies came clean in an instant. I was crazy? They said? Who are they?

"You're a freak, Spencer. Bobby was right. You're a checkup from the neck up."

My heart sank. Not only was there a storm tilting toward full blown outside, inside there was the girl of my dreams calling me a whack job. The brief glimpse of her nipples would surely be the last I would see until I was well into my adult years. I would live the rest of my teens as the butt of many jokes. I thought of the shadow people, of my fear of them. Were they real, or was Sarah right? Was I crazy?

Sarah went to the door. A lump formed in my throat. She was going to hit the switch and plunge me into the blackness of a stormy night. The lights flickered before she reached the switch. I saw her look up, saw the fear in her eyes. Everything went dark.

Lightning lit the room briefly. They were there with us, crawling along the floor, clinging to the walls and ceilings, their bodies long and sharp. I ran for the door, stumbled on the rug and crashed into the wall. I grabbed the doorknob and tried to turn it, but it wouldn't budge. I fumbled for a lock I couldn't find.

I looked back. In the flicker of lightning I could see them closing in, crawling through the closed windows and scurrying over one another. The closet door had swung open. One shadow, much larger than the others and somewhat more three dimensional, came at me. I smashed my hands against the door and screamed, "Let me out! Someone help me! Let me out!"

Its hands wrapped around my waist and lifted me from the floor. Then I was in the air, arms and legs flailing. The weight of my backpack spun me around, and I landed hard on my bottom.

There was laughter—a deep baritone that sounded familiar. In the cacophony of thunder and hisses and my own screams, I couldn't make out why it sounded so familiar.

"Spencer," a voice said. "We're going to eat you."

They knew my name?

I was as good as dead.

The lightning came quicker, giving the room a strobe effect. In those flashes I saw them—so many of them. And there was the other one, so unlike the rest it seemed wrong. Its body stood out among them, not blending with the furniture or the walls but more concrete. And it was laughing.

It grabbed me again, this time by my head. Its hands weren't claws like I thought, and it was very much a physical creature. I swatted at it, a feeble swing of my left hand, but it caught the side of its head. Its head? I was able to strike it? It cursed and shoved me to the floor.

I can't say I didn't see this coming. Deep in the back of my mind I had known all along. I scrambled backward, putting a little distance between us. When the lightning lit the sky next I saw Bobby Jenkins' face as he approached me, arms outstretched.

"I'm going to kill you, Spencer," he yelled.

I braced myself for his fist, my arms over my face and knees pulled up to my chest. I screamed, the sound of a little girl scared of a rubber snake dropped in her lap.

No punches came. No kicks, either.

Just laughter.

The light came on. I looked through the gap between my forehead and arm. Bobby was doubled over, his face red, and tears streaming down his cheeks. He sounded like a crazed hyena.

Sarah stood by the door, her hand on the light switch. She, too, was laughing, her face as red as Bobby's.

"Help me. Someone help me. Let me out." Bobby mocked, his hands near his face as if he were screaming for his life—much like I had. "Geek, you should have heard yourself."

Sarah put a hand to her face and pointed at me as tears spilled from her eyes. Her lips were pulled back, showing her beautiful teeth. But, they didn't look so beautiful. Right then nothing about her was beautiful.

Heat flushed my cheeks and water touched the corners of my eyes. I bit my lip, trying to keep the tears at bay.

Sometimes the world slows, just like in the movies during a critical scene where the hero is in grave danger. That's what happened then. Everything dropped to a crawl. Bobby was on his hands and knees. I thought he would throw up from laughing so hard. Sarah had moved from the door and was holding tight to one of the bedposts. She clutched her stomach.

My dream girl had become my nightmare, and I hated her.

Lightning still flashed outside and the house shook with thunder, but inside the room the storm was so much worse. I could hear their laughter, their words barely recognizable as they tried to breathe.

I thought I would die. I wished I would. Then I noticed it. The closet door still stood open. Bobby had been in there with them, and they had not hurt him. But, something was wrong. Something had changed, and I saw it in the darkness within the closet. I *felt* it.

The world sped back up and through the laughter and thunder and the trip-hammer of my heart pulsing in my ears, I heard their hisses and felt their malice seeping from the open closet.

My legs shook as I stood. Bobby and Sarah were both on the floor by then. She had an arm around his shoulders, and they still laughed. I think she wiped her eyes of the tears on his shirt.

I looked to the closet door, ready to give myself to them, to give up the fight and end the misery of my life.

Piss ran down my leg and my shoulders sagged. I didn't want to die, but I didn't want to live either. I turned back to

Bobby and Sarah. Her shirt was pulled down on one shoulder, the top of her breast exposed.

"Why me?" I asked and looked back to the closet. "What did I ever do to anyone?"

Their hisses became frantic, like rabid dogs set loose on a fox or a squirrel or a little kitten that could never escape those damnable jaws of certain death.

I was the victim ... always the victim. Why couldn't something happen to the bullies for once, to the popular and rich and the good looking who pick on the weak, the poor and those of us not as attractive enough to fit in with them?

Maybe they knew what I was thinking. Maybe they felt it the way I felt them. I don't know. What I do know is I looked into the dark, and I said, "I'll trade you both of them for me." It was a long shot. What if they took them and then came back for me? Or what if the shadow people were like Bobby and Sarah and only preyed on the weak?

Through their hisses I heard the question. "What are their names?"

"B ... Bobby and Sarah."

Again, the hisses grew more intense. I saw the shadows moving, as if they were trying to break free from the darkness, but the light held them back.

I thought it was an answer. I grabbed my pack and slowly backed up to the bedroom door. I looked at the light switch. Was I really going to do this? Let the shadow people take them both and hope it was enough to make them leave me alone.

Then I looked at Sarah's face and felt her stinging laughter. The answer was yes. I flipped the light switch off. The room swam in blackness and their hisses drowned out the thunder. The shapes in the dark spilled from the closet. Like a swarm they went after Bobby and Sarah. Along with their hisses and growls came several voices calling out their names.

I'd like to say Bobby and Sarah stopped laughing long enough to realize the danger they were in, but I can't. Honestly, I don't know if they heard their names being whispered by the gravelly voices. I didn't wait to find out. I swung the bedroom door open and ran through it, making certain to slam it shut behind me.

In the hall—the brightly lit hall—I heard their screams, Sarah's panicked and terrified, Bobby's sounding every bit as feminine as mine had surely sounded to him.

Something thumped against the door and the knob turned. I held it tight, not letting the door open. Sarah screamed, and I think I heard a "Please, help me," from somewhere within the room. I pulled on the knob, afraid to let it open. Or was I really afraid? Maybe I just wanted them to suffer.

I thought of Sarah and Bobby, of the prank they played on me. It had been mean, but did they both have to *die* because of it?

"Spencer, help me," Sarah said. Her voice was weak. I started to let go of the knob, to help the girl I thought I loved. The knob turned in my hands. Her pulled back lips and bellowing laughter resurfaced in my mind. I tugged the knob hard. It snapped off in my hands and I fell back against the hall wall. I looked at the knob, then back at the door. The darkness spilled through the hole where the knob had been.

Hisses and growls came from the room, but the screams had ended. My chest grew tight when one of the black tendrils spilled from the knob's hole. I tried to stand, but my body didn't respond.

"Spencer."

I let out a terrified squeal.

"Spencer."

The door opened, the hinges creaked. A pale hand fell from the darkness. It was Sarah's and her fingers were bloodied where her nails had torn free from trying to fight off the shadow people.

"No," I said.

There was a laugh, deep and hearty.

"Thank you, Spencer," it said, and Sarah's arm jerked away. The door slammed shut.

I got to my feet and ran. The laughter followed me down

the steps and to the front door. I ran out into the night, no longer concerned the shadow people hid in the blackness outside. They were in Sarah's room, and they were eating and laughing.

And they knew my name ...

Chet and Kay's Not So Marvelous Adventure

They meant to leave much earlier than mid-afternoon when they finally got on the road. It was only a couple of hours to Kay's parents' cabin getaway just off Highway 378, but the weather had soured, slipping from the low forties in the morning to just above freezing by lunchtime. Clouds slunk in from the west; a storm threatening to hamper the drive, and maybe the entire weekend.

The first snow flurries fell shortly before two in the afternoon. Chet sat their bags, filled with clothes and necessities on the ground, and looked to the gray sky. "It wasn't supposed to snow this weekend."

Snow. In South Carolina. A once in every ten or fifteen-year event came early, by eight or ten years, Chet guessed.

"Is it really snowing?" Kay asked from the front door.

"A little, at least for now," Chet said.

Kay stepped onto the porch, her hands out in front of her as if she was about to worship or sing praises. Her brown eyes grew wide, her face stretched with a smile normally reserved for children when the white stuff fell from the sky. "It *is* snowing," she all but yelled.

"Do you still want to go to the cabin?"

"Yeah," Kay said, stretching it out, her head twitching as if to say *duh.*

Chet nodded, though his heart was no longer into the trip, not if it was going to rain or snow all the way there. What if they got stuck on the side of the road or at the cabin? What if there was no power? Then what would they do? He shook his head and tried to brush away Mr. Worrywart.

"You're not thinking about bailing on me, are you?" Kay asked. She had approached him and now stood only an arm's length away.

"No. I was just thinking."

"About?" Again Kay let the word stretch from her tongue.

"Our safety. That's all."

"We'll be okay. I promise."

Chet didn't look at her. Instead, he focused on the sky, the gray clouds overhead and the increasing snow, from light flurries to full on snowing, thick flakes falling from heaven.

"Come on, Chet. We've been planning this for months."

"I know," he said, a sheepish tone in his voice, like a child deliberately not owning up to a transgression before finally nodding the truth.

Kay leaned into him, her arms around his waist, a hug that told Chet she really wanted to go. It was always her way of getting him to do things, especially those things he didn't wish to do. "Please, Chet. Let's go. We'll take a few lanterns and some extra blankets. Even if we have to stay inside the entire time, I'm sure we can find something to do with ourselves."

She pulled her head back and looked at him with flirting eyes and a half smile. Chet smiled back. The "something to do with ourselves" comment beamed on her face. He was hooked, and she knew it.

"Come on," he said. "Let's grab the lanterns and blankets, maybe some candles as well."

Half an hour later, they pulled out of the driveway and onto the road, Chet's knuckles already whitening from his tight grip on the steering wheel.

Highway 378 was less than five minutes from the house. Two right turns and a quarter mile, and they were at the stop sign, waiting for traffic to ease up so they could merge in.

"Everyone's in a hurry," Chet said under his breath.

"They want to get home and out of the snow."

The roads were wet, but not covered in snow—at least not yet—making driving still relatively easy. Cars and trucks and a motorcycle or two went by, their riders bundled in heavy coats, one of them not wearing a helmet, his face a brilliant pink, black hair windblown with flakes sticking in the strands.

"Gotta hate it for him," Kay said.

"Yup," Chet replied, eased from the stop sign and into the gap in the traffic flow.

16

Kay's hand settled on his thigh, rubbed for a second then pulled away. "It's going to be okay."

He nodded. He believed her, he really did, but driving in the snow, especially once it started to stick to the roads, put him on edge, much like driving at night in the rain—he hated it, but would do it if necessary. Merging into the slow lane, Chet let out a deep breath. "I know," he finally answered. "Just give me a few minutes to relax, and I'll be fine."

"Do you want me to drive?"

Chet grit his teeth, not from anger, at least not toward her. He licked his lips. "No. I got it."

And he did have it. They went past Lexington County Hospital and the various medical parks associated with it. A few minutes later they passed Interstate 20, cars zooming by as if it was summer and the sun were out.

"Amazing how folks drive in this state," he mumbled. "Someone's going to get hurt or killed driving like that in this weather."

Hurt or killed? Isn't that what played on Chet's mind? Being hurt or killed because they were driving in "this weather?" He wasn't driving fast either, slightly below the speed limit, but fast enough none of the drivers around them would get pissy and honk their horns, yelling for them to get out the way. Chet let out a long breath, focused on the road ahead of him, hands tight to the steering wheel, counting down the miles.

"Are you all right?" Kay asked, her eyebrows slightly lifted in the concerned way of hers.

"I'm ready to be out of the traffic. Once we're out of town, I'll be fine."

Kay frowned and sighed deeply. "You know, why don't we just turn around and go home? We can still snuggle and be cozy there and not have to drive anywhere in this mess."

Chet said nothing at first, the offer playing over and over in his mind. If he was honest with himself, that's exactly what he wanted to do, and the comfort of home just in case of a power outage was tempting. But it wouldn't be fair to Kay. He was sure she had made plans, and even if those fell through because of the snow, she was always good at pivoting and changing courses on the fly—she would come up with something to do.

He shook his head. "No. We're going to the cabin, and we'll be fine."

With that said Chet's mind calmed, as if a switch had been flipped. His grip on the steering wheel loosened. The tension in his shoulders eased, as if speaking the words out loud made his entire body relax, and his mind was suddenly okay with the drive, the danger no longer eminent, or real, for that matter. It was all contrived drama in his head, his little friend Mr. Worrywart trying to ruin a good time.

Highway 378 merged with Highway 1. Eventually Highway 1 branched off to the left toward Monetta and Batesburg, while 378 went right toward Saluda. Four lanes of black top met them, and for the next twenty minutes it would stay that way until the road narrowed into two lanes outside Saluda County, still on the Lexington side of Lake Murray.

The snow fell harder than when they left, coating the world in bright white. Kay commented several times on the beauty of old houses sitting fifty yards off the road, their paint long dulled from weather and time. Tin roofs sat on the tops of the older houses, the yards neatly manicured, a couple of them still claiming fences made of two-by-fours and cinder blocks—redneck picket fences, if there ever were such a thing—and flower planters in the corners made of tires and nothing else. There were some newer houses in this area with red, white, and black shingles on their roofs for effect, and bay windows and real, white picket fences enclosing their meager yards.

This part of the world was still mostly "not grown up," the population consisting of country folk who still talked with a drawl and cooked out over fires on Saturday evenings. They waved to you out here, not a stranger in the bunch.

Still, it was a matter of time before progress really struck this stretch of road between Columbia and Newberry and on down to Monetta and Ridge Springs. For now, the snow accumulated on lawns and in open fields, clinging to trees, pulling branches further and further down as more snow gathered. It was a stretch of road Chet still liked to drive.

"Look over there," Chet said, pointing to his left.

A man in jeans and a heavy coat knelt off the road, a big black truck on the shoulder, white smoke billowing from its tailpipe. The man had a spray can in one hand, his other one on his knee. A boulder the size of a small car sat in front of him. The man walked away as Chet and Kay passed the rock. Glancing in the rearview mirror, Chet read what the man had written: **SNOW? REALLY?**

Chet let out a slight laugh. "I guess he doesn't care much for the snow."

"I guess not," Kay said. "We should take a picture of it on the way home."

"Just remind me to stop, and don't wait until I'm right up on it."

They drove on, stopping only to gas up and grab a coffee at the Conoco station. Another hour, at the very least, loomed ahead for them, and with the snow sticking in places on the road, an hour was bound to be more like two or possibly three. From the Conoco station the road narrowed to two lanes, the speed went from 55 to 45, and most likely after they rounded the next bend, they would be chugging along at 35 or less the rest of the way.

"Crap," Chet said and glanced in his rearview. He tapped the brakes, eased off, then tapped them again.

"What's wrong?"

"There's a truck behind us—he's flying."

Kay turned in her seat, her eyes wide. "Why are you slowing down?"

"If he's going to hit us, he's going to hit us, but I don't want to speed up in this mess. It would be our luck for him to swerve and miss us, and I'd skid off the road."

He glanced back in the mirror. The truck had indeed swerved into the oncoming lane, run slightly off the road and corrected, but not enough to get back over into the right lane. It blew by them, kicking up slush onto the windshield. The car rocked slightly as the truck passed.

"You reckon they're in a hurry?" Chet asked. He shook his head, eased off the brake and lightly mashed the accelerator.

"Chet, I think they're fighting."

"What?" Chet increased the wiper speed, brushing the snow and ice from the windshield much quicker than before. Though the truck was quickly pulling away from them, he could see the two occupants in the rear window. Kay was right. It looked as if the driver was swinging at the passenger, his head facing away from the road.

"This could be—" Before he could finish his statement, the truck edged to the right, its tire catching on icy grass. The driver overcorrected and the truck swerved sideways, the back end sliding off the road and dipping into a ditch. It bounced, then flipped, the passenger's side striking the ground first before rolling onto its top and then flipping several more times. He was vaguely aware of Kay screaming.

Chet mashed the breaks, then instinctively let off of them. The car skidded sideways. He pulled the wheel left, hoping the car would cut back to the right. When it did, he turned the wheel slightly to the right, tapped the breaks, eased off, tapping them again until the car came to a stop on the edge of the road.

His heart sat in his throat, *thump-thumping*, his knuckles as white as the snow on the ground, his palms and shoulders hurting, as was his neck. His breaths came out in rapid bursts.

Kay's feet were braced on the floorboard, shoved down as far as they could go; one hand gripping the bar above her head—the "oh crap handle," as she liked to call it—the other one pressed hard against the dashboard in front of her, as if it would keep her from mashing her face against it, or the windshield or both, if the car flipped.

"You okay?" Chet asked.

"I think so."

"I think I wet myself," Chet said.

Kay looked at him, her mouth hanging open. "Seriously?"

"No."

They both laughed, a nervous tone at first and then full on. For several seconds they giggled like schoolboys farting in a classroom with the girls in pigtails around them all crinkling up their noses and complaining to the teacher.

Chet wiped tears from his eyes, glanced at Kay, who was doing the same and holding her stomach. Beyond her, in a field of grass, down the embankment, and about forty yards from the road, sat the red truck. It lay on the driver's side, one front wheel still spinning. Smoke billowed up from the crumpled hood.

The laughter and smile died almost instantly when Chet realized there was a serious problem before them. "Call nine-one-one," he said and got out of the car. He walked to the edge of the road and followed the trail of dents in the snow-covered ground where the truck had struck. There were pieces of metal and debris strewn everywhere. A toolbox that had once been bolted to the bed of the truck, lay off to his left like a discarded piece of trash. A broken rake and shovel lay near the ditch along with other yard maintenance tools.

Chet wiped his face with one hand and shivered with the breeze blowing snow all around him.

"I'm getting nothing," Kay said from the car, her window down. "I think the weather is blocking the signal."

"Keep trying," he said and carefully stepped down toward the ditch.

"What are you doing?" Kay asked, standing from the car.

"If we can't get the police or EMTs out here, then we need to help them."

"What if they're dead?"

Chet shrugged. "Let's hope they're not."

"Wait for me," Kay said.

"No." Chet turned and put a hand out to her in a stop gesture. "Stay there—keep trying to call for help and flag down anyone if they come by."

"Okay," she responded with a nod, and tried the cell phone again.

He wouldn't tell her—not then at least—but he was worried

about what would happen if they both investigated the accident. The people in the truck had been fighting. That much was certain. But why were they fighting? Chet didn't know, but if the guy who was driving, and clearly striking the woman, was okay or had a gun or something, he didn't want Kay to be down there where she could get hurt. At least if she were in the car, she would be okay and be able to get out of there if anything bad happened.

Snow crunched underfoot. Chet wished he had thrown on his hiking boots before leaving the house. Instead they were at the bottom of the luggage in the trunk.

Chet slipped into the ditch. His pants leg snagged on a stick jutting out from the ground just far enough to be a nuisance. He jerked the leg free and pulled himself out of the trench. The snow stung his hands the way only something cold could—not really burning, but cold enough to make the skin tingle and then hurt, like thousands of needles pricking an open wound. He shook his hands off, and wiped them on his jeans.

The next few steps were taken with his arms out at his sides, balancing himself in case he slipped on the slick ground. He was thankful the snow was still only an inch or so deep, and he could feel solid earth beneath him. The ground slanted, making the trek to the truck a little more difficult. He braced himself, legs stiff, barely bending at the knees, each step deliberate, his eyes focused on the almost blindingly white snow. He slipped once, his foot coming out from under him. His arms pinwheeled, and he tried to right himself, but only managed to look like a person learning how to roller skate for the first time.

The snow soaked through his jeans when he landed on his bottom. A fresh chill raced up and down his body. Chet rolled onto his knees and pushed himself up, one foot at a time, hands on the ground until he was upright. He managed the rest of the way to the truck without slipping and planting himself into the fresh snow.

The truck lay on its side in front of him, the undercarriage a brown and gray mass of metal. One of the back tires was bent in toward the frame. Chet placed a hand on the undercarriage, bracing himself as he walked to the front of the vehicle. The truck teetered slightly as if it could topple at any moment with a strong gust of wind or even by his own hand. From there, he could see the steel bumper was a gnarled piece of metal, once the color of chrome but now a dirty gray with clumps of dirt stuck beneath it. Steam rose from the truck's cracked grill and hood. The smell of gas hung in the air, but not strong enough to make Mr. Worrywart awaken from a nap he was apparently taking.

The windshield was cracked, a spider web running from near the center of it all the way to the top and toward both sides, obscuring the view of the inside of the truck. Chet could barely make out the long seat, a dark blue color that looked wrong for the red pick-up.

"Hello?" he called and then shook his head as if he were an idiot for thinking they could hear him, but repeated his call anyway. "Hello? Are you okay in there?"

A moan came from the truck. *Feminine,* Chet thought and hurried to the window. He slipped, bracing himself on the truck, and pulled his hand away when the vehicle wobbled. Dropping to his hands and knees, Chet crawled around the side. Mr. Worrywart now sat on his shoulder, tapping him lightly and looking around at the truck and the cracked windshield.

One good wind and you're a dead man, Chet, Mr. Worrywart said with a quiver in his voice.

"I'll be okay," Chet replied, but part of him knew Mr. Worrywart was right, if the wind shifted at all, the truck would blow over, and more than likely, crush him.

You need to get out of here. Leave and never look back.

A foot from the windshield, Chet thought maybe Mr. Worrywart was onto something. Leave and don't look back; go to the cabin and enjoy a nice relaxing weekend with Kay, have a snowball fight, build snowmen, warm up by the fire with some cocoa and maybe some soup, make a little love right in front of the fireplace with blankets laid down over the ancient carpeting.

Yeah, that's the ticket. Get out of here while you can, Chet old boy. Go get the wife naked and worship her body for a while. That's what you really want to do, isn't it?

"I can't," Chet said out loud. "At least one person is still alive in there."

The moan came again. *Definitely a woman,* he thought. Chet shoved Mr. Worrywart to the back of his mind, catching only a brief, *You'll be sorry,* like out of a Warner Brothers cartoon from his childhood. He envisioned Bugs Bunny warning someone of impending doom, only to have the character ignore him. *You'll be sorry.* Sorry was always dragged out, like the way Kay extended words when she made a point or asked a question or just tried to get Chet to understand something she said.

At the windshield, he tried to see between the cracks in the glass. He saw a woman lying on top of a man, her blond hair tinged red near the top of the scalp. Her body was twisted awkwardly, like her back was broken. The man was barely visible, his face down, obscured by the woman's hair. One hand held tight to the steering wheel, in what Chet could only believe was a death grip.

The woman's head moved, a hand twitched. She let out a sharp moan, one clearly filled with pain.

Chet stood, using the hood for leverage. The truck rocked, but he pushed on it instead of pulled and it stilled. The passenger's side window was busted out, tiny jagged pieces still clinging to the window frame. Even if he wanted to, Chet couldn't climb through the window or even get on top of the vehicle to yank the door open—the truck was too unstable.

The woman groaned again. She had moved her head. Her eyes were open and staring at him with a very real fear in them. "Help me," she said, her voice muffled through the windshield.

Chet swallowed, glancing around the field looking for something, anything, to help him break the windshield. Nothing—not even a heavy tool from the man's toolbox lay in the snow near them. He guessed all of those were somewhere along the field, tossed from the toolbox and strewn about, most likely already buried in the snow.

He put his hands out in front of him. "Hold on. I'll be right back."

Chet scrambled around the truck, slipping once but managing to stay on his feet. As he rounded the back end and started up the sloped field, he thought he heard the woman call out to him, begging him not to leave her there. He stopped, listened and heard nothing. *Just a trick of the ears*, he thought and scuttled his way to the overturned toolbox. He lifted one end, tilting it on its side then over and upright. The toolbox was divided into three sections, each one with a top that had a keyhole in it.

It's locked, Mr. Worrywart yelled. *You won't be able to open it. You tried. Now it's time to get out of here. Get to the car and get out of here. This was clearly a domestic dispute, and you want no part of it.*

"Shut up," Chet said, angered by the incessant nagging from the part of his psyche he hated most. "Shut up and stay that way." Mr. Worrywart grew silent, and slinked back to the shadows where his bed sat.

True to form, the top to the right side was locked. In the back of his mind, Chet heard Mr. Worrywart giggling. The middle one was locked as well. The giggling grew into a muffled laugh, one stifled only by a hand. Chet almost stopped there, almost listened to the laughter in his head, almost ran to the car for the fast getaway. Instead, he checked the top to the left. It opened easily with a press of the silver keyhole button, no key needed for this one. Inside there were various tools, much of which were useless to him: a small ratchet and sockets, drill bits, but no drill. *It's in one of the other boxes—the locked ones,* Chet thought. It made complete sense. A small ball-peen hammer might work, but it would take too long to hammer out all of the glass. Then his eyes fell on the black crowbar, long enough to do the trick, three feet maybe, and small enough to fit in the toolbox at an angle and against the back wall.

Chet scooped out several tools, dumping them on the ground where they sank into the increasing snow. With both hands, he gripped the crowbar in the center and yanked hard. It came free easier than Chet thought it would and he fell backward, letting go of the crowbar and landing in the snow again, this time much harder than before. A tinge of pain raced up his back. He grimaced as he stood. Another sharp pain raced from hip to mid-back, almost taking his breath away.

The crowbar sat at the bottom of the toolbox. Chet reached in, grabbed it and hobbled back to the truck. Its wheels no longer moved, but the truck still rocked from side to side every few seconds as the wind buffeted it.

Snowflakes as big as nickels continued to fall as the wind picked up, going sideways and sticking to whatever surface they landed on, grouping with other snowflakes and adding to the blanket of white covering the land. Chet's footprints from minutes earlier had already begun to fill in. Deep in the back of his mind he heard, *I told you so. I told you so. I told you so.*

He rounded the front end of the truck. The woman inside beat on the glass with an open palm. Blood had smeared where her hand had struck. A tinge of guilt swept over him for leaving her in such a horrible situation.

"Cover your head," Chet yelled.

The woman looked at him as if she couldn't understand.

Chet showed her the crowbar, its flaked black paint still somehow shiny after years of use. "Cover your head."

Her eyes became big. There was understanding in them. She dipped her head into the man's back, covering it with one arm.

Chet swung the crowbar as hard as he could, striking the glass with the hook end. It cracked, giving at the center, but still held together. A second swing, and small flakes of glass tore free. One piece shot up and struck Chet in the face. A teardrop of blood beaded where the glass glanced off his cheek. The third swing and the hook end caught in the windshield. Chet yanked, pulling a chunk of glass free, leaving a hole about the size of someone's head in its place.

"Hang on," Chet said, certain she could hear him now. He could certainly hear her crying.

It only took two more full swings to take out enough of the windshield to be able to crawl inside and get her, or for her at the very least, to be able to roll out if she were to try. Chet set the tool on the ground and dropped to his knees.

"Crap," he said through gritted teeth, as slivers of glass bit through his jeans and into his knees. He shifted his weight and got onto his feet in a crouched position. "Come on." He held a hand out to her.

The woman moved her arm from over her head. Shards of glass fell away, some of it still clinging to strands of blond. She looked at him, her eyes dazed, as if she didn't know what to do at this point.

"Come on. Give me your hand. I'll get you out of there, but you have to help me a little."

Chet reached forward, grabbed her by one arm. The woman screamed and he let go, raising both hands in the air as if he had done something wrong. "What?" he yelled out, more out of annoyance than anything else.

"My shoulder," she said between sobs. "My shoulder hurts."

"Okay, okay," Chet said. "Does anything else hurt?"

She nodded slowly. "My head. My ribs. I think a few of them might be broken."

"That's not good," Chet stated the obvious, something he was famous for doing and something Kay often picked on him about. *Way to go there, Captain Obvious,* he thought. "Can you move at all?"

"I think so," she said.

"Okay, good. I'm going to need your help getting you out of there. Do you understand?"

"Yes."

"Can you move your legs?"

"I think so."

"Good. Listen. I want you to try and get your legs up to your chest and out the windshield. If I can get you standing without falling down, we'll both be better off. Okay?"

"Okay."

"Give me your hand," he said. She reached for him, took his outstretched hand. "Now lift your legs up and over the dashboard."

She cried out as she moved one, then the other leg. Finally, she rotated on the man's shoulder into an almost sitting position. She extended her other arm out. Chet took it and helped her stand in the snow. He held her around the waist, assisting her to the back of the truck and around it.

In the bright glare of the snow, Chet could see she wasn't an ugly woman, but she was still far from pretty; kind of a plain Jane with a smoker's pallor to her skin. Her blond hair was not smooth and silky like Kay's brown locks, but more of a greasy, almost filthy appearance. Blood trickled from a wound on her forehead, along with other spots on her hands and wrists and face. Jeans—an expensive knock off brand with holes in the knees—clung tight to her legs and hips. Her coat covered most of her upper body, and worn sneakers with holes on both sides covered her feet.

"Are you okay?" he asked, again feeling stupid for asking such a dumb question.

She nodded. "Yeah, I think so."

"Okay, I'm going to help you up to the car before I come back and check on him."

The woman stiffened and snapped her head toward Chet. A scowl covered her face, as if Chet had called her a name or said something about her looks. He cocked his head and stepped back from her, still holding her arm to keep her from falling.

"What's wrong?" Chet asked.

Her head shook from side to side. She stared at the undercarriage of the truck, her face softening, the furrowed brows relaxing. "He's dead," she whispered. "Can you just take me to the hospital, and we'll send the police out for him?"

"What?" It was an odd question, not one he thought he would ever hear in a situation like this.

"I really don't feel too good. Can you just take me to the hospital, and we can call the police from there?"

"My wife is trying to contact the police now, but the weather is causing a problem with the cell. If we can't get a hold of someone, then we'll take you to the emergency room, but I can't just leave—" Chet raised his eyebrows.

"He's my husband," she said sharply.

Her husband? Chet couldn't imagine leaving Kay behind in an overturned vehicle in what amounted to a snowstorm for South Carolina. It would be hours, maybe even a day or two before the police could make it out this far, even though Newberry and Batesburg were just down the road, Pelion a little further out. Historically, the drivers in the south were bad, but throw in a winter storm and they become maniacal, not slowing down in bad conditions, slamming on breaks, *flipping their trucks into open fields.* But even then, at that hour, with the amount of snow already on the ground, the cars passing by had become few, if any. With that in mind, the guy might not be found for a week or more, depending on how long the snow stayed on the ground.

"I'll get you up to the car. You can sit and get warm; Kay might be able to get you wrapped in a blanket or something, okay?"

"My purse," she said and tried to head back around the truck. "I need to get my purse."

"You're kidding, right?" Chet asked.

"No," she said. "I need my purse—it's got my entire life in it."

My entire life in it? Mr. Worrywart slunk from the shadows, his normally frantic, scared face coming into plane view. There was no worry here, but his eyes were shifting slants and his mouth was a heavy frown. *Something's wrong, Chet old boy. Something's really wrong.*

For once, Chet agreed with Mr. Worrywart.

"Stay here," Chet said, and half-slid, half-walked back to the truck. He lost his balance and slammed into the undercarriage. The truck groaned, glass tinkled from the broken windshield. He heard a soft grunt from the other side. Chet stood, a hand on the truck, and hurried to the other side. The man lay still, his head bleeding, something jutting out of his side. It could have been a rib, or maybe part of the gearshift. It was hard to tell.

"Hey, buddy," Chet said and touched the man's head. He pulled away red fingertips, wiped them on his jeans. "I'll be right back."

Again, the grunt came, more of a bark this time than a grunt.

"You're alive?" Chet asked, his heart ramping up a few notches. "Stay put. I'll be right back."

Chet reached into the truck. The purse—a black and white cloth bag that could have been a schoolteacher's tote at one time—sat on the floor, upturned, but the contents sealed up inside, the clasp having done its job and keeping the purse closed. He grabbed it, against his better judgment, and hurried away from the truck. At the back end he looked back toward the front. The man moved his head, something so slight he may not have actually done it. Chet grit his teeth, trying to stave off the anger that was trying to well up in his chest. He thought it insane for the woman to be more worried about her purse than her husband, even more nuts for her to declare him dead, without knowing for certain he was.

Chet went back to the woman, said nothing about her husband, and helped her up the slight hill, placing one hand on the ground to brace himself, while holding her forearm to keep her from slipping and falling. At the ditch, he hopped in, held out both hands to her, aiding her in, then out of the ditch. Not once did he mention her husband was still alive. There was something wrong, and Mr. Worrywart needled him in the back of his mind, telling him to be wary of danger.

"Kay," he yelled. "Give me a hand here."

She left the car, skidding a couple of feet before regaining her balance. Kay took the woman's hand. "Are you okay?" she asked and led her to the car, sitting her in the front passenger's seat. "Sit and get warm." She closed the door.

"Any luck with the phone?" Chet asked.

"No," Kay said. "We have nothing. One bar, if any."

"You have to love these calling networks," Chet said, adding, "Will work even in a cave in the middle of the earth." He let out a dry chuckle. "Sure, it works there but in the middle of nowhere in South Carolina in a snowstorm, you're out of luck."

"Isn't that the truth?"

"It looks that way. I've got to go back down there. The driver looks like he's in pretty bad shape. You watch after her and keep trying to call for help, okay?"

"Okay," she said, and rounded the car. Before she climbed in the driver's seat, she called to Chet. "Be careful."

"I will," he said, and scurried down into the ditch, a nagging sensation still lingering in the back of his mind. He wondered if he should say anything to Kay, if maybe he should warn her in some way to stay sharp and pay attention when she is near the woman. Instead, he continued down the hill. He slipped and slid all the way back to the truck.

The snow came down harder, biting into Chet's face and hands. The wind blew it sideways, and an eerie silence filled the land. He glanced back at the car, barely able to see the woman in the passenger's side window. She stared at him. Though he couldn't see her eyes, he swore they were narrow slits and he would have bet money her lips were pulled down into a frown.

Chet rounded the back end of the truck, dropped to his knees and searched the ground for the crowbar. He found it easily enough, the cold steel sending fresh slivers of ice along his skin. He placed the hook end into the remaining portion of the windshield and yanked it free.

The man hiccupped and then cried out.

"Hold on, buddy," Chet said. "I'm going to get you out of there."

The man's breathing grew loud and wet.

Crap, Chet thought, *I have to get you out of there, quick.*

"Hang in there, buddy," Chet said. He didn't need Mr. Worrywart to tell him the driver was probably going to die. The raspy, wet breathing told him all he really needed to know. He worked the seatbelt latch, but couldn't snap it free. "You're buckled in and the belt's locked. I'm going to have to cut you loose." Chet slipped his pocketknife from the back of his jeans and slid it under the belt, working it back and forth along the edge of the seatbelt. *I should have sharpened this thing.*

"Where is she?" the man asked between gasps, his voice weak.

"What?"

"Where is she? Where is Amy?"

"Amy? You mean your wife?"

The man moved his head, let out a yip of pain. "No."

Not his wife? "I don't know who Amy is then, buddy."

"The woman ... ow, that hurts."

"Sorry. I'm trying to be careful. My knife's dull as crap right now."

The man shifted, using the steering wheel for leverage. It pulled to his right and he let out another yelp of pain.

"Just sit still, okay," Chet said. "I'm going to get you out of here, mister ..." He let the sentence die.

"David," the man said. "My name is David Howser."

"Nice to meet you, sir. It sucks that it's under these circumstances, but still, you know what I mean."

The man let go of the steering wheel, and grabbed Chet's wrist. His grip was firm, one of a working man, a man who hadn't pushed a pen a day in his life, but more like shovels and axes, maybe turned wrenches for a living, fixing cars.

"Where is Amy?" the man asked, his teeth clenched, his face stretched into a terrible expression of miserable pain.

"Who is Amy?" A tinge of fear tickled from the back of Chet's neck all the way to the center of his heart. He remembered seeing him hit the woman just before the truck shot off the road, and his fear grew quickly from a tickle to a searing ache.

"The blonde. The woman who was in the car with me."

"You mean your wife?" Chet asked again, not sure if David Howser had understood him earlier.

"She's not my wife."

"Oh."

"It's not like that," David said, his light blue eyes wet with tears.

"Hey, man, I'm not going to judge you or anything."

"She's dangerous," David spat, a trickle of blood spilling from the left side of his mouth.

"Dangerous?"

"She … she kidnapped me. I stopped for some gas, she came up to me." He coughed, blood spattering his shirt and the side of his face.

A nick formed in the seatbelt. Chet continued to saw through it, making little progress as David talked.

"She came up to my truck, offered me a screw for a few dollars. I told her no, I'm married, so, if I'm going to cheat—" Another round of coughs and David took in several deep breaths. "She pulled a gun on me, told me to get in and drive."

"A gun?"

"It's in her purse. Have you seen it?"

Yeah, Chet thought. *I gave it to her.*

"She has her purse," Chet said, a hole forming in his stomach, a sinking sensation filled with nausea at knowing he gave the woman the purse—the gun—and left her with Kay.

"Where is she?"

"She's with my wife."

The man glanced up, his eyes exactly as he envisioned Mr. Worrywart's. "You need to get your wife away from her."

Chet bit the inside of his mouth, trying to fight back the fear and hold Mr. Worrywart at bay. Though he couldn't see them, he glanced in the direction of his car, at where he left Kay with this Amy chick, the girl with the gun.

"Don't worry about me," David said. "Even if you cut through the belt, my other arm is under the truck. It'll be hell getting me out of here."

Chet went to stand. "Give me a couple of minutes, and I'll be back; I promise."

"Can you do me a favor before you go?"

33

"Sure. What?"

David lifted his arm. A knife with a white handle jutted from his ribs, the blade sunk in all the way to the hilt. "Can you pull that out for me?"

Chet licked his lips, took a deep breath. He couldn't believe what he thought was a rib or the gear shift was really a knife.

"What happened?"

"Just yank it, kid," David said, ignoring Chet's question. "Don't think about it. Just do it."

Chet nodded and knelt back down. "It's going to hurt."

"Just pull it out, please?"

"Okay. On the count of three, alright?"

"Whatever. That's fine, but you're wasting time. Your wom—"

It took little else for Chet to grab the blade and jerk it from David's rib. The blade scraped bone. Chet's hand tingled as if he had swung an aluminum baseball bat and struck a ball directly on the barrel, the impact sending vibrations into his hand, vibrations he would feel the rest of the day, even if they made it to the cabin. Chet doubted that was going to happen, but found himself praying it would.

"Thanks," David whispered through a heavy, pained breath.

Chet set the knife on the ground. "I'll be back." He hurried to the front of the truck, glanced at the car at the top of the hill, the headlamps on, puffs of white pluming from the exhaust. The woman seemed to be talking to Kay, and no longer staring down the hill at the truck.

Hurrying the best he could against the growing wind, the steady snow and slippery footing, Chet hurried up the hill, both hands on the ground, running on all fours like a rabid dog. At the ditch, he hopped over it, slipped to one knee and stood. Amy and Kay both stared at him.

Chet went around to the driver's side. Kay rolled the window down.

"I need the keys," he said, trying to sound as calm as he could.

"What about your set?"

"I can't find them. I must have dropped them somewhere down there."

Kay turned to Amy. "Sorry about this, but I have to turn the car off for a minute." She turned the key and the engine died. "Why do you need them, anyway?"

"Give me a hand for a second. I need to grab a blanket or two."

"Is my husband alive?" Amy yelled through the open driver's side window.

Chet leaned down, took a breath, then released it. "No."

For an instant Amy's face changed, a smirk appeared, one that was triumphant, as if she had won a major game and toppled her biggest foe. It was a look of satisfaction.

"Come here," Chet said and opened Kay's door.

They walked to the trunk. He unlocked it and let it swing up.

"I could have pulled the trunk latch, you know?" Kay said. "We didn't—"

Chet put a finger to her lips, did a quick shake of his head, his eyes getting wide, lips forming the words "*be quiet.*"

Kay frowned, opened her mouth. Chet again did that quick shake of the head and glanced back to the front of the car. He whispered, "Go with me on this."

She nodded.

"Honey, the guy's dead," he said, loud enough for Amy to hear him, but not so loud that it sounded staged.

"Are you sure?"

"Positive." Chet moved a few bags, one that held a bottle of wine in it, another one held Kay's sleepwear—and in this case, her barely there sleepwear, as Chet liked to call them. The blankets sat beneath a sports bag with the rest of their clothes in it. He lifted it out of the trunk. "Grab me two blankets."

"Why?" Kay asked, but complied.

"The guy's dead, but I can't get him out of the truck. His arm is pinned beneath it. We'll cover him up and get out of here, turn around and head to the hospital. From there we can call the police and tell them what happened. But for now, I can't leave him like that."

"And you need my help for this?"

"Not a time to argue, babe," Chet said. "Just give me a hand."

Chet set the sport bag in the car, moved the others back in place and closed the trunk. At the driver's side window, he leaned in a little but kept his head out of Amy's direct line of sight. If she did have a gun, he didn't want to look like one of those cops killed at a traffic stop, putting their heads in to ask for license and registration ma'am and ending up with lights out, sprawled on the black top.

"We'll be right back," he said, went to the back end of the car and helped Kay to the ditch and over it.

A few feet from the ditch, he started talking fast. "Do you have your cell phone?"

"Yeah, but it's useless out here."

"Keep trying to get a hold of the police. We have a bigger problem on our hands than a car accident."

"What do you mean?" Kay asked.

"That woman—"

Kay glanced back, "What about her?"

"Don't look at her. Apparently, she's a nut case."

"Why do you say that?"

"She kidnapped the guy driving the truck at a gas station. She apparently stabbed him, and that's why they were arguing. She's running from something, and now we're stuck in the middle of it."

"How do you know all this?"

"David Howser—the driver of the truck—told me."

"I thought you said he was dead."

"Well, yeah. It's the only way I could keep her in the car and get you out of here. She didn't want me to go back for him—as if she knew he was alive. She might have taken you hostage if she knew he wasn't dead."

"What?" A sharp tone, maybe too sharp.

"I want you to run for the woods. By the time she realizes

36

you're not coming back, you can be well into them. If I'm correct, there are some houses on the other side and you can get some help at one of them."

"I'm not leaving you here," she argued.

"I'm not asking you to," Chet said, as they rounded the front of the truck. Kay slipped, almost went to her bottom, but Chet held her up. "Run and get help. Now."

"What about you?"

Chet pointed at the man. The seatbelt had been cut through and he sat at an odd angle. "I've got to get him out of here."

"Chet."

He bent down, grabbed the crowbar. "Take this, and go."

"But—"

"Do it, Kay. Run. Don't worry about me."

Tears formed in her brown eyes. He leaned in, hugged her tight and whispered into her hair. "I'll be okay. I just need you to run as fast as you can through the woods and get help. Okay?"

She nodded.

"I love you, Kay," Chet said.

"I love you, too." Her voice cracked slightly.

"Now go."

Kay turned and started to run, crowbar in hand. Chet watched her for a couple of seconds halfway expecting her to fall. When she didn't, he turned to David Howser.

"Let's get you out of here."

"Don't waste your time, kid," David said. He had the knife close to the crook of the elbow of the arm trapped underneath the truck.

"I can rock the truck the other way," Chet said. "It won't take too much to get it to tip back onto its wheels."

"What about Amy?"

"She thinks you're dead and that—" Chet's words trailed off, a realization sinking in.

"She'll know I'm not dead if you try and tip the truck back over."

"Yeah, I guess so."

"Kid, just get out of here while you can."

Chet thought about it. He thought hard about it for a minute as the snow whipped around him, and the cold tried to cut through his jacket.

You can leave, Mr. Worrywart said. *He said you could. No hard feelings if you do. Just run. Catch up with Kay, and keep running. You can find one of those houses beyond the woods, and call the police; let them do their jobs. If they get shot ...*

"I'm not going anywhere until I get you out of here."

David let out a long, wheezing breath. "You're hardheaded aren't you?"

"I've been told that a time or two."

Chet stood by the hood, its red paint scratched, clumps of grass and dirt clinging to a pinched piece of metal. He placed both hands on the hood and pushed forward. The truck rocked. David screamed, his voice echoing in the field, intensified by the near quiet world around them.

"Don't yell," Chet snapped, looked in through the windshield. The man held his bicep, tears streaked down his face. "Look man, if we're going to get you out of here, you have to act like you're dead. You can't be yelling like that."

David snapped back. "Try having your arm pinned beneath a truck, and then say that."

"Yeah. Sorry about that, but I can't get you out any other way. Not without sawing your arm off, and I don't think I can do that." He glanced around, his ears perking up the best they could.

"Hey, kid—"

Chet shushed him, and David fell silent. Seconds passed as he listened. Were those feet crunching on snow, muffled footsteps approaching them? When he heard only the beating of his heart and the in and out wheeze of what he thought was David's punctured lung he propped his hands on the truck's hood.

"You ready?"

David nodded, "As I'll ever be."

One shove and the truck teetered toward tipping onto its

wheels. David grunted, loudly, his top teeth sinking deep into his bottom lip, not quite drawing blood. The second shove was harder. Aided by the wind, the truck tottered, tilted. Chet scrambled back, clipped by the edge of the truck, and went sprawling to the ground. The rumble of the truck landing on all four wheels was quickly followed by the crumpling of metal and thousands of shards of glass shifting, rubbing together and falling from the windshield and driver's window. Somewhere, mixed in with all of the other noises was David letting out a stream of pained swears.

Chet got to his feet, trudged through the snow and yanked open the driver's side door. David was breathing hard, his shattered arm by his side, a black, blue, purple mass of pulp that barely resembled an appendage. There may have been fingers still on the hand, but the swelling made it hard to tell.

"David, let's go," Chet yelled and reached for him. A shot tore through the side of the truck, and David went limp in Chet's hands. Chet ducked, his hands going over his head. He peeked over the edge of the truck bed. Amy lurched forward, one of her legs clearly in worse shape than he had known when he helped her up the hill. A pistol was in one hand, the arm extended. She slipped, threw her hands out to her sides and held her balance. Amy leveled the gun at Chet and squeezed the trigger.

A heavy thud as bullet met metal followed the report; a loud, ringing echo hung in the air for several seconds after the shot.

"Are you crazy, woman?" Chet yelled, moved closer to the door so he could look through the window. He hoped if she fired again, the bullet would strike the truck and not him.

"I thought you said you were going to cover him in blankets and come right back."

"I changed my mind."

"You can't do that," she yelled. "You said you were going to do something; that's what you're supposed to do."

"I can't just leave a dead person out here. It's wrong."

Chet listened for her footsteps, gauged she was near the

front end of the truck. He scooted back toward the tailgate, waiting until he saw her again and scampered to the other side. He saw her look in the driver's side door, a grin creasing her face.

"If he wasn't dead, he is now."

Chet glanced up the hill to the car. The keys were in his pocket. He could make a run for it, but, really, how far would he get? Ten yards? Twenty, before she fired off another shot and put a bullet in the back of his head?

She's going to kill you! Mr. Worrywart yelled, his voice as audible and real as the wind and snow around him. *I tried to warn you, but you wouldn't listen. If you would have stayed at home—*

"Shut up," Chet growled, and Mr. Worrywart quieted.

"What did you say?" Amy asked, circling around to the back of the truck.

"I said, I thought he was your husband?"

Amy laughed, and not a, that-was-a-funny-joke laugh. No, it was more of this-woman-has-lost-her-mind laugh, a little bit maniacal, but she was still all there and, in her own twisted way, very much in control of the situation. "My husband? No. Just some guy who laughed at me when I offered him sex."

"Laughed at you?" Chet asked. *Keep her talking. If she's talking, you know where she is.* "Why would he laugh at you?"

"Because he doesn't like women."

"Maybe he's married."

"I don't care if he's married," Amy yelled. She was rounding the truck, but going the opposite direction, trying to confuse Chet. He caught on, backing away, opposite of her.

"Maybe he laughed in a shocked kind of way, you know? Like maybe he didn't think a woman would come onto him like that?"

"Bull crap," Amy yelled. "You weren't there. You don't know. It was one of *those* laughs. One of those looks that men give you when they don't think your stuff is good enough for them."

"Maybe it's not," Chet blurted out and immediately cringed at what he said.

40

The sounds of feet on snow quickened—she was all but running around the side of the truck. She appeared to his left, gun pointed. Chet stooped down as she squeezed the trigger, the bullet barely missing his shoulder. He scrabbled on hands and feet to the front, to the busted grill and bumper that looked like it could have been made of plastic instead of metal. He slipped, fell onto his chest and rolled onto his back. Amy, with madness in her eyes, rounded the front of the car, the gun shaking in both her hands.

The snow became brighter, the flakes took shape, much like the cutouts kids make at school with scissors and folded pieces of paper. The gray sky grew darker. The color stood out on the truck. Amy's cheeks flushed red with anger, her blond hair streaked with blood, her shirt and jeans—still look-ing old though somehow sharper in color—were caked with blood and grime, as if they hadn't been washed in weeks. The gun—more importantly, the barrel of the gun—stood out on the backdrop of the world, a black hole that was meant to do one thing: kill.

Amy yelled something, but Chet didn't understand any of it. It was like she had slowed down with the rest of the world.

Just as quickly, real time kicked in, and the end of Amy's tirade was clear in his ears.

"... I'll teach you, you little liar."

Chet saw Kay behind Amy before he realized she was there. Amy's mouth hung open, a look of confusion in her eyes. The confusion faded and Amy smiled, her bloodied gums missing one of her front teeth. She turned as Kay swung the crowbar.

The gun went off, its deafening roar lingering behind. The bullet struck the crowbar, and Kay screamed. The crowbar connected with the side of Amy's face, her jaw shattering. Both women fell to the ground. Three teeth joined the other one in their exodus from Amy's mouth. She twisted toward the ground, landing face down. The gun dropped from her hand and landed in the snow several feet away.

Chet got to his knees and crawled to Kay. He saw the blood before he saw anything else. "Kay?" he yelled, his nerves suddenly on end, every hair standing. Tears formed in his light blue eyes. He tried to scream again, but her name came out as a hoarse whisper.

The snow on the ground, the bite of ice through his jeans and on his bare hands, the wind blowing, even the real cold of the late afternoon faded, leaving only Kay, lying on her side in the snow, the blood seeping from a wound somewhere close to her midsection. Amy and the accident, David Howser, who was most likely dead, and all of the events that led up to that moment didn't matter. Only Kay mattered. Only the blood turning the snow red beneath her mattered.

"Kay," Chet said again, his arms and legs weak and refusing to move forward, his mind not allowing them to, the defense of his sanity firmly in place. He blinked tears away, and they slid down his face. One hand crept forward, then the other, then a knee. The other one followed and he crawled, like a baby tentative in those first few shaky moments of walking before full out stumbling forward, momentum seizing control, and he was by her side.

You dummy, Mr. Worrywart was back, and he was mad. *You should have listened to me. You should have put your foot down and said traveling in the snow was too dangerous. But, no, you couldn't do that, could you?*

"Shut up," Chet said.

Even if you didn't want to listen to me then, you should have, at the very least, listened when I tried to warn you about that psycho. Even David What's His Name tried to warn you, but you wouldn't listen to him.

"I said shut up," Chet growled.

His mind became quiet, but Mr. Worrywart didn't leave. He stayed, his foot tapping on the hardwoods of Chet's soul, arms crossed, scowl on his long face.

"Thank you," Chet said, his eyes never leaving Kay.

Chet's fingers twitched, his hand shook as he reached for her, his heart slamming while his breathing was on hold. He touched her arm, carefully rolled her onto her side. He stared at her chest, waited for a moment. Then it happened. Kay's

42

chest heaved, a deep breath, not a shallow dying one, but a full tilt deep breath, maintaining life in the lungs.

"Kay," he said, his voice higher.

She opened her eyes, blinked several times. "Chet?"

He didn't mean to, but he couldn't help himself. Chet laughed, his heart lifted, the heavy feeling of it breaking replaced by the even heavier feeling of relief.

"I'm not dead?" she asked.

Again, he laughed, this time louder. "No, babe. You're not dead."

She tried to sit up, fell back to the ground, a whimper in her throat. Chet knew she wouldn't allow a scream to live, not Kay Wilmington, a woman who knew how to be a woman, but also was tougher than most men he knew.

"Where does it hurt?" Chet asked.

"My arm."

The blood had made it hard to tell, saturating her coat at both the stomach and the sleeve of her right arm. Chet crawled around to her other side, and lifted her arm. Her face pinched into a grimace, and her breaths came in quick gasps.

"She shot you in the arm," Chet said, more to himself than Kay.

"You think?"

Chet glanced up at her, the seriousness in her expression, the sarcasm in her tone confusing him for a moment. Then it dawned on him.

"Well, duh," he shot back. "Captain Obvious strikes again, huh?"

This time Kay laughed, a soft singular chuckle. She nodded. "Umm ... yeah."

"Let's get you up and out of the snow, back to the car where we can try to stop the bleeding."

Chet helped Kay to her feet, and held the back of her jeans at the belt loop as they went up the hill. Kay held her wounded arm tight to her chest, clutching it with her other hand, keeping it still. Halfway to the ditch, Chet stopped and turned. Snow crunched under foot as Amy charged at them, crowbar in hand. Her face was a shattered wreck, the entire left side from cheekbone to jaw swollen, her lips fat, bright red dripping off of them.

The battle cry of the insane lifted from her throat as she swung the crowbar. Chet put up his left arm. The bone snapped just below the elbow as the crowbar struck home. Heat followed by blinding pain shot up his shoulder and all the way to his fingertips. Unlike Kay, he did scream. He spun, like a matador away from a raging bull, the blow knocking him off kilter, but he managed to stay upright.

Amy came at him again, the second swing just missing. The over swing sent her skidding in the snow. Her free arm waved at a nonexistent crowd of onlookers. Chet charged at her, his arm jarring with each step, sending fresh daggers through the shattered bone. Amy looked back, the madness in her eyes, a swollen grin on her busted face. She swung as she turned. Chet, thankful for all of those years of playing sports, dodged the swing and caught her wrist.

They struggled, trying to remain standing, fighting for the crowbar. Amy shoved her shoulder into Chet's broken arm, sending him back, his good hand releasing the weapon. Amy swung it quickly, striking the broken arm again. Another bone, this one near his wrists, popped, crumbled under the impact of steel on flesh. Chet fell back into the snow, his arm now a broken mass of useless bones and muscles.

Amy stood over him, the crowbar at her side. Chet had never really seen the look of a truly insane person before, but staring into her eyes he knew, without any doubt, this woman was crazy enough to kill them all and walk away as if nothing had ever happened. She laughed, seeming to revel in her victory. "You got your butt kicked by a woman."

The words dug deep into Chet's ego. Anger flared, and even with Mr. Worrywart screaming in the background to keep his mouth shut, Chet spoke calmly between clenched teeth. "You're not a woman. You're just an ogre with breasts pretending to be a woman."

NO! Mr. Worrywart yelled, and ran to the darkest shadows

of Chet's mind, his back to the outside world, afraid to see his own ending.

Amy bellowed, her eyes narrowing. She raised the crowbar over her head.

Out the corner of his eye, he saw Kay running toward her. He wasn't sure what she held in both hands, but he was positive Kay meant business. Amy looked to her right, and steadied herself to swing the heavy black bar at Kay when she was close enough. She would win that battle, Chet was certain of it. Kay held a rake, not a flimsy one by any means, but a wooden one nonetheless, and wood on steel was bound to lose every time.

Kay screamed, then ducked and fell to the ground at the thunderous boom. The rake fell beside her. One hand went over her head.

Amy staggered backward, the crowbar slipping from her fingers. Her mouth hung open as if she was trying to breathe but couldn't; her eyes were wide. Blood sprayed from her neck. One hand covered the wound, but her life's fluid spilled from between her fingers. Amy took a step backward, turning her eyes away from both Chet and Kay. She fell, face forward into the snow. A patch of red blossomed around her head.

Chet looked toward the truck. A badly wounded David Howser was on one knee, Amy's pistol in his trembling hand. Smoke rose from the barrel. David Howser coughed once, then fell to the ground.

Minutes. Only minutes had passed from the time Amy was shot and killed, to the time Chet and Kay reached the car. They held each other around the waist, their legs moving together as if marching until they reached the ditch. Carefully, Chet climbed down, helped Kay and then climbed back up using his good arm, stifling a cry of pain when he slipped and bumped the broken one. Once Kay was out of the ditch, they walked the few feet to the car and Kay sat down inside. David followed behind, holding his stomach and grimacing with each step he took.

Chet cranked the car up, and turned the heat all the way

up. He dropped his head against the steering wheel. "You try your phone again?"

Kay was looking down, the phone already in hand. She laughed, exasperated, maybe even a little out of relief.

"What?" Chet asked.

She held the phone up for him to see. "We have bars."

The Scarring

On the bed lay the drunken man, his eyes wide and blood-shot. They darted from side to side. His mouth opened and closed like a fish out of water, but he only managed a few strangled croaks. His arms and legs were bound to the bed-posts with ropes. He was as naked as the day he came into the world.

"Do you hate?"

"Yes."

The first scar came at the age of eleven, courtesy of an angry father and a bottle of whiskey. He had ducked when the old man threw the bottle. It shattered against the wall, slivers of glass spraying back at him, along with the remainder of the caramel-colored liquid.

He probably wouldn't have been scarred if only small pieces of glass had pricked his skin. If not for the old man's follow-up to the bottle toss, he would have been just fine. But the old man chased the broken glass like a beer at a drinking party, and the smack to the back of the head was unseen. He—Nothing was his name—went sprawling backward, hands out behind him, a heavy sting on the side of his face. A gash appeared from mid-forearm to elbow when he landed among the shattered glass.

Nothing bled. He cried, and as he did so, his father wailed on him, telling him to "clam it up, boy, or I'll clam it up for you."

Mom stitched him up with a sewing needle and thread as thick as fishing line. Nothing wasn't sure which was worse, the initial slice of skin by glass or the constant poke of the needle and tug of thread.

The skin puckered over time, leaving a pink welt of flesh that grew as he grew, never shrinking, and a constant reminder.

###

He stood in a brightly lit room, a young lady in front of him. She used to be afraid of what she was about to do, but no longer. He knew of her fear, of how the blood made her squeamish at first. Her blue eyes held determination in them, or maybe it was desperation. If Nothing had to wager a guess, he would bet the house on desperation, a fear of the heart keeping her there with him. For that he could love her forever.

"Do you hate?"

"It's all I know."

His name hadn't always been Nothing. He couldn't recall what it had been before the whiskey bottle incident. He just knew how his father thought of him, how he spoke of him, what the bastard called him all those years of his childhood.

"You're nothing, boy. You're nothing to me. You'll always be nothing."

Nothing. Nothing. Nothing, you son-of-a ...

"I am Nothing," he told himself. "I will always be Nothing."

"Do you hate?"

"It's what I do."

He looked down at his naked body. A road map of grooved indentions and pink puckered skin riddled his flesh, as if they were mountain ridges and deep valleys on a meat map. He could recall where each one came from. The one on his right forearm to the elbow was obvious; the four on his right knuckles came from a set of braces in another kid's mouth a couple years later. The one on the middle finger of the same hand was from a bottle opener he lost his grip on. The one to the left of his stomach—on the fleshy part of his side—came from a bullet. The exit scar on his back was twice the size. He wished he had died from that one. The several scars on the left of his jaw and neck and shoulder and both palms of his hands were from the windshield he went through. No seatbelt or airbags and a lot of anger led to the telephone pole. His car lost the game of chicken; his body took the brunt of the damage when he was propelled from his seat, through the glass and onto the top of the car. The ones on his legs were self-inflicted. Knives, glass, nails, whatever was handy at the time. The ones on his backside were all Dad-induced.

The last of the scars, the ones on his left cheek, right calf, and below his right eye were put there by the girl—Lena—a lost soul like himself, searching for love in all the wrong places, never finding it until Nothing came along. Even then, what

48

was love without pain?

He hid the scars growing up. Long shirts, even during the summer months, kept them a secret. His shirt would never come off at Grover's Pond, even when cute little Sally Evans wanted to skinny dip with him. He walked away, embarrassed by the marks left by belts and plastic and PVC pipes and rose bush switches, complete with thorns that tore ragged holes in the backs of his legs and torso and arms ...

"Why do you hate?"

"It's who I am, who he made me to be."

That was then, when he was a scared kid, hiding from a drunken dad with crazy eyes and a quick temper. Now ... now, he wore them proudly, his face like tanned leather with the exception of the areas that were pink or white and raised or sunken in. They were like tattoos for him—ones with no ink and hurt far worse than any needle could.

"They give you character," Lena said on their first night together.

They were in the dark. Though unseen, they could be felt, and she ran her fingers along the ones on the side of his face, even after he said, "don't." He could love her for that, too—for not being afraid the way so many others were.

"Let me see."

"No."

"Why not?"

"Just no."

He stared at her. Inside, he felt something, but outside ... outside he showed nothing. She stood in front of him and waited for him to tell her what to do. She had helped him before, all because he wished her to. Yet another reason to love her.

"Are you ready?" Nothing asked.

She nodded.

He handed her the nail ... and he remembered her reaction ...

It took a year for him to show her everything, the scars given by others and the ones done by himself. Her reaction was everything.

She didn't look away. She didn't blink or flinch or gag in disgust.

Lena wept.

And he fell ...

"Do you love?"
"No."

Mom died from fourteen blows to the head and body by a crowbar. There was hair and blood and bone fragments on the walls, floor and ceiling, as well as the couch where she had been sleeping when Dad came home drunk and angry. Nothing saw the rage, the purple of his face, the crazed eyes; Mom's flesh as it tore away, and the blood ... so much blood.

Dad left the house—staggered, really—and came back later with a friend, some trash bags, tape and shovels. They left with her body wrapped in the liners and taped shut. Before he came back though, Nothing had touched the ruined flesh of his mom, poked a finger into a shattered eyeless socket. When he pulled it away, he sliced the tip on fractured bone. Pain followed, sharp and sudden. Nothing stared at the jagged wound. He marveled at the glistening red fluid seeping down the finger to the hand and passed the wrist.

Three weeks later a white indention remained.

"Do you love?"
"No."
"Why not?"
"Love is weak."
She took the nail. The tip had been sharpened.
"Are you sure?" she asked.
"Yes."
A nod. A smile.
She lifted the nail.
Nothing turned his back to her.
"Are you ready?" he asked his father, the man who could only feel hate and taught that lesson well. Dad shook his head, a shaky side-to-side gesture, and tugged at his bindings.

Nothing picked a bottle up from the table, an amber liquid inside. He smashed it on a cinder block on the floor. The world danced a slow waltz as glass exploded, and whiskey splattered. For a moment, he was a kid again and ducking away from a thrown bottle seconds before he would get his first scar. He lifted the broken bottleneck to his face, stared at the jagged edges. He stepped on the shards and felt no pain.

"Do you love?" Lena asked.

50

"No."

The nail pierced his left shoulder. The pain was instant and blinding. It took his breath away and made his knees weak. He swung the bottleneck down, a reaction to the immense pain, opening a gash in Dad's left cheek.

His old man screamed.

"Do you love?" she asked again.

"No," he growled.

The nail went into his left shoulder again, striking nerve and bone. He screamed and swung the broken bottle down. Dad's chest opened, the white of the breastplate showing through blood spray. Dad's turn to scream.

"Do you love?" she yelled.

"No!"

Pain—hot and blistering—ripped through his left bicep. He followed it with another slash of the bottle.

"Do you love?"

"No!"

Pain.

"Do you love?"

"No!"

Blood.

"Do you love?"

"No!"

Torn flesh.

"Do you love?"

"No!"

His blood was hot and sticky and rolling down his back and side and arm. With each heartbeat, pain traveled through him. With each driven nail, he brought the bottle down harder, scarring his father's body in strokes of hurt and anger until the old man's screams tapered off, and eventually ceased.

"Do you love?"

He looked at the mutilated body of his childhood tormentor. Dad was unrecognizable except for hateful eyes that blankly stared through Nothing. The sheets and wall were blood soaked. As was the floor. Suddenly drained of all energy, he blinked away a life full of pain and scars.

Nothing turned to her. Like him, she was naked and covered in red.

He smiled, one of relief, of a weight having been lifted, stretched across his face.

"Yes."

Claire, The Movie

Her hands shook. She hated when her hands shook.

From her cushiony seat with all the stars surrounding her, Claire's nerves danced along her skin. Her mouth had grown dry, and the butterflies in her stomach were the size of rabbits, and they thumped at her insides with their large feet.

She glanced to her left. Was that George Clooney? She would swoon if he walked up and talked to her. Not likely to happen, even though she was a young actress up for an Oscar. Johnny Depp passed by only a few feet away, his hair floppy and unkempt, his suit not really a suit at all, but a purple dress coat and dark slacks.

Claire took a deep breath, still not believing where she was and how she got there. She pinched her forearm and winced with the slight pain.

"Don't do that, Claire," her father said from her right. She looked at him. He was clean-shaven—a rarity. Jack Edgecomb liked his whiskers, even if his wife didn't. Claire hated them. His brown eyes were shadowed by his forehead and the dim lights of the theater, but she didn't need to see them to know what they looked like, to know the hard squint and knitted brows.

"Sorry," she said. "I'm nervous, and I keep thinking this is a dream."

"It's not," Jack said. "We've made the big time." He paused. "Just don't blow it for us."

We? Us? She said nothing, but pondered those two words. After a minute, she realized maybe he was right. Maybe this was a 'we' moment. He did play a significant role in her acting career, as short as it was, and they *were* at the Oscars—the Oscars! —hobnobbing with the big names in the business.

"Daddy," she said, her voice a shaky whisper.

He stared off, not paying much attention to her. In the distance, three women were walking toward them, their tops dipped in low V's, their dresses hugging their hips. A smile creased Jack's face.

"Daddy," she repeated.

"What?" he said sharply, barely looking at her before turning back to the myriad of blondes, brunettes, and redheads all walking around in screw me dresses, all trying to outdo the other actresses, yet stay cordial with each other in the process.

"If I win, will you walk up there with me?"

His face lightened. His lips went from pulled down in an angry frown to somewhat of a smile, the most she's ever gotten from him. He chuckled and rubbed his newly shaven chin. "Of course. I was planning on it."

Planning on it? That's nice. In truth, it wasn't. She didn't want him to walk up to the stage with her during her one shining moment. At least not at first. But as the nomination came down and the possibility she could actually win an Oscar, her thoughts changed, her desires changed. The more she thought about it, the more conflicted she became. She could thank all the people in the world in a scripted statement or thank the one person who molded her the most in person and up on stage. And the more she thought about it, she leaned toward thanking the single person. Yes, that was the best thing to do. It would be electric and something she didn't believe any other performer had done.

"Thank you," she said and let him turn back to his women browsing. She watched him for a few seconds, the way his eyes seemed to glisten, even in the shadows of darkness, when a sexy woman walked by.

Claire spread her fingers out on her lap. Momma's moon ring hugged her right ring finger. The dark blue dress was silky, and she liked the way it felt. She could get used to the way gowns flowed and made her skin cool and how it made her *feel* pretty. Pretty? In this place with all of these women, some with their fake boobs and plastic smiles and wigs and spray on tans? Others as natural as the day they were born. That beauty just couldn't be created with a scalpel, implants, liposuction, or injections.

She wondered if men would leer at her the way her daddy did the actresses surrounding them. Claire suddenly felt vulnerable. She crossed her arms over her breasts and tried to conceal the small amount of cleavage showing. She glanced around nervously, looking to see if anyone gawked at her. When she was younger, it wouldn't have been so bad having a boy stare. Just having one notice her through the baggy clothes Daddy made her wear would have been nice. Now, here in this large room filled with bigger than life people, the discomfort level of not being pretty enough, of all things, was high. Not just high, but at its apex. She wished she had kept her hair long instead of cutting it for the awards show. At least that way, she could let the brown locks cascade over her shoulders and cover the top parts of her breasts.

Claire's skin prickled. Her bladder tingled, and she wanted to find a restroom. Doing so meant walking up the long aisle, passing by the beauties and the men with roaming eyes. She wondered if her dad would look at the way the dress hugged her hips and would smile. A deep breath, followed by a second and a third, and her nerves began to calm.

She tried to focus on the murmuring conversations going on around her, but could only catch a glimpse of what this woman said, or the joke that actor told. There were too many voices, too many words rolling through the air.

Claire swallowed hard and stared down at her blue silk covered legs. There was a dip in the material where her legs were parted slightly. She closed them all the way, but the dip remained. Claire gripped her small black purse in both hands, the feel of false leather, shined to an almost impossible brightness, calmed her hands.

Daddy patted her knee, his rough hand heavier than he probably intended. He rubbed the top of one thigh, and Claire froze. Her eyes grew wide, and she looked straight ahead, afraid to look down at the hairy hand, afraid to see the cleanly manicured nails, the silver wedding band he never took off, even long after Mom left him. Her heart sank at the thought of her mom, gone in the middle of the night with no note or even consideration for her teenaged daughter. What was she thinking, and why didn't she take Claire with her? Claire's fingers pinched tight along the purse's closed flap, and she bit down on the inside of her mouth to keep from screaming.

Music began to play, the soft tones of violins and pianos and a couple of horns she couldn't discern. The lights dimmed, and thankfully, the crowd clapped. Daddy moved his hand and clapped along as well, his hands making thunderous booms that seemed to lift over the rest of the applause.

The opening announcement came from all around her, the smooth voice of a man who had spoken similar words time and time again was like the voice of a god. Claire looked around as people scampered to their seats. The announcer spoke on:

Put your hands together for ...

The applause grew louder as some comedian she had vaguely heard of came on stage. His jokes were received with laughter and some applause, but Claire mostly forgot the words as soon as they were out of his mouth. Her nerves held her tight, twisted her stomach into knots. A wave of nausea swept over her, and she swallowed it down.

The stage was an elaborate affair with stairs leading up from both the left and the right toward its center. Two glass podiums with long microphones on bendable coils jutting up stood on either side of the stage. Beige curtains—not just any beige, but this color seemed to dazzle in the bright lights mounted somewhere overhead—ran along the width of the stage and behind the podiums. A cinema screen sat back from the front and it was there where clips of movies and skits would play throughout the night.

The lights dimmed, and the comedian appeared on the screen. Reenactments of old movies played out with the comedian taking on several roles. Many laughed, but Claire's chest tightened and her breaths grew shallow.

Then she stood along with everyone else, her hands clapping of their own accord, the smile on her face forced. She sat back down, straightened her dress, and awaited the next award announcement.

With each passing award, bands played and clips were shown and there was a moment where Claire felt fine—just fine, thank you very much. Her hands still shook. She hated when her hands shook.

The night passed by too quickly, with other awards handed out, speeches given and music played. Politely she clapped and smiled, doing what everyone else did, all the while wondering what secrets this actor had or what pain this actress dealt with, because, surely, knowing pain was part of being a good actress. At least that's what Daddy always said.

Daddy … She glanced to her right to see him. His brown hair was unusually neat and that clean-shaven face, it unnerved her, even if she did hate his whiskers. The suit made him look less like Daddy and more like one of the many actors who sat around them, their trophy wives at their sides and fake smiles plastered on their faces. She wondered if any of the losers genuinely were happy for the winner. She doubted it. After all, second place is just the first loser; another thing Daddy liked to say.

The words from the male presenter drew her attention from her dad to the stage. She knew who he was, but her mind refused to tell her. Her heart sped up, and her hands shook worse than before.

"The nominees for best leading actress are …"

Claire stopped breathing. She was aware of it, but could do nothing to make her lungs push the air from them and fill themselves back up afterward. The nominees were announced, each one with a short clip from the movie they were in. Part of her hoped Nichole Kidman would win it this year. She always liked Nichole Kidman.

Then she heard the last nominee and her stomach fell into her feet. "And for her role in *Daddy's Little Girl*, Claire Edgefield."

On the silver screen behind him a scene played out in gritty black and white. The teenaged girl, Josie Ledson, lay crying in the bed. A bruise closed one eye, and her hair was matted on the side of her face. Stains—black on the grainy screen, but everyone knew in real life they would have been red—dotted the white sheet. Josie, played by Claire Edgefield in her debut role in an independent film, no less, pulled the pillow from beneath her head and slid it between her legs. She pulled her hand back and blood covered three fingertips. The eyes, full with fear, grew wide. Her jaw worked up and down, but she neither spoke nor made any sounds other than a whimper that came from somewhere deep in her throat.

The brutal scene ends with her putting the bloody hand over her eyes and crying into the mattress. For anyone who saw the movie, they knew she had been raped, and not by a stranger.

Silence filled the audience as the scene clipped off.

"And the winner of the Oscar for best leading actress goes to …" The female presenter who stood next to the guy she couldn't place, pulled the flap open on the golden envelope, slipped out the golden card and looked at the audience, her face holding a slight bit of shock to it. "Claire Edgefield, for her role as Josie Ledson in *Daddy's Little Girl*."

Jack stood quickly, pumped one large fist in the air, and then extended a rough, calloused hand to Claire. She stared at him for a moment, not sure what she had heard. The applause and whistles did nothing to help her comprehend what the actress had said.

"Come on, Claire," Daddy said. "We won."

"We … we … we won?"

"Yes," he said, taking one of her hands and helping her to her feet. She clutched the purse tight to her stomach as her legs, which felt like lead weights, began to wade through those seated to her left until she came to the red-carpeted aisle. Her breath caught again, and she thought she would die before she could take another step. But Claire didn't die. No, she took a step and followed it with several dozens more until she reached the stairs that led to the half C shaped stage.

On her heels was Daddy, the suit making him appear dignified and distinguished. For one moment, Claire was okay with that. They went up the steps, though her legs threatened to give out on her halfway up, and reached the stage. The lights were hotter than she thought they would be.

The presenter—was his name, Owen?—leaned in, gave her a hug and whispered a "congratulations" and a "well deserved." The female handed the Oscar statuette to her. The award was cold in her overly warm and sweaty hands. For the briefest of seconds, she thought she would drop it. How embarrassing would that have been? How angry would Daddy have gotten? She could see his scowl, the way his lips tucked into his mouth. He wouldn't say anything with the entire world watching, but later, in the hotel room, he would say plenty, the least of which had anything to do with embarrassing him.

Claire stepped in front of the microphone and looked out at the many people. To her, it looked like millions, but in reality it was only several hundred and surely not much more than that. She wavered for a second, set the Oscar on the podium. She steadied herself with one shaking hand and took several deep breaths.

"Ummm ..." She hadn't prepared a speech. There was no need. She honestly didn't believe she would win. Not with Nichole Kidman in the lineup. But she had, and there were so many people to thank, and she couldn't remember anyone except for Daddy.

Claire glanced at him. His brows lifted, a "what the hell are you waiting for" expression crossing his face. He put on a fake smile. How many times had he rehearsed the expression in front of the mirror in the bathroom?

Turning back to the crowd, she focused on the one person she idolized, the person she thought would beat her out. Her red hair was pulled up. Strands of it spilled from whatever clip held it in place and fell alongside her face. She wore a dark green dress with just enough cleavage showing Daddy probably noticed her easy enough. Her lips were red—and oh, so bright—and her eyes dazzled.

"I ... I ... ummm ... Wow. I can't believe I won."

Daddy's voice entered her thoughts. *I? Really, Claire? You know it was us. It was always us.*

She bit back tears threatening to slide free, and no, they were not tears of joy, but hot, hateful tears of pure anguish. Her first words came out cracked and unsteady, but her voice grew stronger, or at least as strong as she could make it.

"There's so many people I need to thank, but I'm drawing a blank right now." She rubbed her forehead with two fingers and a thumb. A headache was forming and those bunny rabbit butterflies were back and kicking the tar out of her stomach. "And, I'm so sorry I can't remember anyone's name right this minute. But there is one person I do remember and need to thank ..."

Claire realized she still held the purse tight in her other hand. She was thankful she hadn't left it in her seat.

"Daddy," she said, as the tears brimmed in her eyes. "I just want to say thank you. Without you, I wouldn't be here."

He nodded and mouthed *You're welcome.* He may have even been sincere.

Claire turned back to the audience, took a deep breath and spoke the only words she thought mattered.

"They say experience makes the person. It molds us into who we are."

She paused. *Am I really going to do this?* She bit down on her bottom lip, gave an inward nod and continued.

"Daddy, I have a gift for you, and I know I only have a couple of minutes to do this, so please, don't play the music yet."

Claire opened her purse and reached in. She turned to her Daddy, Jack Edgefield, the man who had raised her since her mother left. The man who had shown her what real talent was, how to act and show true pain.

She slid the pistol out, let the purse fall to the shining floor. Claire stretched her arm toward Daddy—Dear Daddy—and swallowed as if she had a mouthful of sand. His eyes widened, and he put his hands out in front of him.

There was a murmur of words from the audience, several loud gasps, and even a few screams, but no one moved. Not even the security guards at the entrances or along the edges of the backstage.

"Don't move, Daddy," she said. "Do you know why I took the role of Josie in *Daddy's Little Girl*? You don't? Let me tell you. If not for you raping me over and over when I was little, I wouldn't have known how to show the type of fear portrayed in that movie. It reminded me so much of you. And me. The pain and shame Josie felt—that was all me. The hate she felt for her father throughout the movie was all me.

I never understood why Momma left us until I saw the way you manipulate women. I never understood, until I saw you strike that one girl. You know, the one you buried out in the shop before you put in the concrete floor."

She gave a laugh—an exasperated, pained sound everyone could hear, even all the way to the back of the room.

"Where's Momma, Daddy?"

He shook his head, mouthed, *I don't know.*

"Come on, Daddy. Yes, you do. You know where Momma is, don't you? Go ahead, tell me the truth."

He shook his head and glanced behind Claire. His brows lifted as if saying *help me* to someone, but no one moved. No one made even the slightest motion to help him. They were all as stunned as Claire was when they announced her as the best leading actress. Really? She was good. She had experience, and experiences made the person and she had pain within her. Oh, yes, she had plenty of pain buried deep inside her.

"Claire, this isn't funny," Daddy—no, Jack—said. His hands were still out in front of him, and he shook his head.

"I'm not laughing."

"Come on, now. Let's put the gun down."

He took a step forward. If he wanted, he could take a second one and be within arm's reach of her, and she had no doubt he would.

"Don't move," she growled.

He stopped, a sudden, startled action.

"Where is my momma?" she asked again. "I know where

she is, Daddy. I know where you hid her body. But, I want you to tell me."

Claire had never admitted her mother was dead. To do so meant facing the truth and no longer harboring the bitter pill of anger deep in her heart—a pain she had been able to act out quite well as Josie Ledson. Now it was out, now she had confessed to herself the truth she had always known. The bitter pill grew tenfold for Jack, the man whom she called Daddy as recently as five seconds earlier; a man she would never recognize as a father figure from that day forward.

Jack's jaw slackened. Recognition dawned bright on his face. His eyes seemed to shrink in their sockets, just as his body seemed to deflate. He took a deep breath, turned his head slightly to one side, his eyes remaining on hers.

"I know you killed her," Claire whispered, but with the microphone just to the side of her, the audience heard every painful word. "Just admit it, and everything will be okay."

Neither of them moved. The audience held their collective breaths, all of them hanging on each movement, each word spoken, much like a well thought out and acted script. Their bodies were tense, some had hands to mouths while others stared on in what many would later say was horror, too scared and engrossed in the events unfolding to move even the slightest muscle.

Then Jack's hands fell to his side and he nodded, a simple up, down and back to center. "Okay," he said. This the audience didn't hear, but Claire did. "Louder," she said, gritting her teeth. Her jaw hurt from clenching it tight.

"Claire."

"Louder," she yelled. He flinched. Claire wanted to laugh at him. How many times had she jerked awake to his hand on her thigh or cupping a breast? How many times did she almost scream when he entered her room with an odd look in his eyes, the one that said we're going to pretend you are not my daughter tonight? How many times had she cried herself to sleep and hurt deeply the next few days after one of his visits?

"Claire, please."

She laughed. Please? He sounded like she did when …

Claire extended her arm to fully straight, tightened her grip on the pistol, her finger touching the cold steel of the trigger. Tears rolled down her face. "Louder!"

He took another deep breath, but something wasn't right. Jack Edgefield opened his mouth to speak. Instead, he lunged for her, arms extended, hands like desperate claws. The anger on his face was evident and washed in defiant determination.

Claire screamed, pulled the trigger and threw one hand over her head as she ducked. Jack's hand grazed the side of her face as he fell. A neatly manicured nail sliced her cheek. He rolled onto his back and put a hand to his chest. Blood bloomed on his white shirt, and spilled through his fingers. He opened his mouth. His eyes watered.

Vaguely, Claire was aware of the sounds of screams and crying and people rushing the stage.

"Put the gun down," a disembodied voice said from somewhere in another world.

She looked to her left to see a uniformed police officer, his weapon drawn and pointed at her. To her right, stood the stunned presenters.

Claire set the gun on the floor, put her hands on her face and cried. A moment later, she felt the warm arms of a man, holding her tight and whispering *everything will be okay*.

But, would it? Would anything ever be okay again?

She stared at Jack. His hand had fallen away from his chest, and the patch of blood on his shirt had swelled and run down one side, pooling on the floor beneath him. His eyes had already begun to dim. She was in trouble. She knew it, but she didn't care. The weight of the last few years of living with her dad—living with Jack—had lifted.

"No more acting lessons," she said and closed her eyes. Her hands no longer shook.

Black Storms

I'm not so sure about this whole end of the world thing. All those post rapture parties and looting and all the trash talk that went on about it. I'm not going to lie and say I wasn't intrigued by it—I think that's the right word at least. It's not the first time someone went and predicted the end of the world and all. None of those other folks had anything solid to back up their beliefs. I ain't so sure this guy did either, but at least he didn't try to poison anyone with the red Kool-aid.

May 21, 2011. That's the date he set forth. Starting with a massive earthquake, the world would be in ruins, and all those who were good Christians were going on up into Heaven, their physical bodies left behind for the spiritual ones they would claim. He even gave us a time. Six p.m. Eastern. I wondered a little about that. No, not the earthquakes and the rapture and all. Okay, maybe I did wonder a bit about all of that, too. But, really, I wondered about the time. This guy said he knew the exact time. If you think about it, that's kind of scary. Kind of like a death sentence for the world and six-oh-clock was the time the switch would be thrown. My question is simple; who had the clock that would read the right time? If it were six-oh-two at my house, it very well could have been five-fifty-nine in someone else's. The clock in Momma's room was set seven minutes fast. Was her six p.m. the time the earthquakes were to hit and end the world or was it someone else's? Was it six in the evening in Australia when it would happen? If so, it wouldn't be six here in my neck of the woods.

I didn't rightly know, and I don't think anyone else did either. Including the religious radio guy claiming all this.

I live down here in the south in a little town where there are no stoplights, and people can still park on the street without feeding a meter all their hard-earned coins. We all know each other, and we all look out for one another. It's the way things ought to be: one big family caring about one another, even if a couple of them folks weren't liked too much to start with. Like Billy Johansen, a transplant here in Briar's Ridge who arrived as a drunk, but got him a bit of the Holy love, and he done become a changed man. There's Billy's brother James, as well—a couple years older and a lot meaner than Billy, even when he wasn't drinking. Ain't anyone in town cared much for James at all, but we tolerated him because of Billy. Well, Momma liked him some. She said all bad people have good in them and all good people have bad in them. The good just didn't shine through with James.

You may be wondering what I'm getting on about and I plan on telling you, but you have to understand, not many folks in the cities or even the larger towns have it all figured out yet. Me, I think I do.

You see, the whole May 21st thing—that fellow might not have been so wrong after all. He just had some of his facts all mixed up. Kind of like back in 1994 when he said the world would end then. Remember that? He said he was wrong because of some math'matic error in his figures. That's just as well, I reckon. Momma said it wasn't no math'matic error made him wrong, but God had said no man would know the day or hour. If anyone would know what she was talking 'bout, it would be Momma. I ain't never seen anyone with the Holy up in them the way it was with Momma. She taught me the ways of righteousness, and I ain't never really gone astray too much. Maybe when I was a little younger and needed some of them wild oats tended to, but after I matured a little I stayed on the straight and narrow. Momma could put the fear in a person, and I didn't like it when she put it in me.

The fellow who went and predicted the end of the world was so certain it was coming he got him a bunch of followers and they spread the word like it was wildfire. They believed, that much is for certain. And you have to give them credit for their beliefs. If a few more people would have went and believed old Noah, then they might have survived them rains and the flood.

Here's the thing. Remember, he said he knew the time and the date. Well, maybe he got it part right. You see, I think he had the year all wrong, but the rest of it, and in what manner it would happen, was just a little off. No, it didn't happen in 2011 like he said it would. It didn't even happen in 2012 or 2013 or 2014. But I'm a reckoning, it just may have come in 2015.

Just stick with me here, okay?

The earthquake didn't quite rumble like they thought, starting out at one part of the world and shivering its way throughout the rest of it. And it didn't happen *when* they thought. But there *were* some tremors on May 21st of the good old year of 2015. Might have been caused by all them storms out this way at the time, but I know the ground went and shook. and I ain't the only one who said so. Mary Marie Mackey said the storm rattled her windows something fierce and a couple of her good china fell out the cabinets and broke on the floor in her dining room. And down at the fill station, Mr. Harvey told me (while rubbing that bald head of his with a greasy rag) the sign went and fell from the door and clattered on the front stoop. Teddy Jones' hounds barked their fool heads off a few minutes before the earthquake started and right up to the last tremor. Then they hushed up and went under his porch where they stayed the rest of the night.

Then the storms started. From what I heard at the grocery store, Teddy Jones thought his dogs were dying by the way they brayed and howled and ran around in circles. Down my way in the little shack I shared with Momma and Aunt Louisa, lights flickered a few times before going all the way out. I had my matches and candles and lanterns all ready, seeing how we had a bunch of storms before the quake. Just before those lights went out, the black sky was streaked all yellow and the thunder came down like a giant foot trying to squash my house. My old legs trembled, and I fell to the floor and bumped my knee mighty hard. Don't you think I didn't look down at my watch just before them lights went out? It was one before six, according to Timex. And don't you think I didn't wonder about the man and his prediction right then. I did, and I just knew the world had finally met its end.

Momma, she was asleep at the time—getting in her mid-evening nap—and I didn't think nothing of it when she didn't come running all fired up, heart thumping and her cane out in front of her. Aunt Louisa—she ain't really my aunt, but the woman who cared for Momma and had since I can remember way back when—came tumbling out of her bedroom, her shirt hanging off one shoulder and sagging just enough to show me the top of one of her wrinkly breasts when I lit the lantern. I pulled the light away and looked toward the parlor room window.

"That's some rumblin' out there tonight," Aunt Louisa said and got up right next to me. I could smell her joint cream and the stale odor of cigarettes on her breath.

"It ain't night, yet," I said back.

"It's awful dark out there for it not to be night."

I could hear her yellowed nails scratching on dry skin. Later on, she would put on some more ointment and go to bed, but the sound of nails on skin 'bout made me want to scream for her to stop. I didn't say anything, though. I just stared out the window at the big dark world beyond it. There was no more lightning or thunder, and the rain that usually came with these evening storms in the south never arrived. It just stayed dark, like night decided to show up early and tell day it could take an extended rest.

By then it was after six—had to be well after in some places—and guess what? The world hadn't ended. I stood there as right in the head as I am now. Aunt Louisa stood beside me, her stale breath and lotioned skin still stinking up the room. There wasn't no real earthquake, and we didn't get raptured away. No, all was the same, except the darkness outside.

"I reckon the world ain't gonna end tonight," I said and left the window. Aunt Louisa mumbled something about believing such nonsense and headed back to her room.

I thought nothing else of it.

The next morning, I woke to Aunt Louisa screaming from down the hall. I sat straight up in the bed and tried to get to my

68

feet. My head was woozy from sitting up too fast, and when I stood I crumpled on down to the floor. I reckon the sheets all bundled up around my feet were the main culprit, but the racket going on between my ears couldn't have helped none.

"Jeddy," she screamed in her old crow's voice. Jeddy ain't really my name. It's Jed, but Momma called me Jeddy when I was a little tot, and it kinda stuck.

I struggled to stand, my legs hurting and my head all dizzy. I got to my feet and staggered out the room and along the hall. I had to use one hand against the wall to keep from toppling over, but once I reached where Aunt Louisa stood screaming, nothing would have kept me from dropping to my knees.

Momma lay on her bedroom floor, one side of her head pressed against the hardwood, ringlets of gray hair covering her face. I didn't need to walk over to her and check for any heartbeat or feel for breath coming from her mouth. I could tell from the doorway she was as dead as she was going to get. Momma's skin was all black, like she had been tossed on the fire pit for a few minutes—just enough to dust the skin with a coating of ash.

Aunt Louisa, knelt down in the corner, her hands to her face, her eyes all big with croc'dile tears in them. And, Lordy, she screamed. She screamed until she went hoarse and then tried to holler some more. I walked on over to Momma, got down beside her and brushed some of the gray from her face. Her skin wasn't dusted like I thought, but smooth like it always was. The color had just changed from milky white to dark as night, but, it was her eyes that made my bowels almost re- lease. They were missing. No, not poked out or burned out or anything like that. Just missing. Inside her skull I could see a mass of something I reckon was brain, or it may have just been where her eyes may have rolled off to. At any rate, those green eyes that were Momma's pride and joy were missing, and it scared me something awful.

I gathered Aunt Louisa up, helping her out the room and back to her own. I laid her in the bed and put a cold rag on her forehead. Eventually her crying became sniffles and she dozed off to sleep. I went out to the porch stoop and sat for a spell in my rocker. A smoke of tobacco would have been nice right 'bout then, but I didn't have no desire to go back in the house for my smokes. Momma was dead, and as far as I was concerned, the preacher man had been right for the most part—my world had just ended. I don't reckon that's what he meant, but that's what it felt like.

I had to set to burying Momma, but it was the Sabbath day. Ain't no one supposed to work on the Sabbath day, though I think the Bible did allow for burials if needed. I went down the hall to Momma's room to check on her. Nothing had changed. She still lay dead on the floor, her face still all smashed on the hardwood. I closed her door, and my spine set to shaking something bad. It's like someone took an ice cube and ran it from my tailbone to the back end of my skull.

From there I eased on down to Aunt Louisa's room. She lay asleep, her back to me. I let out a quiet breath, releasing a bunch of stress that had grabbed hold of me since the day before. I closed her door and went to the front porch again. The morning was already hot, and my skin grew sticky from standing at the top step looking out at the risen sun and cloudless sky. I wondered if it would be all right to miss just one Sunday scripture lesson, then thought I might want to just go on in and get closer to the Lord. He would hear me better in His house, or so Momma always said.

My Sunday best didn't consist of much: a pair of overalls with only one hole in the right knee, a button-down shirt I had to roll up to the elbows so no one would know it only came to my forearms, and my old work boots—the ones I got right before they retired me from the rock quarry when I was forty-two. I donned my best and grabbed my old King James from the coffee table in the first room—what city folk call their living room.

I don't drive none. Not since retiring with these rickety knees always wanting to sit me down when they needed some rest. The folks at the traffic department said I was unfit for driving. So, I walked the mile or so to the church house.

70

By the time I got there my legs were all angry and wanting to quit their working right then. Sitting on a wooden pew near the back was a welcome relief.

Preacher Harry was there, he with the dashing white hair and salesman's smile, as Momma always put it. She used to say, "If'n he can make it into Heaven, the devil can." I never quite understood what she meant, but I figured if the rapture did happen the day before, well, surely Preacher Harry would have been lifted up with the others. Or maybe Momma knew what she was talking 'bout.

Here's the thing; everyone showed up who normally showed up. Well, except for Momma and Aunt Louisa. Billy Johansen was there with his shock of red hair and in his gray wool suit. Now certainly if the world had come to an end and the saved had been lifted on up into Heaven, Billy Johansen would have been one of the first to go. With him sitting in his usual spot near the pulpit, I reckoned the prophesy of the apoc'lypse just wasn't true, and I reckoned my wondering mind ought to give it a rest. That prophesy was four years beyond its happening anyway.

After services, Preacher Harry came up and asked about Momma and Aunt Louisa. His hand was all sweaty, and he brushed a lock of hair from his forehead as if it were a fly buzzing 'round.

"They're not themselves today, Preacher-man," I said.

"Are they sick, Jeddy?"

I shrugged. "I reckon so."

"We'll be praying for them," Preacher Harry said, clapped me on the back, and turned his attention to pretty little Mary Marie Mackey.

I made my way home, my heart heavy like it was full of rocks. I went in and checked on Aunt Louisa, and she ain't budged none. After I mourned Momma's death for a while, I made my way round back to the shed where Pop's pickaxe and shovels were. I picked a spot near Momma's garden and set to burying Momma. It was mid-evening before I had the hole deep enough to bury her in, and by then I was plum exhausted. I ain't all too proud to say I didn't go ahead and bury Momma, but my bones ain't never been all that strong, and they were feeling as brittle as ice out on Corley's pond in the winter. I sat down, meaning only to take a small rest, and fell asleep. It was morning before I woke.

My back and legs and arms were stiff, and it hurt to move. It took a while to get going. Even then, I only made it as far as the couch before having to sit down for a spell. I finally got going again and made my way back to Momma's room. I put her in an old sheet and dragged her out to the grave. I tried to be gentle. There ain't but a couple ways you can get a body into a hole: pick it up and carry it in or roll it down, like it was a log. I hated rolling her in, but it was the only way I could get her in by myself.

Filling the hole was a lot easier than digging it. I placed a cinder block at the head of the grave until I could make her a proper cross. Sweat soaked my clothes and poured down my face. My legs and arms shook as I went back inside, sat at the kitchen table, and drank a cup of ice water.

Aunt Louisa didn't get out of bed that day, and by the next— that would have been Tuesday—I was a little worried. I went into her room to check on her. She hadn't moved from the day before. She also had a smell about her, like something dead being trapped in a box that sat out in the sun all day. Unlike Momma, who died of something I didn't understand at the time, Aunt Louisa died of something more natural; I think of a heart attack or the stress of having found Momma like she was.

My shoulders slumped, my heart dipped. All the family I had died in around four days. My bones and muscles hurt from digging the first grave. Now I needed to dig a second one. I went outside and drove the pickaxe into the ground next to where I buried Momma. It was slow going—much more so than the first time—and the heat was an oven cooking my skin and insides.

I didn't think much of the time when I finished. The sky had changed. Clouds bumped together, blocking out the sun and making the world look like night, all early like the past Saturday. Lightning lit up the undersides of those black clouds and thunder followed close on its heels. I set the tools back in Pop's shed and closed the door before the wind got to picking up. The rain started coming down halfway back to the house, but there wasn't no hurrying for me—my body was mad and the muscles were crying out. Even though I was under the porch roof, I ducked at the sound of hailstones coming down.

"Gonna be another rumbler."

An hour or so passed, and when I looked at the clock it read five fifty-nine. I thought it had been much later. I stood and headed for the kitchen. The house got dark as the lights went out. I stopped, my hands out in front of me. Then another one of them bright bolts filled the outside world again, lighting up the room in its magnificent yellow. The floor shook and the windows rattled as the thunder followed close behind it. The wall kept me from falling to the floor.

Just like that, it was over. No more rain or hail. No more wind. The lightning and thunder was gone, leaving behind the dark. A chill crept up into my bones. Though I knew I needed to bury Aunt Louisa, I no longer wanted to go outside, not with the blackness swallowing up everything out there. I went to the window and stared out for a while. I saw nothing beyond the glass in front of me, not even the porch.

That night I didn't bury Aunt Louisa.

I got up early the next morning. The sun burned off the rain and dew left behind from the night before, and steam rose from the ground like a wet fog. By then, Aunt Louisa was ripe with the stink. I didn't bother with getting another sheet or a blanket. I just pulled the ones from her bed and wrapped her in those. I ain't gonna lie none, I 'bout threw up several times until I got her folded away and those sheets sealed up with duct tape. I dragged her from the house, carefully going down the steps, and set her on the lip of the grave. I rolled her in, and, just like when I buried Momma, I felt all sick inside for not placing her in the ground all gentle-like. She landed with a slight splash in the partially water-filled grave.

When I was finished, I went inside and showered for the first time in several days. I didn't realize how bad I stank until I peeled off the clothes and the reek of sweat and odor hit me. The water was cold on my skin, and I washed, rinsed, and stood there until I felt clean, though only on the outside. The inside needed more than just soap and water. It needed hard prayer, and I set myself to getting dressed.

'Round suppertime, I made my way to the church for the Wednesday night prayer meeting. A lot of folk were there, but one person was missing: Billy Johansen. Just 'bout everyone noticed. Preacher Harry even commented on it during the service and made sure to lift his name up in prayer.

After services, I made my way 'round the corner so I could talk to Preacher Harry 'bout Momma and Aunt Louisa. I found him standing awful close to Mary Marie Mackey, almost pressed up against her. Her blue eyes were wide, and she looked scared. I didn't hear what Preacher Harry said, but I saw Mary Marie's face screw up like she was 'bout to scream. She slapped the side of his face with an open palm and pushed by him, tears in her eyes.

"Mary Marie, are you alright?" I asked, as she hurried by. She didn't answer. I turned to Preacher Harry.

"She just got some bad news, Jeddy," he said with his car salesman smile. "She'll be all right in time. Don't worry none about her." He walked off, leaving me there, slack jawed and confused and worried. I had seen him pressed all up against her, and why would she have slapped him like that? Momma's words came back strong. "If'n he can get into Heaven, the Devil can."

I didn't get to talk to Preacher Harry before he was gone out the door and chasing him just wasn't happening. Instead, I started my walk home. Halfway there, I reached the crossroads which would take me into town if I chose one way, or toward Billy Johansen's place if I chose the other. Billy never missed church. If them doors were open, then he's there, rain or shine, hot or cold. It never minded none to Billy. He used to say, "If I ain't in church, then I've done been called home." I don't reckon many folk thought much about that, seeing how the locals say sim'lar things, but they didn't mean it the way Billy did. Billy believed when the roll is called up yonder, he'd be there, singing and praising and having him a right good time.

The walk to Billy's home took me a mile out the way. My poor legs were going to be fussing for a few days, but I reckoned after the previous events and all the extra work I had done burying Momma and Aunt Louisa, it wasn't going to hurt any to go and have a chat with Billy. I strolled up into the yard as the sun was going down. Wasn't much to the place: green grass lined with dead flowers in tire planters. The white paint on the house flaked, and the shutters were closed over the windows.

The first step creaked beneath me, and I heard a voice call from inside, "Who's there?" It was James, and he didn't sound like he wanted company.

"Jeddy Sanford from down a ways," I called back.

"Go away."

I stood on the first step, part of me saying I should get out of there before James came out the front door. The other part, though, it told me something was wrong, and I should stick around, try to help if I could. It told me James wasn't going to hurt me none at all.

"James Johansen is your brother, Billy, home?"

James didn't say nothing at first. I made to call to him again, and just as I got his name out my mouth, the door opened up. James stood there, whiskey bottle in hand, hair all a mess. His eyes were swallowed up in blue and gray puffs. He leaned against the jamb. "Billy ain't here no more."

I frowned. "What do you mean?"

"What'd I say, boy?" James took a couple steps toward me, staggering from side to side like he was 'bout to fall down. He reached the porch column at the top of the steps and looked down on me. Even in the dying sunlight I could see the tears on his face.

"What's wrong, James?" I asked. I ain't gonna lie, I was

scared. I had seen that type of look on a few of the boys' fac-es at the quarry before they lost their jobs. It was madness, and it looked like it had hold of James.

"Why don't you just go away, Jeddy Sanford?"

I backed away, gave a nod, "I reckon I could, but I really would like to know where Billy went and ran off to."

"Billy ain't ran off to nowhere," he said, looking back to the front door. "He's in there."

"But, you just said—"

"I know what I said!" James yelled, throwing the bottle at me. I barely got out the way as it struck the ground behind me. He stumbled backward and slumped against the wall. Then that big old boy started sobbing like a little girl who done got her ponytail pulled.

"What's all the fuss, James?" I asked and went up the steps. I stopped at the top one, not sure it would be safe to go much further.

He looked up at me, his eyes all pulled down right along with his lips, making his face look sadder than any I had ever seen. "It's Billy … he ain't gone nowhere."

"Is he inside?"

He shrugged, pointed with his thumb toward the door. "I reckon you can see for yourself."

Fear saddled up beside me, laughing in my ear as it ran one of its fingers along my skin. I hurried passed James, afraid he might take a swing at me, and went into the house. Billy sat on the couch in the front room, his chin on his chest, arms down at his sides. His skin was all black, like Momma's had been. I inched a little closer and knelt down to look into his face. His eyes were missing.

I stumbled backward, landing hard on my tailbone. Pain went up my back and down into one leg, and I rolled onto my belly. Though I was hurting, I got to my feet and all but ran out of there. James didn't try to stop me as I hobbled down the steps, my heart in my throat and skin tingling. Somewhere in the back of my head I heard Fear laughing at me, a hoarse, raspy sound, and I ran harder up the road.

It was plum dark when I got home. My legs ached, and the spot on my tailbone where I landed pulsed as if it had a heartbeat of its own. Once inside, I sat on the couch. It was tough to breathe, and that laughter came and went, came and went, like it was part of me and not something in my head.

My mind was a mess, thoughts coming and going, not sticking 'round long enough for me to really grab hold to. Snot ran down from my nose. I wiped it away with the back of my hand. As I sat there with those muddled thoughts, I got scared even more than I had been. What was going on? Momma had been all black, the same as Billy Johansen, and it wasn't the color of a dark man's skin, but something more like the shade of dirty marble. Their eyes were missing, and this bothered me more than anything. I didn't know why, but for some reason, those missing eyes were trying to tell me something.

I went on to bed, my body shaken and unnerved, my mind sluggish from all that had happened. I didn't think I would ever sleep again, but I was wrong. Sleep found me soon enough, and I went willingly.

It was afternoon of the next day before I woke. I didn't get up to do much more than take a leak, then crawled back beneath the sheets and hoped and prayed the world would straighten itself out, and things would get back to normal soon enough. That day turned to night and then another day. I didn't do much then either, just laid in bed.

Sunday came and I stayed in bed for a while. Come the afternoon, I got up. Toast and coffee and a long shower and I still didn't feel all that great. I knew what I needed to do. Ain't no better place to pray than at the Lord's house.

I left earlier than normal, wanting to get to the evening service before all the other folks. Maybe Preacher Harry would be there, and I could talk to him about what I had seen, about what I thought. Exhaustion grabbed hold of me pretty good as I reached the double doors and went inside. The preacher wasn't anywhere to be seen. I left the sanctuary and made my way down the hall to the Sunday School wing.

I heard voices and followed them. Rounding the corner, I

stopped. In the hall right near to the preacher's study stood Preacher Harry and Mary Marie Mackey. He had her pinned against the wall, just like on Wednesday night, a hand on one of her breasts. Tears streaked her face, and she let out a big sob. Her eyes caught mine, and she called my name.

Preacher Harry, he turned 'round to see me, his face all full of shock, and red blossoming on his cheeks. He moved his hand right quick-like, and let Mary Marie off the wall. She folded her arms across her chest and got behind me. I figured out right quickly what Preacher Harry was doing or 'bout to do, and Mary Marie didn't want no part of it. Momma was right again. If he was getting into Heaven, the devil was, too.

Preacher Harry put his hands out like he was 'bout to give me some excuse as to what had happened. He got out, "Jeddy, listen ..." before the rumblings started outside. I knew what was coming, and I just wanted out of there. Preacher Harry could do his 'splaining some other time and to the church board. I grabbed Mary Marie by the hand and we hurried back to the sanctuary and looked out the double doors. Clouds had rolled in, and the wind whipped the trees across the way. Lightning struck one of them, and it split in half.

I closed the door and pulled Mary Marie toward one of the pews. She pulled against me, shook her head when she saw Preacher Harry. "I wanna go home."

I looked up at the clock on the wall just above the doors. I ain't so sure why, I just did. It red five fifty-one.

"Mary Marie, I don't think we ought to go anywhere right now. That storm's coming in pretty quick.

She looked toward Preacher Harry and started crying again. "Please, Jeddy. Please, get me away from here."

I gave a nod and let out probably the deepest sigh I ever had. "Okay, Mary Marie, let's get you on home."

"It's about to storm," Preacher Harry said. "Y'all don't want to go out in that."

Mary Marie looked at me all doe-eyed and scared. I couldn't deny her what she wanted, even if I thought it was best. I took her hand, and we bolted right out the door and into the pouring rain. The wind whipped us from side to side, but we ran on like our lives depended on it. The hail came as we reached the shade trees. A big gust of wind pushed me backward, and I let go of Mary Marie's hand before I fell. She stumbled a few more feet and …

You remember what I said about the preacher who claimed the end had come and the rapture was supposed to have taken place on May 21st? Remember how I said he might not have been off by much, just maybe had some of his facts all wrong? Well, when I fell down and Mary Marie staggered further on down the road, one of them bright bolts of lightning streaked the sky, making the world all yellow 'round us. Thunder rumbled long and loud, and it shook the earth something fierce, and I couldn't get to my feet on account of the world shaking.

When the lightning struck, Mary Marie, she stopped her scrambling for the shade trees. In that moment, while the world was all yellow, I saw the truth of what the preacher man had spoke of. Mary Marie's body shook right along with the ground, her hands down at her sides. Then, from out the sky came something black—a shadow with wings, all dark against the yellow of the lightning. It wasn't large at all—maybe the size of one of them red hawks that frequent the woods out here, but it wasn't no hawk or any other bird. The creature had legs and arms and a head like a person. It landed on Mary Marie's chest, its hands gripping tight to her face.

As the lightning's yellow glow faded, the creature grabbed Mary Marie's eyes and yanked them right out of their sockets. Mary Marie didn't scream at all. And the creature, it took off, its wings flapping and sounding like the heavy wind. It took with her Mary Marie's eyes and … trailing after it was something all white that flowed right out of Mary Marie's sockets. It went straight up into the black. I watched it go until it was no longer there.

When I looked back at Mary Marie, she lay on the ground. I crawled over to her, and I didn't need no light to know her skin was the same awful black as Momma's and Billy Johansen's had been. It was like when the creature pulled out her eyes and took to flying, it pulled her soul right out her body, and her soul ... her righteous soul, was the light that made her what she was, and with it gone, all that was left was black.

I don't know if I screamed, or if I bawled like a kid. I do know after a while I ran. I ran like there was no tomorrow, and in truth, there may not be many tomorrows left. At home, I crawled up in my bed. I stayed there for several days, my Bible all clutched to my chest, my little prayers like whispers to God in hopes I don't get left here with the likes of Preacher Harry and all those bad people who do bad things to others.

My hand's cramping real good right now. I reckon I've been writing this the better part of the day, but I want to get this done and over with.

I get out of bed every once in a while and look out the windows, watching for the storms. There's been three more since Mary Marie died. Each time I hid in my closet, all scared of the creature. I ain't so sure it will come for me like it did the others, and I ain't so sure it was an angel or the other type of creature. All I know is it comes at the end of the storms and it takes your soul. I hope and pray it takes them on up into Heaven.

Right now, it's a storming pretty bad outside. I can feel the wind and the thunder rock the house. This storm's a little rougher than the others. It may be time. It just may be the end of the world. I can say this for certain: ain't no one knows the time when it will happen. Maybe the radio preacher man was on the right track. Maybe he had the date right for the *beginning* of the end. And maybe all the saved are being taken up one soul at a ...

Anymore

We'll be back together again one day.

"It's time, B."

"I know."

"Let's go."

"I'm not ready, H."

"You never will be."

They sat in his car—a beat up Toyota, the red flaking off in places—in the parking lot that led to the small town's Riverwalk. Day was giving way to dusk. In another hour or so the sun would be down and about an hour later, the moon would start its nightly ritual of rising high.

It's amazing how deserted this place can be in the winter, but in the summer ...

His thoughts were cut off by her hand taking his. When he looked at her, B had tears in her blue eyes. His heart sank.

"Come on, B. You can do this. I know you can."

"I can't." She looked away from him and out the window. A man and a little boy walked passed her door. The boy wore a ball cap that was too big for his small head. It was cocked to one side, the local university's logo clearly visible. The man held the boy's hand in one of his. A leash was in the other hand, a dog tugging on it as if saying, faster, faster, faster.

H touched her arm. Her skin was clammy, as if it were spilling tears right along with her eyes.

"We can go," he said, dropped his hand from her arm, and put the key in the ignition. The motor turned over, but H didn't put it in gear. Instead, he watched five people not much younger than he and B walk by them—two boys three girls, all wearing bathing suits and carrying inner tubes. He couldn't hear them, but he could see them clearly. One of the boys said something, and the other four laughed. One of the girls—a brunette with her hair in a ponytail and wearing a one-piece bathing suit—tilted her head back, her mouth wide open. He wondered, briefly, what her laugh sounded like.

It wasn't like he wished he knew. It was just a thought. Nothing more. Nothing less. It's just the way his mind worked. He was inquisitive by nature.

Not as beautiful as B's, he thought.

He stared out the window, his mind slogging through the nothing of his thoughts. Everything had stopped when he looked at B and saw the tears rolling down her face. He shook his head and then put the car in reverse. He let off the brake and let the car roll back as he looked behind him.

"Stop," B said, her hand grabbing his forearm.

H mashed the brake, and the car lurched to a stop.

"What?" he asked, and hated how it sounded when it came out.

"Let's stay." She smiled, but it wasn't her usual shine. Sure, her dimples showed, but her teeth were hidden and her eyes told of sadness and fear and … regret? Yeah, regret. Maybe that's what held her back all these years.

"Are you sure?"

She nodded, a jerky motion, but still it was a commitment.

H put the car back in gear and pulled into the parking spot again. He shifted into park, turned the key, and the engine shut off. The car shuddered when it did. They sat quietly for several minutes. More people passed the car on both sides, making their way to the concrete sidewalk that led to the river and off to either the left or the right. There were two women in yoga pants and girly tank tops, their arms swinging from side to side, their elbows out as if they were going to take flight. There were three mop-topped teenaged boys on skate boards, each one wearing torn jeans and Converses and shirts with the names of punk or ska bands scrawled across the fronts. There were couples and kids and families and even an old man with a cane hooked on his forearm pushing an old lady in a wheel chair. A brief thought came to H that would have tickled him any other time: *I wonder if he is going to roll her right into the river.*

"What are you smiling about?" B asked.

"Huh? What?"

"You're smiling. Why?"

Sweat beaded along his forehead, and his face suddenly felt hot. "I ... I ... ummm ... I didn't know I was."

B gave a quick nod. "Sure, you didn't."

"Really. I didn't."

B almost laughed. H saw it in the sudden flicker in her eyes. There was a smile on her face, though he thought she tried to hide it. There was no hiding the dimples. No matter how hard she tried she would never be able to conceal the truth those dimples always spoke. B took a deep breath, blew it out and up. The air blew through the few strands of blond hair that dangled in front of her eyes.

"If we're going to do this, let's do it now."

H's smile faded, and then he was out his door and rounding the car where he met her as she stepped out.

"Are you sure?"

"Are you trying to talk me out of it?"

"No. No. No. I just ... let's go."

"Forgetting something?"

"What? Forgetting ... what?" His eyes widened as he realized what she meant. H went to the back of the car and popped the trunk. Inside, among the jumbled tools, flat spare tire, and old clothes he would probably never wear again but hadn't thrown out yet, was a cardboard box, its flaps folded one over the other to keep it closed. He lifted it out, carefully keeping it level. He elbowed the trunk shut.

"Got it," he said and held the two-foot-wide box out so she could see it.

B smiled. It wasn't quite real yet, but H saw it as a good sign. *She's on her way back.*

On her way back? She hadn't been the same since ... he shook his head, forcing the thoughts and memories away.

They walked together, not quite hand in hand, but with her

hand slipped between his elbow and ribs, as if he were escorting her to a seat at a fancy ball or wedding. The sidewalk sloped down and forked thirty or so feet from the river. To their left was the bridge that connected the sleepy town to the not-so-sleepy city. A small dirt path led down an embankment to the river directly in front of them. The river, itself, was a rolling mass of water white capping along the rocks and filled with people on inner tubes or kayaks, riding their way to calmer waters four or so miles away. If they went beyond the bridge, they would have come to an amphitheater where a large crowd had gathered to hear a local duo play their brand of music in support of a new album. To their right, the sidewalk extended those same three or four miles through the woods. They went right, following the path as it winded, first through an open expanse of grass on one side where some kids played with a soccer ball, and the river rolled on the other, and then into the once thick woods that had been trimmed back within the last three years since the Riverwalk was developed.

Just before entering the trees, B stopped. She chewed on her lower lip, a sure sign she was nervous.

"It's okay, B."

"Right around the corner," she whispered.

"Yeah. I know."

She slid her arm all the way around his and clung a little tighter to him as they entered the wooded area. The temperature dropped and the sun disappeared, only poking holes in their gray surroundings where branches and leaves had parted above them. They walked slowly until they came to where the sidewalk went straight, and a dirt path bent further toward the river. Again, she stopped and bit her lip. Tears shimmered in her blue eyes, and she sniffled. She started to speak, but stopped. H didn't ask what she almost said. He knew if he did they would be backtracking out of there.

Finally she did speak, and her voice cracked and faded in and out as she did so. "I can't. This hurts too much." Tears spilled down her face.

H looked away from her and toward the dirt path. Less than fifty yards and the past would be right in front of them. Less than fifty yards away is where they lost Dorian. B was right. It hurt, but turning around and running from it would continue to drag her down, to destroy the person he loved more than life itself. Eventually ... eventually it would destroy her, just like it did Robert.

H said the only thing he could think to say: "B, we have to unite them. It's what Robert wanted."

They stood in silence for several minutes. A bike rider zoomed by them calling out 'On your right,' as he did so.

"Okay," B said, sniffled again and then wiped her eyes with her palms. "Let's go."

She slid her arm back around his, and they stepped off the path. His legs shook as they made their way to the edge of the river. He could almost hear Dorian and Robert, B's friends since grade school. He could almost hear their laughter, their joking around. He closed his eyes for a second, trying to force the sounds from his mind. When he opened them they had stopped and were standing at the edge of the embankment and the downward slope that led to the water.

"Do you remember what happened?" B asked.

"Yeah. I don't think it's something I'll ever forget."

"We were drunk, weren't we?"

He shrugged. "They drank a lot more than we did. I wasn't going to take you home to your parents drunk, so no, we weren't loaded. But Dorian ..."

"She was my best friend."

"I know."

B sniffled. An audible sob came from her. H knew if he looked at her he would probably cry as well, so he looked straight ahead. Guilt washed over him, and he wondered if it would go away with the passage of time, or maybe it would linger forever, just as it had done for B and Robert over the last four years. Or maybe it would claim them all. It had already taken Robert, thanks to a rope and a sturdy light fixture in the basement of the house he and a couple of buddies had rented.

And just like the snap of fingers, it came rushing back. They had been drinking, but H told the truth, Dorian and Robert had a lot more than B and H. At one point there had been some dancing and probably a little more than some heavy petting going on. Day turned to night, and the little stretch of land that would become part of the town's Riverwalk a year or so later grew dark. The moon hid behind thick clouds. There was the promise of rain in the air, thick and sticky, but it never came.

I'm going for a swim.

Dorian, I don't think that's a good idea.

H had said that. Robert intervened, just as he always had when it came to Dorian.

She'll be fine, man. I'll be out there with her.

H remembered thinking, *that's like the blind leading the blind,* but he didn't stop them, and maybe that's on him. Maybe if he would have been more assertive…

There was plenty of splashing and laughing from the unusually calm river that night, even as the wind picked up and the current most certainly did as well. H and B sat back on the blanket she had brought. They were young—just out of high school—and maybe they were in love. They were definitely in like, but H wasn't sure then. If he was honest with himself, he wasn't sure now either. At least, he wasn't sure of *her* feelings. The last four years had been strained, yet they remained close, and he *thought* she loved him, but …

He shook his head, again pushing his inquisitive nature aside and allowing the force of the memories to take him back to that night, to when the splashing and laughter stopped and the screaming began.

Dorian? Dorian! Where are you? Dorian?!

At first they weren't sure if Robert was playing around, but quickly realized something was wrong.

Dorian!

In the dim moon light H saw Robert dive beneath the water, come up, scream for Dorian again and then disappear back beneath the surface. He came up again, spun around, slapped the water with both hands and started to go back under. He stopped. Something clearly caught his eye not too far away from them. H saw it. B did as well.

"Dorian," she screamed and ran for the water.

"Where?" Robert yelled. "Where is she?"

"Over there," she yelled and pointed further downstream. And Robert dove under. H didn't think he had seen her. He though Robert was swimming blindly. Turns out, he was right. But H saw her. She bobbed up once and then a second time, but she wasn't fighting the suddenly strong current pulling her further away.

She's dead, he thought as the breeze ruffled his hair. She had to be. She didn't struggle or scream or even try to swim. And the water pulled her further away, even as Robert swam and dove and came back up, whipping his head around, screaming her name between breaths of air.

It was less than seven minutes, but in that short time, Dorian and Robert went from playing in the water to Dorian sucked in an undertow and pulled downstream.

Bobbing, half-submerged in the water, her ankle caught between two stones, they found her. But that wouldn't be until morning after the sun came up and the mist rolled off the river, and the police had long since arrived. As had their parents.

Just as quick as that snap of the fingers, H was back and B was staring at him. He was vaguely aware of the tears on his own face.

"Are you okay?" B asked.

H nodded. "It's time to let it go."

"Yeah. It is."

They made their way down the path, two adults left over from a quartet of teenagers who had lost all innocence on a mid-spring evening. At the edge of the embankment they stopped. The water lapped at the ground with heavy slaps. H sat the box on the ground, and pulled at the flaps, opening it. Inside was a wooden boat, the center carved out. A mast and sail lay on top of it. The boat's hull was painted red and on the side were the words **DORIAN & ROBERT 4EVER**. A black urn sat beside it, the top taped shut.

It only took a couple of minutes for H to get the mast up and in a hole close to the bow. He straightened the sail with a guidewire that ran through the boom and hooked to either side of the boat. He handed it to B, pulled the urn from the box and placed it on the ground. He was careful while pulling the tape free and even more so as he slowly poured Robert's ashes into the hollowed out portion of the hull. He bent down to grab one last item in the box: a lighter.

"You ready?" he asked B.

She nodded. "It's time."

And it was. After four years and Robert's suicide, it was finally time to let go. The sun had begun to sink faster, and night was setting in. The croaks of frogs and the mating song of crickets and cicadas hummed in the night.

H waded into the water, sliding his feet along the ground, letting it bump over rocks and mud. He took the boat, handed B the lighter, and went further in. B followed, her arms out at her sides, the lighter held high, her head down and staring at the water. He stopped when B was hip deep, recalling how she and Dorian were about the same height.

"This is good enough."

"Are you sure?"

"Positive. We have enough of a breeze to push it along before the flames engulf it."

H set the boat in the water, held the bow with one hand. He gave B a soft look. She nodded.

"Robert, tonight we set you free. Go be with Dorian." It wasn't flowery, but it was all he could think to say.

B reached forward, flicked the lighter's wheel. It came to life on the first try. She set the flame to the extended boom. When it caught fire, H let the boat go. The breeze did its job, puffing out the sail and pushing the boat away from them and toward the center of the river.

H took a step sideways, put his arm around B. She leaned into him, her head on his shoulder. She sniffled, wiped at her nose. H did the same thing, but he didn't bother wiping away the tears falling from his eyes.

They watched as the boat sailed away, the flame gradually increasing. The sail caught fire, and shortly after, the boat was engulfed. A few seconds later, the boat and the flames disappeared into the water. It was then H knew this was just as much about him as it was B. How much guilt had he held in all of this time? The weight of it lifted, and he let out a long breath, one filled with relief.

"Let's go," H said and took B's hand.

They waded out of the water and then up the embankment, holding hands like long time lovers, or maybe first time lovers. Though they were soaked they moved along without caring about how they looked. They reached the car and got in. Before H could crank it up, B put her hand over his.

"I love you."

He smiled. Though she probably couldn't see it in the dark, he hoped she felt it. "I love you, too, B."

H turned the key. The motor sputtered and then caught.

"H?"

"Yeah?"

"I wonder if that old man pushed his wife into the river."

Crisp Sounds

When it's cold sounds are crisp.

Dave's dad told him that when he was a kid. They had been staring out the window as the snow fell outside. It was a rare occurrence, so watching it in the middle of the night was both exciting and calming for Dave (exciting because he wanted so bad to throw on his warmest clothes and go play in it, and calming because, from inside the warm house, it looked peaceful outside).

"You notice how quiet it is, Son?" Dad asked, his hand on Dave's—Davey back then—shoulder.

Davey listened. Other than the wood crackling in the fireplace there were no other sounds to be heard. He nodded, "Yeah, it is, isn't it?"

"When it's cold sounds are crisp. They are either not there or very loud and distinct."

At the time he had no clue what his father meant. But now, as he sat behind a tree in a neighborhood he had never been to, he had a feeling he *knew*.

Before we get to that, let's go back to the night before.

He woke to the sound of men talking. They weren't very far away, maybe even just a few feet, at the mouth of the alley. Cardboard and trash bags comprised the bed he lay on. A ratty old teddy bear was his pillow. He was behind a dumpster in the alley between Brewster's Bar and the little Italian eatery, Mia's. It protected him from the wind tunnel of the main street thirty or so feet from him.

Dave didn't move when he heard the voices. Another man, far wiser than he, and one who had been on the streets much longer, once told him something important about being homeless. 'At night stay as quiet as you can once you find a place to lay your head. If anyone hears you they will do one of three things: arrest you and throw you in the pen for a day or two, run you off and take your spot, or kill you and take your spot.' So, Dave, having remembered what the old buzzard said, stayed as still and quiet as he could, even with the cold eating through his jacket and chilling the exposed skin of his face, and the shivers threatening to come on him every few seconds. He tried to relax his cold-tense muscles, but found in doing so he shivered more.

The voices—three, he thought—were all distinct, but one of them more so than the other two. It sounded scared.

"I'll have your money, Johnny. I promise. I just don't have it right now."

"You know it's not my money, Reuben," one of the non-scared voices said. Dave thought it was the one Reuben called Johnny.

"Can't I have a few more days?"

"We've already given you an extra three weeks, Rube."

Dave didn't know who that voice belonged to. He listened, hoping to find out. For him it was like listening to a radio pro-gram when he was a kid back home in his bed, hands behind his head, eyes focused on the white ceiling above him. He could still hear Jay 'The Voice' Manning's deep baritone as he narrated the adventures of some poor sap who had the unfortunate luck to enter the town of Homesick. Dave never thought it was a great name for a town, but it didn't matter as a kid or even right then, when he really was sick for home and the carefree life of a child.

"Welcome to WKRH, radio 88.7,' Manning always start-ed, his voice soothing and god-like. *'Welcome to the town of Homesick, South Carolina, where tonight we find Reuben in a back alley and things don't look so good for him."*

"You know Mackey ain't too happy with you, Reuben," Johnny said. He had a distinct old school mobster sound to his voice, not quite deep, not quite high-pitched, and some-what dramatic (like the characters on the radio show Dave loved so much as a kid). It was almost as if the words were rehearsed.

They probably were, Davey, he heard his father whisper into his ear. *This probably isn't the first time they've done this.*

"But … but … but Mackey doesn't need to know I don't have the money right now."

"If you ain't got the money for us, what are we supposed to give him when we get back?" No Name Voice asked. He sounded like a real nice guy, if nice guys were rattlesnakes.

Dave could almost see them in their dark coats, derbies from the later '20s or early '30s on their heads. No Name would have his cocked sideways, probably more to his right, shadowing one eye. And they held guns.

"Just give me until Friday. I get paid then. I'll give you my whole paycheck, Johnny. You know I'm good for it."

"If you were good for it, we wouldn't be having this conversation, would we, Reuben?"

"Things have been tough lately, Johnny. Jimmy's been sick and Laura lost her job and—"

"Not our problem, Rube," No Name said. He sounded like a weasel, one ready to strike, maybe one wanting to prove his worth to Johnny and Mackey. Move on up the ladder, why don't you? No Name had an agenda.

"You have to understand, Johnny. You, too, Wade. You have families."

Wade? He doesn't sound like a Wade to me. Dad's whisper held surprise in it.

"We don't play the cards like you do, Reuben. We ain't gambling men," Johnny said. Dave could almost sense compassion in his words. He didn't want to be there anymore than Reuben did, but he had to be. He had to take care of things or Mackey—probably the big boss man in their operation—would take care of them, and not in a good way.

"I just got a little in over my head. I can make it back."

"See," Johnny said, probably shaking his head. "You don't get it, Reuben. You're still itching to play the cards."

"That itch, you can't scratch it,' Manning said in his deep voice, pausing briefly between itch and you for emphasis."

"Johnny ..."

"No, 'Johnny' man," Wade said. "You can't talk your way out of this one, Rube."

"Shut up, Wade," Johnny said, and a sound, crisp like Dad had said those sounds were when it was cold, came. A meaty slap of hand to face. There was no doubting the distinct sound. It was like a wet kiss—once you've heard it, you never forget it.

Dave didn't realize it, but he smiled when Johnny silenced the weasel.

"Wade glared at Johnny, one that intoned anger, maybe hate. The side of his face burned and red welts formed where Johnny's fingers made contact. His nose crinkled and the left side of his lip curled up for a second, but then, just as quickly as his anger surfaced, he nodded and backed away a couple of steps. This was Johnny's deal and to interfere would only end badly for him."

"Johnny, listen to me, please."

There was a deep sigh, presumably from Johnny, then, "You got two minutes, Reuben."

Dave pictured the scene playing out. Johnny standing with his hands in his coat, his head down, trying not to stare at the man he would soon kill, and yes, he would kill him, but not because he wanted to. No, he didn't want to. This much was clear by the deep sigh he released. He had to. It was either Reuben or Johnny and Wade. Someone was going to pay up. His gun was probably in one of his pockets, the butt of it cool in his hand. Wade probably stood next to him, but maybe a couple of feet away now. A stinging face and a little bit of embarrassment will make a guy back off. It'll also piss him off, and Dave had a feeling if he could see Wade's face then he would see a scowl, the red fingerprints, maybe one eye squinting but not the other one. It would be shadowed by the cocked sideways derby. His hands would be fists, something Johnny would probably have taken notice of, something that would let him know Wade was stupid enough to try something with him.

Then there was Reuben. How old was he on Dave's picture screen in his mind? Late thirties? Early forties? Fifty? No, not fifty. Too young sounding to be fifty or older. He was probably not a little guy. If he was a gambler, then he probably had his fair share of winning and the gluttony that often follows winning. It didn't matter how big Reuben was, he was probably on his knees, his hands behind his back, maybe. His eyes were wet with tears, his lip trembling, his breaths were quick and raspy, the sounds of a terrified man. White plumes of mist rose from his mouth with each of those breaths. And he was begging. Yeah, begging for his life.

Manning the radio jockey would have paused for station identification and a commercial break before going on. The break would have lasted so much longer than the two minutes Johnny claimed Reuben had. Then he would come back, his voice grave and deep.

"We return to the back alley on this cold winter night. Reuben was on his knees, his eyes wide and pleading ..."

"Johnny, don't do this, man. We've been friends since second grade. Doesn't that count for something?"

Not in business, Dad whispered. Johnny said nothing. But Dave could almost hear Johnny tapping his watch when he said, "Your time's wasting, Reuben."

Reuben must have seen the tap, and he certainly heard Johnny's statement. He began to ramble, his words flowing together. "Johnny you can't do this, man. I promise I'll right this. Just give me two more days. That's all I need. I promise, man. I promise."

Dave heard the shifting of feet and the click of something. A bullet being chambered? He could almost see Reuben's eyes grow wider. What color were they? Green? Blue? Hazel? He imagined saliva spilling from Reuben's bottom lip. He licked at it. That's what Dave saw. What he heard was the fear in the helpless man's voice.

"Don't. Don't do this, Johnny. Please. Don't kill me, man."

And Manning paused. There was a new character added to the story, one he probably didn't know was there as he read the script straight from the paper in front of him. Then he began again, his voice almost a whisper.

"Dave could move. He could make the smallest of sounds,

maybe even a cough. Anything to spook the two men. But would he? Would he risk his life for a stranger? Or would he sit quietly and hope they didn't find him out?"

And dad was there, too.

You have to help him. You can't let the man die.

What am I supposed to do? They got guns.

Make a noise. Move your legs. Anything to let them know they may not be alone.

That didn't make sense. Dad would never say that. Dad would want Dave to be as quiet as he could. Dad would want Dave to stay out of harm's way, at least if he could help it, and right then, he absolutely could help it. The words of the wise homeless man came back to him, loud and strong. *At night stay as quiet as you can once you find a place to lay your head. If anyone hears you they will do one of three things: arrest you and throw you in the pen for a day or two, run you off and take your spot, or kill you and take your spot.*

He was fairly certain the guys in the alley—Johnny and Wade—weren't going to arrest him and run him in for a couple of nights. And he didn't think they would just run him off and take his spot. They probably weren't really interested in a place to sleep anyway. But kill him? Yeah, he thought they would certainly kill him if they knew he were there and listening in on the conversation taking place right then.

So, Dave, homeless for less than six months, stayed quiet. He clenched his teeth to keep them from chattering. He let his body stay tense, though it hurt to do so. He was thankful for the worn teddy bear he used as a pillow. It kept his neck from being at an odd angle and kept him from having that good old pain called a kink. Surely, if one of those formed, he wouldn't be able to sit still.

But son ...

You're not my dad. Be quiet.

And the voice did. But the voices outside his head didn't cease. At least, not right away. Reuben rambled on, the clock in his head probably tick ticking away and soon the two minutes would be up, and there would be a loud gong and ...

"Johnny, I have a family for crying out loud."

"Maybe we'll pay them a visit when we're done here," Wade said, getting one more contempt-laced jab in. "I hear your wife's a hot ticket."

There was silence in the alley for several seconds. It was thick and loud and painful to hear.

"Johnny …" There were tears in Reuben's voice. "Please?"

"I'm sorry, old friend," Johnny said, and Dave thought he meant it. "Business is business."

The sound of the gun going off was deafening. It was crisp, like no other sound on a cold winter night could be. No amount of trying to be still could keep Dave from jumping. His knee struck the dumpster and one hand went over his mouth, stifling the scream he wasn't sure he let out or just heard between his ears. He didn't know if they heard it over the gunshot, but tears formed in his eyes from fear of being found and having them do the same thing to him they had done to poor old Reuben, the gambler with the family who would probably get a visit from Wade the Weasel at some point in the near future.

"What was that?"

Yup, they had heard.

"I don't know," Johnny said. "It sounded like it came from over there."

"Johnny pointed toward the trash-laden corner where the dumpster sat, the terrified Dave Jennings behind it. Wade the Weasel made his way toward him but stopped at the sound of ruffling in the trash against the wall."

Wade let out a startled cry.

"It's just a rat, Wade," Johnny said.

"I can see that. I should blow its head off."

"No, you shouldn't. One gunshot is enough. It was really one too many."

"He had it coming."

"Did he?" Johnny asked.

"Mackey said get the money or end him. He didn't have the money, so we ended him."

"We?"

"Yeah, *we*."

"Shut-up, Wade," Johnny said.

From behind the dumpster, Dave heard their footsteps as they walked away. Eventually, they faded all together.

"They exited the alley, two men having pulled off the execution, two men who went about their way as if nothing had happened."

Dave slowly began to relax, releasing a breath he hadn't realized he had been holding. He stretched his legs and rolled from his side onto his back. His muscles were stiff and his bones hurt, more from the cold than from sitting still, tensed up like a rubber band wound too tight. Though his hands were gloved, they felt like frozen blocks of ice. He rubbed them together knowing there would be no warmth coming to them any time soon. He slipped the stuffed bear from beneath his head and stared at it. Though it was dark, he could see one glass eye. The other one was missing, with only a few strands of thread jutting from a dip in the fabric where the eye used to be.

"We're going to get out of here, okay, Pillow?" He paused, not really expecting an answer. "We're just going to wait a few minutes to make sure Johnny and Wade are gone."

Dave rolled back onto his side and then onto his stomach. He shoved himself up to hands and knees, his joints groaning and popping as he did so. Caution was the word of the day for him, and with it, he eased from around the edge of the dumpster, peeking out just enough to see Reuben lying on the ground. He wasn't old—forties, so yeah, Dave was right about his age—and he wasn't big, so, no, he wasn't right about that detail. Reuben's hair was brown, peppered with sprinkles of gray. His face was clean-shaven, and his eyes had been brown. This he knew because Dead Reuben stared his empty eyes in Dave's direction.

He jerked away and sat on his bottom, his back to the dumpster. Though Reuben was no longer in his sight, he could still see him. Even when he closed his eyes for a few seconds, Reuben's face was clear in the dark behind Dave's lids.

"It's not my fault," he whispered, but when he poked his head from behind the dumpster again, the dead man's eyes told him otherwise. They pled to him, asked him, *Why didn't you do anything to help? I have a wife and a kid for crying out loud!*

"There was nothing I could do," he said as he stared at Reuben. There was a neat little hole in his forehead where blood oozed out and into his hair. Dave was certain if he looked, the back of Reuben's head wouldn't be so neat and part of the skull would be missing (and if the alley wasn't so dark where the walls of the two buildings that formed it were, he would have seen a spatter of blood, brain tissue, and hair on the wall to his left, the wall to Brewster's Bar). In his head Dave got a clear snapshot of the scene just before Reuben took the bullet. Reuben had been looking up at Johnny, his old friend from second grade, his eyes pleading, much like they were right then. He saw the look on Johnny's face, the gun raised to his head. He probably saw the gun recoil just after the trigger was pulled and just before his lights went out for good.

"Time to get out of here," he said and grabbed Pillow, the teddy bear. He stood, his knees creaking and joints aching. He grimaced as a shard of pain went from his right knee down into his ankle. For several long seconds, he held tight to the edge of the dumpster, his foot off the ground, his teeth clenched together and his breaths deep and raspy. The pain eased, but he knew it would never fully go away. It never did, not since the fall down the stairs at work that shattered his knee and ended up costing him his job (and, no, they didn't fire him right away. They waited until he went back to work and couldn't perform his normal duties to do the deed). Dave rubbed his knee and then put weight on his leg. The pain came back, but not as sharp and unbearable. He took a step, then another, releasing the dumpster as he did so.

Several more steps had him standing next to Reuben. He

started to pass by him, but realized, the man might have his wallet on him, and if there was a wallet, there might be money.

He knelt, the pain suddenly bolting back into his leg. He dropped to his knees, let out a cry of pain and then clamped his hands over his mouth. If he could have, Dave would have plopped onto his bottom, but the fresh pain held him firm, like a vice, to the spot where he knelt.

That's what you get for trying to steal from a dead man. Dad was back and what Dave heard was disgust. And why wouldn't he be disgusted? Dave didn't help the dead man at his knees. Dave didn't even try. Even so, Dad was right. He had thought about stealing from Reuben, hoping there would be at least a little bit in his wallet, but not really believing there would be. If he would have thought it all the way through before trying to bend down, he would have realized if Johnny or Wade had thought Reuben had any money on him, they would have checked his pockets, and they hadn't. He was sure of this. If Wade had tried to check, Johnny probably would have smacked him again and the wet, meaty sound would have reverberated in the alley, in the *cold*.

"Get up, Dave," he whispered between clenched teeth. He reached for the wall and fell forward. His hand struck the brick, but he couldn't catch himself before sprawling out in the trash left behind by other homeless folks. The pain was still there and stabbing at his surgically repaired knee, running down his leg and into his ankle. A hot poker of heat brought tears to his eyes. As he lay on his stomach, the one hand touching the wall, a darkening fact swept over him.

"I gotta get out of here," he said. "They might come back."

Dave pushed up with his hands and onto one knee. He crawled like a three-legged dog to the wall and placed one hand on it, the other stayed on the ground. Trying to keep his right leg straight he lifted himself up, placed his foot beneath him. The pain intensified as he bent the knee to gain his balance. He bit his bottom lip as tears fell down his face. Once standing he put his weight on his good leg and planted his back against the wall. Through his jacket he could feel the cold bricks. A shiver rippled through his body, causing his muscles to spasm.

A deep breath was followed by several more, and then he put weight on his right leg. The pain was bad, but fear had a hold of him. He took a step, then another. He leaned over, careful this time not to fall to his knees. Fingers wiggling, he reached for Pillow, almost had the stuffed bear on the first try, but only managed to graze it. He stretched a little harder, this time reaching for its nose. Between the thumb and two fingers, he pinched Pillow's nose and began to stand. He wavered for a moment, almost tipping over. Dave balanced himself the best he could with his other arm slightly behind him, fully believing if he fell he wouldn't be able to stand again. He would be forced to crawl back to the space between the dumpster and the wall, and Dead Reuben would be there through the night, his eyes glazing over and frost covering his skin. By morning he would be a block of ice and Dave would have to try and pass him then, in the daylight, when people could see him leaving the alley. He had to go, and he had to go right then.

He gained his balance and stood for several seconds, waiting for his leg to give out and hoping it wouldn't. With Pillow tucked beneath one arm, Dave limped toward the alley's entrance. He could see the light of the street lamp across the street, its yellow glow like a beacon at sea. He focused on it, making it his goal. If he could reach the street lamp he could walk a block further and make a left at Hundredth Avenue and then limp another half block to the alley between Devin's Décor Emporium and The Fabric Shop. There wasn't a dumpster back there, but it was narrow and the wind didn't reach the middle, and someone had put up a privacy fence years ago at the opposite end. If anything, he could lay low for a few hours until morning, or maybe he could get busted by the police and have a warm cell to sleep in for a day or two.

Dave reached the mouth of the alley and stopped short of walking into the street. He looked around. Less than a block away he saw what he was afraid he would see: two men arguing. They both wore long coats, but neither of them wore derbies on their heads. One of them was easily half a foot taller than the other, and his not-so-short blond hair whipped about his face. The other guy was lean with a rough beard that hadn't taken full shape yet. His hair was brown and he looked angry. Truthfully, he looked furious. They both took a step toward Dave, and then stopped. The blond said something, and the beard started yelling. Though Dave couldn't quite hear what he said, he knew the two men half a block away were Johnny and Wade, and they were on their way back to the alley.

Looking around, Dave thought he could just hobble his way across the street. "No, they'll see me, and I'll end up like Reuben."

He glanced down, and his eyes grew. On the toe of his right shoe was blood. It wasn't much, just a smear, but it was there. And Dave wasn't about to try and bend down and wipe it off. To do that would be suicide. It also meant he wouldn't make his way toward the two men arguing. Dave turned and lurched back toward the dumpster as fast as he could.

When he reached Reuben, he looked down at the body. Though there wasn't much light, he could see where he had knelt and where his foot had disrupted the puddle, leaving an indention in the thickening blood.

If they see that, they'll know.

And the radio disc jockey came back in full throttle then.

"What will become of our hero? Will they find him in the dark alley? Could this be the end for Dave?"

At this point, the disc jockey clearly cut to a commercial, leaving his captive audience on pins and needles.

"I hope not," Dave whispered. He started to go behind the dumpster, but stopped. They almost found him the first time. If not for the rat in the jumbled trash on the ground, he would surely be dead already. He looked down at the ground, at the flat of cardboard he laid on earlier. Getting down there would be easy enough—painful, but easy—but getting up would be near impossible, especially if he had to stay there for a while.

"As our hero contemplated, Johnny and Wade continued to argue, their voices growing louder ..."

Dave looked around. The trash on the ground wasn't so much he could hide beneath. Behind the dumpster was ruled out already. Maybe inside ... The thought made him want to gag. Laying in the throw-away of everyone else was less than appealing to him. But, in reality, wasn't that what he was already doing? Wasn't he just a throw-away of the world? A throw-away person?

The dumpster itself was more long than tall. There was a place on either side where the trash truck could put the lifters in and pick up the dumpster and, well, dump it. They weren't too high, he thought.

I could get one foot in it ... but what about the other leg? Suck it up, Buttercup. Pain is better than dying.

He could hear Johnny and Wade. They were closer. At any moment they would round the corner and they would see him, and one of them would kneel him down on the ground where the pain in his leg would be the least of his worries. A bullet would end the pain and everything else for him.

Dave, fearing the worst, tossed Pillow inside the dumpster and grabbed the lip of it. He lifted his right foot, fighting against the screaming pain that throbbed up into his thigh now. The foot went into the hole where the lifter would go. With everything he had, he pushed up with the foot, his knee threatening to give out, and pulled with both hands until he was waist high with the opening. The other leg went up onto the lip and he slid his right foot free, letting himself tip into the garbage.

"We're going to dispose of the body, Wade, and that's the end of it," he heard Johnny say from the opening of the alley.

Crap!

Dave pulled several bags from around him, and a tattered piece of cardboard and placed them on top of him. The cardboard went over his face, and then he slid an open bag of garbage over it. Some of its contents, including a foul-smelling liquid spilled out. Dave gagged but held himself together, trying to stay quiet, but terrified the duo of killers had heard him. He strained his ears, and what he heard were footsteps and a brief conversation.

"What are we going to do with him?" Wade asked.

"Put him in the dumpster."

"Seriously?"

"Yes. Grab an arm and a leg. We'll just haul him up and over."

Dave had been scared when he climbed into the dumpster. Now, he was terrified. They were about to dump Dead Reuben on him. Though he couldn't see them, he could picture them next to the body, the radio host narrating right along with their actions.

"The two men looked at each other. Wade shook his head, his eyes like slits, the hand print from the slap earlier still on the side of his face, though not red but a light blue and purple shade, the beginnings of a bruise. They both grabbed an arm and a leg and lifted the already stiffening body, Wade with a grunt, Johnny quietly."

"Man, he's heavy."

"He's dead, Wade. What do you expect?"

"I didn't think he would be like lead to pick up."

"It's called dead weight. Just get him in the dumpster, okay?"

Dave listened as the two men struggled to lift Reuben's body. Their shoes scuffed across the concrete, and Wade let out several more grunts. He was kind of a wimp is what Dave concluded. And lazy. Being a wimp could be forgiven in most cases, but being lazy, especially in disposing of the body of the man you just executed could be the difference of going free and being caught. If Dave had figured out anything, Johnny probably didn't like Wade, and not just because he was an obnoxious mouth, but also because he was lazy. And lazy was bad.

Something clanged hard against the outside of the dumpster. Dave held his breath, hoping he didn't make any noises or jump from being startled.

"Get his leg up," Johnny snapped.

"I'm trying. He's heavy."

The clang came again, then another and then the sound was different. It was still a clang, but it was less hollow, less on the outside and more at the top of the dumpster.

"His feet went over the top of the garbage container, the heavy soles of the boots clanking hard against the steel. They lifted a little higher and his legs went over the lip of the container. With ..."

"One more shove," Johnny said.

There were several grunts, and then the clatter of the boots on the inside of the dumpster. This Dave knew, but he didn't have a chance to brace himself for the body landing on him and rolling slightly to the side. He couldn't see Reuben, but he could feel the garbage he had covered himself with had moved somehow, had shifted beneath the weight of the dead man. He was certain if he opened his eyes he would be staring up at the two killers, and one of them would have a gun pointed at him. Then, as if to confirm his thoughts, he heard Wade say, "Have you used this alley before, Johnny?"

"First time, Wade. And the last. Why?"

"There's another body in there."

"Really?"

"Yeah, look."

This is where it ends, Dave thought. *They'll see I'm still alive, and then I won't be.*

There was some shuffling beyond the dumpster, and then Johnny spoke.

"Looks like someone beat us to the punch."

"You ain't kidding."

"Let's go, Wade."

"Wait, you don't want to know who it is?"

"No. Why would I?"

"He could be someone we know. Maybe Mackey put the hit out on another punk who couldn't pay up."

"Maybe so, but I don't care."

"Why not?"

There was a long pause and a very audible sigh. Dave, with his mouth pursed tightly closed to keep the foul liquid that had spilled onto his face from getting into it, listened to a silence just as loud in the bitter cold as sounds were. That's something Dad never mentioned—how strangely loud silence could be. The erie quiet crept up his spine as he strained to hear anything. Almost any sound would have been a welcome relief to the deafening quiet.

Then Johnny spoke, his voice edgy. What he said were words that were anything but a welcome relief. "Wade, why don't you go ahead and take a look? Hop on in and search the body for some I.D."

"Really?"

"Yeah. Go on ahead. Maybe he has a few bucks on him. If so, then you can keep whatever you find. Won't even mention it to Mackey."

"Seriously?" Wade suddenly sounded hopeful, and this was not what Dave wanted to hear. Inside, he groaned.

"Seriously."

But there was something wrong with the way Johnny talked. He was saying all the right things to get Wade to stop being annoying, but there was something else in his voice, in his tone, something that made a million red flags pop up in Dave's mind. Before he could put his finger on it, the sound of Wade's shoes hitting the side of the dumpster brought him from his thoughts. Dave's heart sped up, and he was suddenly sweating.

I'm about to die.

He was almost right.

The gunshot was so much louder inside the dumpster. He knew he jumped, and he hoped he didn't scream, but he thought he had. But it wasn't Dave who was dead. It was Wade. He slumped over the side and fell forward, landing on both Dead Reuben and Dave.

"Man, how can someone be so annoying all the time?" Johnny asked to no one. "Good riddance." Then came the sounds of his footsteps as he walked away. It would be awhile this time before Dave moved from the trashcan, even as the liquid seeped between his tight lips. When he finally moved, frost had formed on the bodies on top of him and the liquid felt like it was trying to freeze on his face.

He pushed Wade off his chest and tried to move his right leg, but it was too stiff to bend much more than a couple of inches. He wiped at the liquid on his face and found it had dried, leaving a sticky residue behind that clung to his sleeve and smeared against his cheeks and nose and chin. He tried to sit up in the garbage and managed to shift trash bags and nastiness around, but didn't really move much in the way of getting out of there.

"Come on, Davey," he whispered and was startled to hear his dad in his own voice. He lay there quiet for a few more seconds, and then spoke again, this time listening to his voice, "Get up, Davey." There it was again. Dad, right there in his own voice. He smiled at this. Dad had been a good guy, even when Dave had gone wrong.

"Get up," he said again. "Get out of here. Get your life back together." It was Dad, and Dave was certain he was speaking through him.

He struggled to move, the cold having set deep into his muscles and bones. Still, he shoved with his hands and pushed with his good leg until he was sitting up. He then pushed Wade completely off him, rolling him onto his side. But before he could get him onto his stomach, he saw the man's face. The front of his skull had been blown out by the exit of the bullet. His eyes were still there and they were open and full of surprise, as if his last thought before keeling over into the dumpster was *I can't believe he shot me*. Then Dave had him over onto his stomach, and the horrible expression was no longer staring at him.

He struggled, but managed to get his right leg free. The pain was mostly gone, replaced by numbness worse than the hurt he had felt earlier. Dave pushed Reuben over, glad he hadn't landed with his face toward him.

He reached for the lip of the dumpster, but stopped. Instead, he looked at Reuben's pants. There was a bulge where his wallet should be. There could be money there. He could get a ticket home, or at least a decent meal. He hated the thought of it, but what good was the money going to do Reuben? He was dead, and by the time his wife and kid found out, well, it wouldn't matter then anyway. Dave reached for Reuben, stretched his fingers into the back pocket with some effort. *I'm not copping a feel*, he told himself as his gloved fingers first touched the wallet and then gripped it. The billfold slid from the pocket with relative ease.

Dave opened it. Inside was a picture of a woman, maybe six or seven years younger than Reuben. Beside her was a boy, his brown hair neatly combed. They both smiled. Dave shook his head as he considered the fold where money would go. Seven dollars—two ones and a five—was all Reuben had on him. He started to take the money out, but then folded the wallet and slid it back into Reuben's pocket.

He didn't climb from the dumpster. Not right away. He scooted along the trash until he saddled up to Wade. Blood still dribbled from the wound in his head, but it was beginning to clot. He patted Wade's bottom—there was a wallet there. Like with Reuben, he worked his gloved fingers into the pocket, pulled out the wallet and unfolded it. Unlike with Reuben, there was more than seven bucks there—a lot more. Dave pulled out the handful of bills, fourteen in all, and counted out 827 dollars. He licked his lips. That was more than enough to get him a meal and get him home.

The bills went into his front pocket and he reached up to the dumpster's opening. He grabbed it, started to pull himself up, and then stopped again.

Get out of here, Davey.

"I can't," he said in his dad's voice. "I can't just leave him here. His family … they'll be worried about him."

What are you going to do?

Dave considered this. He had heard Reuben begging for his life. He had been a witness to the stranger's final minutes—a little more than two of them— of life. The woman in the picture looked like a nice person, the child … the child reminded Dave of himself when he was a kid. His smile was full of innocence, just as Dave's had been at that age. Life hadn't tainted the boy. Not yet, at least. But it would when he learned of his father's death.

"The right thing."

Dave plucked at Reuben's pocket again, pulled out the wallet and shoved it into his coat pocket. He searched the dumpster and found Pillow. Dave tossed the stuffed bear out and knew he would regret it when he went to pick it up later. Then he pulled himself to a standing position and worked his bad leg over the edge of the dumpster. It felt sore, but the cold kept it numb and stiff. He lifted himself out, trying not to fall too hard to the ground, but failed. The pain in his knee was like an explosion, and he let out a cry of agony.

"Deal with the pain, Davey. Deal with it, and get out of here," he growled through clenched teeth.

He did, on both counts. He rolled onto his side and saw Pillow.

"Hi there, Pillow. You ready to get out of here?" He grabbed the dirty stuffed bear and held onto it as he tried to get to his feet with the help of the dumpster. Then he limped up the alley, careful to avoid the pool of blood where Reuben—Rube to the now deceased Wade—had died. At the sidewalk, he made a left and hurried in the opposite direction he had seen Johnny and Wade coming, and the way Johnny surely went alone.

It took a couple of hours, but he made his way to the bus depot. The sun was coming up, and the blackness of light had given way to the gray of predawn. He stopped for a bite to eat at a little restaurant where one of the waitresses gave him a dirty look when she saw the dirty teddy bear. She barked at him about not wasting her time if he didn't have the means to pay. He flashed her a fifty and went to a different table where a younger waitress worked, ordered a meal and gave a thank you when she returned with a fresh cup of coffee. Unlike the older lady, she didn't give him a look of suspicion or assume he couldn't pay for his meal. When he was finished he paid for his meal, left a tip that equaled the bill and limped out, Pillow in hand.

The bus station was in the middle of downtown, something he always thought was convenient if you were homeless and had the money to catch the Greyhound to wherever you were trying to get to. It wasn't so convenient if you didn't have the money, but had the desire to get out of there and go anywhere else. But he had the money and he made the long walk from the diner to the bus station, the throbbing in his knee making each step more and more painful.

It was a nice station, as far as he was concerned. Renovations had been done over the last year. The once white façade had been replaced with a beach sand stucco look and there were benches along the front on the outside where there hadn't been before. Those benches were currently occupied, mostly by other homeless people using them as beds.

At least the police haven't run them off yet.

There were two service windows, like at the movie theaters, both with thick windows, more than likely bulletproof, with intercom holes in them so the people on either side can hear what the other is saying. A waist-high counter started where the window ended, and there was a slot on either side, one where money went from one side and a ticket came out from the other. Dave smiled at this. *You can never be too safe, can you?*

He walked up to the window. Behind it sat a woman with graying hair and crow's feet around her hazel eyes. A couple of hairs poked out just to above the right side of her lip. Dave couldn't help but wonder if she realized there was this thing called a razor.

"Good morning," he said, trying not to sound too anxious.

Hair Lip regarded him with all the boredom of an eight year old in algebra class. "What can I do for you?" she asked, not too kindly.

"When's the next bus heading to Century Falls?"

"Not until tomorrow morning around eight."

110

"Really?"

"Really."

He nodded. "How much is one ticket?"

"Twenty-eight dollars."

"I'll take one, please."

"You don't need one for your friend, there?" Hair Lip said and eyed Pillow.

"No, I don't think he'll need a ticket. Thank you, though."

She rolled her eyes. "Slip the money in the drawer, and I'll give you the ticket."

That's typical, he thought and slid a fifty from his pocket and placed it in the metal drawer.

"Is this real?" she asked.

"Yes," he said, the aggravation clear in his tone.

A minute later the drawer opened on his side. He took the change and his ticket. "Thank you," he said and walked away.

Back on the street, he had time to think about the rest of the day, about what he would do with the next twenty-four plus hours. Then he thought of Reuben, dead in the dumpster right along with one of his killers. He reached into his pocket and pulled out the wallet, unfolded it and stared at the woman and child.

You should let them know he's dead.

"Yeah. But how?"

Reuben's driver's license sat behind the picture of his family. It was coming up on expiration. Two more months and he would have been at the DMV trying for renewal. Dave read off the address, and then went back to the bus station and back to the window where Hair Lip sat, her face as dour as her mood.

"Excuse me, Ma'am."

She gave him the same bored look. "What can I do for you this time?"

"What time does the city bus run through here?"

She shook her head, rolled her eyes and let out an impatient breath. "It doesn't come this way. It stops two blocks down—all of them stop on Senate Street, so pick your favorite, and go for a spin."

"All of them?"

"That's what I said."

"Thank you." He didn't wait for her to respond. He thought she wouldn't. If he would have waited an extra five seconds, he would have known he was right.

He was halfway to Senate Street when he stopped. Dave looked up at the sky, eyes squinting. The sun was up now, and traffic had begun to fill the streets. Adults going to work, kids going to school, young adults going to college, all of them going about their daily lives without a clue of what happened in the middle of the night where three men went into an alley and only one ended up leaving. They were oblivious to one of the men having a family, for crying out loud, and his friend from childhood had put the bullet in his head, ending his life. They didn't know that Wade wanted to pay Rueben's family a visit when they were done with him. After seeing what she looked like, Dave guessed Wade would have paid her a little more than a visit.

They also didn't know about the man who witnessed it without seeing anything. He had *heard* everything, seen the bodies, and there he stood on the sidewalk in the early morning, his knee angry with pain and swelling, and money in his front pocket he stole off of one man and the wallet he stole off the other.

No one knew about any of it, other than Johnny and Dave. So how was he to tell Reuben's wife?

"I can't."

You must. It's the right thing to do.

"They'll think I killed him."

You don't have a gun.

"It doesn't matter. They'll think I was involved, and since I didn't stop them, I was."

Don't be a coward.

That ended the debate, one that was half-hearted, at best. It didn't end the *how* he was going to tell Reuben's wife of her husband's death. That came a few hours later as he sat on a park bench watching a man walk his dog, a big black lab with a booming bark. In one of the man's hands was the handle to the leash. In the other was a paper bag, the top folded shut and clenched tight in his hand.

Dave stood from the bench. Though the pain in his leg had subsided considerably, it still hurt enough for him to limp along at a slower pace than he would have liked. He made his way to a convenience store, purchased a bottle of water, a pen and a small notepad. When the clerk asked if he wanted the items in a bag, Dave said, "Yes, but can I get a paper bag?" The clerk said nothing, though he eyed Dave the same as the older waitress had. He produced the paper bag from beneath the counter, put the three items in it and handed it over to Dave.

Then it was a short bus trip to the area where Reuben had once lived and where Wade never got to pay a visit. Dave found the house with ease. It was a little brick and vinyl siding structure with a chimney sticking out the roof and a heavy wooden door with a small square ornate carved window about head high. There were no bushes lining the house, and all the curtains were drawn in the windows. A privacy fence closed off the back yard to the public. There were no cars in the driveway, and he suspected Reuben's was probably in a pond somewhere or maybe in a parking lot at the airport. It didn't matter. He would never drive it again, and she would probably never see it again. What did matter is his wife had to be home when he delivered the package at night.

Dave left the little neighborhood, hoping no one saw him come or go, and if they did, they would think he was just some nobody passing through, which was more truth than they would ever know. He found a little park on the edge of another neighborhood a mile or so down the road. He sat on one of the three unoccupied benches. He looked at the childless playground and wondered if Reuben's son ever played there, if Reuben had ever slid down the slide with the boy or pushed him on one of the bank of four swings, or helped him get across the monkey bars, holding him by the legs and laughing as he did so. Dave's heart started to hurt as he thought of the dead man he left in a garbage can in an alley with another dead man who had participated in killing him. He thought of his son and his wife and the worry they must have been going through. Tears fell from his eyes, and he leaned forward on the bench, putting his face in his hands.

Dave wept. When he finished, his chest hurt, his eyes were puffy, and snot had run from one nostril and over the top of his lip. His gloves were wet with tears.

It took a couple more minutes for him to compose himself, but when he did he slid the glove on his right hand off and picked up the paper bag he had carried with him. He set the bottle of water on the bench beside him and then pulled out the pen and the notepad. He flipped the cover and started to jot down a quick letter on the first page. He was only two sentences into it when he looked it over and almost ripped the page out to crumple it up. Dave stopped short of doing so and flipped the page to the next one.

A second time he started the note and read it, only to turn the page and start again. For over an hour he sat on the bench, the wind blowing gently around him, his bare hand losing feeling from the cold. His nose, which had started running when he cried, still dripped. He sniffled every few seconds. Dave placed the pen in his lap and flexed his fingers. Then he picked it up and wrote the letter to Reuben's wife.

Dear Mrs. Reuben,

You don't know me and I don't know you, but last night I put a gun to your husband's head, and I pulled the trigger. I was with my partner Wade, who I also killed. I dumped them both in a dumpster in the alley between Brewster's Bar and Mia's. To prove to you I'm serious, I'm giving you his wallet. I hated killing Reuben—we were friends since second grade—but he owed Mackey a lot of money, and that's a bad thing. I just thought I would let you know, not because I want to taunt you or hurt you, but because I hate what I've done. I'm sorry for your loss, but now you don't have to wonder about Reuben. He's dead, and I killed him.

Johnny

Dave read over the note several times before tearing it out of the pad. He tucked the pad into his back pocket and then put the note in the white bag. He flattened the bag out and wrote, in his same chicken scratch handwriting, *For Mrs. Reuben.*

He put Reuben's wallet in the bag, made sure the note was inside and folded the top down. And he sat on the bench, staring out at the playground. As he did so, he swore he could hear the laughter of a little boy and his father.

"Did you hear that?" he asked Pillow. The stuffed bear didn't answer. "I didn't think so."

The sun began its slow trek from high in the sky to out of sight. The day grew colder as it turned to night. Clouds had gathered during the afternoon. It would be a long evening, he thought. Dave stood, and as he did so, his knee groaned and popped and that tingle of pain was back.

"Let's get this over with."

He began the long walk back to Reuben's neighborhood and hoped he could find it in the dark. He did.

From across the street he could see a car in the driveway. It was nothing special, just a Chevy, and not a newer one. He could see a light on in what he thought was the living room window and another light on to the right.

She's home,

He looked around, saw no one, no car lights. Hobbling, he made his way across the street, stopped on the sidewalk when he thought he heard something and then hurried up to the front porch.

Manning, the DJ, piped in, his voice almost a baritone whisper. *"Will Dave make it to the door? Will he leave the note? And will he be caught doing it?"*

Before he could go any further, the first flurries on a coming winter storm fell from the sky. *Hurry,* he thought and went up the steps to the front door, wincing as he did. He didn't know how much time he would have from the time he rang the doorbell, which had a glowing white light, but he hoped it would be enough to get him out of sight, at least to the tree across the street. The bag went onto the porch, *For Mrs. Reuben* facing up. He then rang the doorbell several times.

RUN!

He didn't think he would make it across the street without slipping in the freshly fallen snow or before the door opened, but he managed to make it onto the opposite sidewalk before the front light came on. It was another few seconds before the door opened, but by then, he was behind the tree, his back to it, and breathing hard. Snow fell harder around him, catching on his coat and in his beard. He clutched the teddy bear tight to his chest with both hands. His leg throbbed, and he put one hand to his mouth and bit on the glove to keep from screaming.

"Hello?"

Dave peeked from behind the tree, not far, just enough to see Mrs. Reuben on the porch. She bent and picked up the bag. She looked around before opening it. She pulled out the wallet and the note. He watched as she read it. She dropped the note and put an empty hand to her face.

Mrs. Reuben wailed, and it was nothing like he had ever heard before.

He stopped watching her and leaned his head against the tree, clutching Pillow to his face. It stank of mildew. That didn't keep him from hearing the eerie echoes of her screams. In that moment, Dave understood exactly what Dad had meant.

"When it's cold, sounds are crisp. They are either not there or very loud and distinct."

Dave had never felt as cold as he did right then, and no sounds were ever crisper and more distinct.

And the disc jockey became quiet.

Numbers

He's out there, beyond the door of rusting metal on the outside and dried gore on the inside. He calls.

"Open the door, Dane. You can't stay in there forever."

On the other side of the room, in the corner of a doorless closet, Dane shrugs, her arms wrapped around bruised, bare knees, and the voices—the voices that are in there with her—laugh and whisper sweet destruction. She wants to put her hands over her ears, but fear keeps her from doing so.

"Dane, I'm coming in."

"Not!" she yells but knows he won't understand what she means.

Not? Not what?

Sweat beads along her brow, and Dane looks from side to side, her head twitching all the while.

"Dane?"

Her name is four letters. Four-letter words are bad, not like three or five or seven or even nineteen. Those are odd numbers and odd numbers are safe. Even numbers, those are different.

He calls her name again and she cringes.

The doorknob turns.

Dane tries to shrink deeper into a closet filled with only her.

A skirt lies on the floor, tattered and blood-stained. Its owner was thirty-eight and her name was six letters long: Aubrey. A double whammy. She didn't understand the laws of the numbers, didn't see the way the demons licked their lips each time she said an even-lettered word, each time she stressed Dane's name in her speech.

On the floor, in the center of the room, a pair of sunglasses, twin mirrored lenses, reflect a double image of the skull lying near them, skin and hair still attached to the crown. He wore a suit, and his name was Steven, six letters. Forty-four years old. A double whammy. The sunglasses didn't belong to him.

The skull did.

The knob turns. A knot forms in Dane's stomach, and vomit swells in her throat. She swallows it down, tears filling her eyes as she, again, searches the room.

Blood-spattered walls box her in. The carpet, once only blue, is now lined with maroon spots.

"Dane?" He pokes his head in. Older than the others, head full of gray, glasses on the bridge of his nose. Distinguished. Lines crease his face from the sides of his nose down past his lips. Another head shrink who thinks he can help her. But she knows, she knows there is no help coming, not for her. Not for him.

"Please," she says and covers her head with her hands. Six letters.

A pinprick of a hole appears in the ceiling. She hears it—a hiss like a snake—and tries to think of words with letters in odd numbers only.

"Dane." He steps fully in the room. Dressed in a sports coat and gray trousers, he carries a pen and pad in one hand, a folding metal chair in the other. One look around the room and most people would run, fear in their throats, their heart hammering much too hard for comfort. Not him. He closes the door, sealing his fate.

"Dane?" His voice is deep, soothing, rehearsed.

At the sound of her name the pinprick widens a little, the hisses intensify.

He's cautious, careful not to step on the bloodstains, careful to avoid any portion of flesh not devoured by the demons that haunt her.

"Dane?"

She cringes. "Leave," she says.

"I can't do that." Odd-lettered words outnumbered by even ones.

"You ... can not ..." She grinds her teeth. How many days has it been since the demons came? Three? Six? Six is an even number, but an odd-lettered word. Safe? She's wondered this about the numbers themselves. Two, five, six, eight, nine, ten, eleven, and so on ... those words and numbers with both properties of even and odd. Time has done little to help her figure things out, other than to know—beyond a shadow of a doubt—that odd-numbered words are safe and even ones aren't.

"I can't do what?" He unfolds the chair and sets it on the floor a few feet from the closet, blocking her view of the glasses and the skull with its hair still attached. She still sees the skirt, still remembers the woman, her soft voice, the way she tried so hard to help Dane. Her screams ...

The demons always leave mementos behind. For the lady, it was the skirt; the young man, the skull. She can't remember who the sunglasses belonged to or whether it even matters.

"You can not ..." she pauses, knowing the word is four letters, but having little choice, "stay."

They howl in delight.

She shoves her palms to her ears and shakes her head.

Behind the man, the hole grows larger. She could stick two fingers in it if she wanted.

He sits and crosses one leg over the other knee. "Why not?"

She lets out a long breath. Relief. Three and three, both odd.

"I can not ... explain why," she counters, runs the words back through her head to make certain they were all odd numbered.

"What happened here?"

She squeezes her eyes shut. Tears spill from them. "Odd numbers."

"What?"

The hole widens.

She hiccups and sucks in a deep breath. "Use odd numbers."

He squints, confused by the request. "Why?"

She swallows. What should she tell him? Thoughts scramble across her mind. He'll never believe her.

The demons whisper, mock her, dare her to tell the truth

when they know lies are all he'll believe.

"You can not ... believe the truth." The math is right. She lets out another breath, her body sagging, knees still clasped to her chest.

"Let me be the judge of that."

She laughs, though nothing is funny. She can't help it.

The hole widens.

He shifts on the metal chair, causing it to squeak and complain, clicks his pen, then writes on his pad. He speaks without looking up, "Well?"

"What's?"

What's? Dane's mom, an English teacher, taught her better than this. She would have rolled her eyes, corrected Dane, and reminded her of proper grammar. It was one of the things she hated about her, but missed the most after she died.

He lifts a brow, and Dane wonders if he's related to her mom somehow. An uncle, maybe?

He says, "Are you going to tell me what it is I won't believe?"

Too many words to keep track of. The math runs together, but Dane knows he has used a combination that will surely bring the beasts from their Hell. The hole expands then shrinks, repeating the process as the demons giggle maniacally, taunting her with their whispers.

Her eyes roll up, and she counts letters. "Believe ... the thing ... I say ... and you ... survive."

"Survive?" Both brows are lifted now. "Survive what?"

Idiot. Dane wants to blurt out the problem, but if they hear, they will come for him, come for her; but if they only hear him, like the others, they will only take him. She bites her bottom lip. She liked the woman, but not the man nor this new guy, this older man with his false sense of distinction, his air of arrogance—no she doesn't like him, and she wonders for the first time ...

"What's ..." A combination of words tick through her mind, but none of them perfectly odd. The mixture could be safe, if the odds outnumber the even. She decides to take the chance, knowing her mom would have hated the way she speaks. "What's your names?"

"My names?" He smiles, this time letting out a chuckle. He thinks she's playing with him. It's on his face, the smug smile of a head doctor tracing upward on one side of his mouth. "My name is Charles. Doctor Charles."

Though the rest of the words are even numbered, his name has seven letters. Seven is lucky and "lucky" has only five letters. Safe.

"How old are you?"

Charles tilts his head to one side. "What does that matter?"

Four plus four plus four plus six. All even numbers.

The hole in the ceiling widens. A brown hand pushes through, its nails yellowed and cracked, hair on the knuckles. The hiss becomes a low growl.

If the demons wanted, they could grab "Doctor Charles." But where would the fun be in that? If Dane has learned anything since they first appeared, it's they like their fun and unless they are particularly hungry, they will have their fun.

Dane counts the words on her fingers, nods, "It's important."

"How so?"

A tingle traces up her spine, like a sliver of ice. She shivers, shakes it off, repeats, "It's important." What more can she say without using even-numbered words?

"I hardly think my age—"

"How old are you?" Dane yells, spittle shooting from her mouth.

He drops his pen. It hits the pad before toppling off and landing on the floor. He keeps his eyes on her as he leans down and picks up the pen.

And she knows ... she knows...

"I'm sixty-two, young lady, and you will speak to me with respect." The smoothness is gone from his voice, replaced by shaking anger.

Dane remembers what the other guy said, the one whose skull lies near the wall, reflected in the sunglasses' lenses.

"Why are you angry?" he asked.

"Not," she responded.

"Yes, you are. Why? Don't you know that anger is a secondary emotion? It's not real. It's not a true emotion."

"Not angry," Dane repeated.

And then she argued, and they came, and he went, leaving behind the skull with the scalp of hair.

But, the sunglasses. Dane can't remember where they came from. She tries, but nothing, not even a vague resemblance of a face comes to mind. A "mind block," the first guy said.

Now, Charles sits in his chair tapping his pen on his pad, his lips pursed as if he's going to kiss Dane, as if he—

She remembers something, and her eyes widen. A man. Stubble-chinned and dark-haired. His breath stank. Always stunk. He liked the dimples in Dane's cheeks when she smiled. He liked the shirt she was wearing, the color of purple brought out her eyes. Those magenta ringed orbs fascinated everyone who came in touch with her, except for the doctors.

The doctors wouldn't listen to her when she spoke of him, how he would touch her leg while riding in the car, the way he leered at her when she walked by, or sat on the couch reading a book, or ate her supper, or while she slept.

"So, are you going to talk with me?" Charles grows impatient; his sentence ends with a sigh, as if he knows the answer and is resigned to it.

"Yes. Why not?"

"That's what I'm asking you. Why won't you talk to me?"

"You can not believe ... is why." The one word makes her look beyond Charles' shoulder toward the hole. It hasn't changed, but the arm, the brown mass of flesh, waves, trying to wiggle further from the hole.

"Why don't you stop playing games and tell me what happened here? Why did you kill these people? What did you do with their bodies?" He's faster to anger than the others, this self-esteemed man with the pad and pen.

The demons laugh, and Dane can almost see them licking

their twisted lips, can almost smell their fetid breath.

"I did nothing wrong. You … you …"

"I what?"

The air in the room grows thick.

Pain blossoms in her temples. Heat rises up her face, and big tears blur her vision. "Leave. Now. While you can."

"Are you threatening me?"

He's not leaving. Not now. Dane sees it in his expression, in the way his lips pull down at the corners, the way his brows knit above his nose. He leans forward, and the chair creaks and groans under his weight.

Dane wonders if he knows anger is not a true emotion, it's secondary and not real at all.

The hand disappears back into the hole.

It's only a matter of time now.

Dane bares her teeth and squeezes her eyes shut—a grimace that makes her look as if she's in pain.

The demons' laughter becomes cackles, and the hole opens further. The brown hand appears again, this time along with a white one, thin with no hair, and laced with bruises. One of the new hand's nails is broken.

Dr. Charles stands, sets the pad on the chair and takes long strides toward Dane.

Her heart speeds up, a steady *thump, thump, thump,* in her ears.

He stops at the doorless closet and glares down at her, his hands on his hips.

"Come out of there."

Dane shakes her head from side to side. "Not."

"Not what?" His voice is higher now.

Her head shakes faster. She knows what's coming. She tries to melt into the wall, to shrink away, her legs pulling tighter into her chest and her arms gripping around her knees.

"Not comin' out." For a second, she fears she added the G in there, but she didn't. She's safe for a little longer.

"I think you are."

The cackles lessen at this sentence. All odd-numbered

words.

"Not comin' out."

"Yes, Dane. Yes, you are." Doctor Charles bends down. He looks different up close. The crow's feet around his eyes are deep, and his gritted teeth show through slightly parted lips. His forehead is wrinkled. A vein bulges on one side of his neck. His hands are so much larger up close than they were when he was seated at the chair, his pad on his knee, and the pen tapping against it.

"No!" she screams.

The demons' laughter goes unnoticed. The doctor grabs one of Dane's wrists. He's strong, and he jerks her arm free from its grip around her legs. A sharp pain runs up her forearm and into her elbow. He ignores her cry of pain and lifts her from her seat in the corner of the closet. Dane lashes out with her other hand, dragging her fingernails across his face.

His grip loosens slightly, but he doesn't release her. Instead, he hefts her body off the floor.

Dane's legs remain bent, and she falls forward as he backs away. He tries to lift her up again, but she forces her weight to the floor. She may not be a large girl, but she's learned through the years how to become a heavy rock.

Though the numbers scare her, they become her only salvation, the only thing keeping her and the demons in this room.

Doctor Charles bends down again, grabs both of Dane's wrists, one in each of his hands. He is speaking, but she doesn't hear him.

All she sees is his face, reddened from anger, a scratch along the cheek, where the nails dug into his skin.

He tries to lift her again. She falls forward. Her knees drag across the carpet, and then she lands on her stomach.

"I will pull you out of here if I have to." Doctor Charles' lips are peeled back in a snarl. Sweat beads along his forehead.

Memories flood her, and she screams. Then the words spill from her mouth like water from a cracked urn. "They did it. They killed them all, not me."

124

The hisses echo in her ears.

The hole grows and a face peaks out. Singed hairs cover charred skin. Blue eyes, the color of faded navy, stare out from deep sockets. Cracked lips expose rotten brown teeth.

"*Who* are *they*?"

The demon dips back into the hole—two odds and one even, and she knows there is strength in the numbers, in any of the combinations, as long as there is more odd than even.

"I'll tell you. I'll tell you everything."

Doctor Charles releases her.

Dane drops onto her hands. She rolls onto her bottom and scoots backward.

"Don't go back in the closet." His chest heaves up and down, up and down.

Dane stops short of the closet entrance, and rubs her wrists where bruises are forming in the shape of fingers, and for the first time since all this began, she understands a little more.

"Talk," Charles says.

The demon's eyes grow larger. A strand of drool drips from her mouth, and soaks into the carpet. Both of her arms stretch out from the hole and she places her hands on either side as if she is going to push her way free.

"Uncle Barry ..." Dane pauses.

"What about him?"

"Uncle Barry liked me." Three odds, one even. Safe.

"Of course he liked you. He was your caregiver after your parents died."

"No." She flinches. Even. "Barry liked parts ... liked certain parts." She puts her hands to her breasts for emphasis. She glances down to her crotch, then back up at Doctor Charles.

A light bulb turns on—she can see it in his face, the way a child's eyes light up when he finally learns something new he's been working hard to understand. The doctor's eyes soften, and he relaxes. He had been wrong about her. "Did he touch you?"

She bites her bottom lip, looks down at the floor, and whispers, "They didn't like what he did."

Six words, five even-numbered.

The hole widens, exposing the demon's upper torso, void of clothes, small breasts drooping the wrong way.

"Who didn't?"

"I called them. I brought them here." Keeping her head down, she stares up at the doctor through her bangs.

The demon pushes herself further from the hole, her hips free, legs soon to follow.

Dane waits for Doctor Charles to ask the inevitable.

"You called who?" Two to one, the odd over the even.

"Them," she says, intentionally even, her voice flat.

The demon drags one leg out of the hole. It's battered and bruised.

"Who?

She searches for just the right words. "My family."

"Your family is dead."

The demon pulls the other foot from the hole and drops to the floor. She stands straight, directly behind the doctor.

"Four," Dane says. "Eleven. Thirteen."

"What?"

Dane stifles a laugh. Her lips turn up. Her eyes shine in anticipation. "Zero is even."

"I don't understand."

The demon creeps up behind him, her hands outstretched.

"My family. They're here."

"What? What are you— "

"Even numbers kill," she whispers.

Doctor Charles' body jerks as the demon—a member of the family she cried out for—sinks a clawed hand into his back. He tries to turn his neck to see what has his heart in its decaying hand but can't.

A scream freezes in his throat.

He is pulled backward as the others reach down, their arms outstretched, their laughter clinging to the air like thick smoke.

The doctor grabs hold of the folding chair, but it won't help him. He looks up, his eyes bulging. His face is red and snot flies from one nostril.

He sees what is happening, the demons' hands and arms charred black and blistered, the nails curled around the tips of fingers, browned in the flames of a fiery car crash.

Doctor Charles' foot strikes the sunglasses and they skitter across the floor. He screams again as Mom and Dad lift him by the hair and shoulders.

Dane stares at her dead parents. They exchange knowing smiles and then disappear into the ceiling, the hole closing up behind them.

Dane releases the breath she was holding, and then crawls back to her closet. As she sits down, her eyes catch a glimpse of the pen lying on the floor, fresh blood smeared along its barrel.

"Thank you, Mom. Thank you, Dad."

Dane lowers her head to her knees. Maybe next time she'll allow the even numbers to be safe.

To Bleed

I am pain. To know me is to feel me. To feel me is to hurt. To hurt is to bleed. To bleed is to live ...

Kimberly sits naked in the center of the crumbling house. Flickering candles encircle her. She clutches a knife in both hands. The blade touches the floor—a splintered hardwood.

The house groans, its roof sagging. Dry rot has set in on several spots in the floor. Brown patches of mold cling to the ceiling. The walls, miraculously, are not damaged with holes. Only Time's wicked finger has caused buckles near the ceiling that push outward in places. Images, offered up by many others, line the room from corner to corner, intertwining with each other; visages move and swirl, as if breathing. Prophets clutch tight to Bibles, graffiti gangsters hold old school boom boxes, music notes spilling out in whites, blues, yellows, and oranges; a knight in dull armor sits on a hobby horse, its stick drawn with a splintered end, and an angel with black wings, a white shock of hair and blue eyes.

Outside, rain pours, lightning flashes and thunder bellows. Wind batters the ancient house, racing through empty windows and forcing a cool draft through the halls and beneath the door of the room she is in. Her hair stirs as a puff of wind blows through the room. Somewhere someone is calling, but the voice is too far off for her to care, for her to listen to the pleas of a distrustful lover.

I am pain. To know me is to feel me ...

"I feel nothing," she whispers. "I want to feel again."

She lifts the knife, its blade glistening yellow/orange in the candles' dancing flames. A distorted reflection of herself looks back at her from it.

Feel me ...

The cool blade slices through the skin of one thigh, but only deep enough to draw tiny beads of blood. Kimberly's breath hitches, eyes enlarge. Her lip quivers as the pain tingles, then subsides, leaving only a slight sting in its wake. A smile forms as her leg begins to itch. She wants to scratch it, but to feel … to feel anything is better than the nothing she has felt since …

The once distant voice rings out, closer, calling.

Kimberly glances at the door, a bolt holding it closed.

I am pain. To know me is to feel me … Feel me …

Kimberly slides the blade across her other thigh, deeper than the first cut. Her teeth are gritted, her lips spread in a grimace. Skin peels aside as blood spills down the sides of her leg. She shivers as the wave of pain dies off as quickly as it was born.

Focusing on the painting of the angel with black wings and blue eyes, Kimberly brings the knife from knee to hip, this one deeper than the previous cut. A cry escapes her as muscle pares from muscle and blood cascades from another wound. The angel's wings shimmer, its chest heaves, eyes twinkle. His white hair seems to blow with the cool draft in the room.

A prickle of fear creeps through her, sending goose bumps along her skin. Her nipples harden, and the fine hairs on her arms stand on end.

To feel me is to hurt …

The angel steps from the wall, tearing away from sheetrock and walking inches above the floor. In his wake is a yellowed outline. His white hair billows around his head.

Do you hurt?

A tear spills down Kimberly's cheek.

"Always."

Her eyes once sparkled when she thought of Daniel.

"It's over?" she asked as she stared across the table at him. Everyone else in the restaurant had disappeared in the seconds before her questioning reply to his statement. The waitress vanished, the parents with the snot-nosed kid who couldn't stay in his seat for more than three minutes evaporated, the older couple behind them grew silent, all of them no longer there as her world fell apart.

"I don't love you anymore," he said, not looking at her. He seemed very aware of the people still there.

"But, we're getting married."

"No. No, we're not."

He placed his napkin on the table, stood and walked away, leaving her sitting in the restaurant, their meals untouched. She stared at the Italian dish with its marinara sauce and Parmesan cheese covering the almost heart shaped piece of chicken breast.

Hours passed with her sitting there, the world still invisible to her. She left at closing time. Head down, she walked in the rain until she found herself in front of the only house on Wayley Street, a tiny dilapidated structure with no inviting characteristics. The door opened, and she heard the whispers ...

To hurt is to bleed ...

Kimberly's heart breaks all over again—a hurt she had forced aside—and she brings the knife across her bicep. Tissue severs, pulls from bone. Her arm throbs and blood covers it in red, dripping off her fingertips and blending with the dust and grime of the floor. Her vision blurs. Breathing becomes harder.

The angel kneels, dips his finger into the blood pooling around her legs and licks his finger. The other images cry out and hiss in both anger and elation. One of them—one of the Biblical prophets with hollow eyes—extends a hand, ripping it from the wall, but he can't break free.

"Kimberly!" The voice yells for her. Sharp raps echo through the room. "Kimberly, open the door."

He's here, whispers the picture of a snake stretching the four corners of the room. The other paintings writhe on the wall, struggling to break free from a canvas that holds them tight.

"I can't live without you."

"You've lost your mind, Kimberly."

The phone went silent, then beeped as she listened, stunned by his apathy. She clicked the phone off, then back on. Kimberly dialed, waited. Daniel's message service followed two rings. She bit her lip, almost hung up, but instead spoke. "If I can't have you, I don't want to live." Before hanging up, she spoke the words she heard when passing the house on the far side of town. "*I am pain. To know me is to feel me. To feel me is to hurt. To hurt is to bleed. To bleed is to live ...*"

Calmly, she recited the address, hung up the phone and set it on her nightstand.

She awoke with knife in hand, candles lit, and the house whispering to her. Her body was numb, her mind a heavy fog of memories that no longer felt real.

Kimberly's vision clears as she flays away part of her forearm. Skin falls to the floor and her jaw quakes with a fresh pain that sears her senses. Her blood seeps into the rotting wood beneath her. Tendrils sprout from the floor, crawl into her legs, rapping around bone, rooting her in place. The paintings screech and groan, howl with lust as she pulls the blade across her palm and smears the blood on her abdomen.

Outside the room, Daniel yells for her, beats on the door. Several heavy thuds rattle the frame until the bolt splinters wood, and the door slams open. She sees him, smiles weakly.

"You came," she whispers.

In three long strides, Daniel is across the room and kneeling in the circle beside her. "What are you doing, Kimberly?

Trying to kill yourself?"

"Trying to live," she says, her green eyes staring up at him but only seeing a vague semblance of Daniel.

To bleed is to live …

Daniel spins, loses his balance and lands on his bottom. The angel stands in front of him, ethereal features swimming on its body, wings dripping crimson and hate in its eyes.

"What the Hell?"

"I am pain," the angel speaks.

"To know me is to feel me," Kimberly says and drives the knife into Daniel's back, between two ribs and into his heart. His hands go up as if he was surrendering to someone with a gun in front of him. His head turns. His mouth is open, eyes large, with tears spilling from them. She pulls the blade free, stabs him again and again, even after he slumps to the floor, blood soaking into the dry rotting wood.

"To bleed is to live," Kimberly sobs.

Images pull free from the wall, creeping forward, reaching for Daniel's blood, lapping it up with starving tongues. The snake swallows his body slowly, its jaw unhinging, then it returns to the wall, satiated for the time.

Kimberly brings the knife across her right breast; a deep wound sends slivers of hot pain coursing through her body. She trembles, slices her left breast, deeper … deeper each time, shaving flesh from bone. With each cut the pain heightens, though her senses dull.

To bleed is to live … Live, my angels …

The images converge on Kimberly, their hands and claws pulling at her, teeth nipping into ruined flesh, tearing meat away as her blood flows into the floor. She doesn't scream as darkness takes her into its arms, folds her away.

One by one the pictures retreat, taking their place along the walls, blending with the once white interior, until lastly, the angel takes his place among the dead, nearest a fresh image, still wet, its artwork and artist forever one. The woman cradles her lover in red tinted arms, his eyes are full with fear, his heart sitting in her open palm.

A trickle of blood seeps from the heart, tracing down the wall and pooling on the floor beneath the image.

And the angel whispers one last time, *To bleed is to live. To live is to die ...*

Not Like You

"There is evil in those who do nothing," Pastor Michaels said from the pulpit. He waved his Bible over his head, his gray peppered brown hair neatly cut, suit wrinkle free. "Those slothy people who do only for themselves, and sometimes not even that much—they are the devil's tools. They get under the skin of hard workers, causing the sins of gossip and jealousy, causing anger and frustration to the righteous. Oh, yes, there is evil in the lazy ..."

Brian's ten-year-old mind took in the sermon, soaked up every word as if Pastor Michaels talked directly to him. He focused on the yelling man behind the pulpit, the rest of the world shut out, the church, his brother and sister's constant wiggling, the grandparents on either side of the trio of siblings, the choir behind the preacher and the constant cough from Mrs. Hagler in the second row, her seventy-three-year-old hack more like a dog barking than an old woman clearing her throat and chest of phlegm.

A nudge and a hollow voice brought him from his trance. "You ready to go?" Granddaddy asked. He stood, slightly hunched over, and waited for Brian to respond.

"Yes, Granddaddy," he said, his voice still holding childish wonder in it, even through several years of neglect, of little food and filthy diapers, unchanged for two and three days at a time, blood from the rash dribbling along the floor when he crawled or walked through garbage and roaches. Six years in the past, the effects of being alone for hours, sometimes days, still lingered.

At home, he sat on the bottom of the bunk beds he shared with his little brother, who was only a baby when they came to live with Grandmomma and Granddaddy. The room was crowded with a long dresser, a television sitting on top of it, and a tall shelf unit where toys and excess clothing went. A mirror sat opposite Brian, hanging on the closet door.

He scooted further onto the mattress until his back touched the wall. He stared at himself in the mirror. His brown hair was cropped close, blue eyes centered his face, small nose and thin lips didn't look right sitting above a prominent chin.

You look just like your daddy, Grandmomma said once. At the time, Brian had been happy to have something from his daddy. If he couldn't be with him, why not look like him? He held onto that thought, hoping one day to be like his daddy, a man, grown and able to make his own decisions in life.

"I don't look like Daddy," he said, and the words of Pastor Michaels came back to him. *There is evil in those who do nothing.*

"Brian," Grandmomma called from the front room. He scooted to the edge of the bed, his eyes focused on the mirror, taking in every inch of his face, the way his hair stood up on the sides, the light brown blemish on his skin near his right ear. Brian was big for his age, not fat, by any means, just big, like his parents, tall and *thick*, mountainous, as someone else from church once marveled. He flexed his fingers, watched the hand curl and uncurl, fascinated with the simplicity of movement.

Grandmomma appeared in the doorway, hands on her hips, orange hair crowning her skull. "Brian, did you hear me calling you?"

"Yes, Ma'am," he mumbled and shrugged, a habit of his, shrugging and answering a question, but not looking up at the person he addressed.

She shook her head. "You're as hard headed as your daddy is."

"No, I'm not," he said, his tone sharp.

Grandmomma raised her eyebrows. "Speaking of your daddy, he's here if you want to see him."

Brian's disdain for his father vanished in the blink of an eye, his heart lifting. "Daddy's here?"

"Yes. He's a little late, but he wants to give you something for your birthday."

"All right!" Brian yelled and slid from the bed. A wide smile stretched his face. He brushed by Grandmomma and ran down the small hall to the front room. His daddy stood near the front door, talking to Brian's sister. A scraggly beard covered the lower part of his face; hands stained with grease dangled by his sides.

"Hey, Daddy," Brian said, and tugged on his dad's dirty flannel coat. Daddy smelled of cigarettes and grime, like he hadn't bathed in a few weeks. Brian crinkled his nose but said nothing. Last time Brian mentioned how he smelled, Daddy didn't come around for a month.

"Hey, Brian," Daddy said, his voice deep. He tussled Brian's hair. His stench wafted in the air.

Brian held back a cough and smiled. It was Daddy, after all.

"I wanted to tell you happy birthday," Daddy said, squatted and gave Brian a hug.

"Thank you," Brian responded, then like any other child, "Did you get me a present?"

Daddy stood, put his hands on his hips and shook his head. "Brian, right now money's kind of tight, and I just didn't have any extra to—"

"Didn't you just buy a new computer?" Granddaddy asked from the kitchen doorway, his arms folded across his chest, eyes narrow, lips turned down. Grandmomma had said on more than one occasion it was their son's fault that Granddaddy's hair was the brilliant silver of a very old man instead of the natural gray of a man just losing the color in his strands. Right then Granddaddy looked a little bit older than earlier, when he smiled down at Brian after church services had concluded. It was as if Grandmomma was right. When Daddy was around, Granddaddy became much older.

Daddy's mouth dropped open and then snapped closed. The air in the room changed. Brian's mood swung with it.

"Brian, why don't you go on outside for a little while?" Granddaddy asked and rubbed Brian's shoulder.

"But I want to go somewhere with my daddy."

"Brian, we're not going anywhere today," Daddy said. "I have some things to do at home."

Brian's heart sank into his stomach, his mind slowed. The rest of the world dimmed, vanished, leaving only Daddy and himself. But he was no longer Daddy. He was the man who lived next door who never came out to play or say hello or even yell to 'get off my lawn'. No, he was now the lazy, filthy sinner Pastor Michaels spoke of. He was a sloth.

"Come on, Brian," Mary said, tugging his arm. He glanced at his older sister, her blue eyes magnified behind the lenses of her glasses. "I think Granddaddy and Daddy are going to talk."

They made their way past Granddaddy and to the back door. Brian glanced back and waited for his father to say goodbye. When he didn't, Brian went outside, sat by the door, crossed his legs and put his chin in his hands. Tears touched the corners of his eyes, and he took a long, deep breath.

"Let's ride our bikes," Mary said from the end of the porch.

"I don't want to," Brian said, not looking up. His eyes traced the cracks along the concrete porch. He counted the planks of the wood deck that extended out fifteen feet from the back door. The benches lining the rails all held some item or other on them: a fish tank, rocks in a white paint bucket, Christmas lights that hadn't been put away and probably never would be. A cat hopped on the rail, glanced down at Brian and strutted away, tail in the air, head held high as if he, the cat, had better things to do than to be around Brian, the boy, whose own father didn't care enough about him to buy him a birthday present or spend even an hour with him playing in the front yard.

Brian stood, pushed the back door open and listened to Granddaddy and Daddy arguing. Daddy said little. Each time he spoke, Granddaddy spoke louder, angrier.

"You're just making excuses, just like you always have," Granddaddy said.

"It's not an excuse."

138

"Sure it is," Grandmomma interrupted. "You spend your money on anything but your children. You do all you can for you, but can you be depended on to provide food for your kids? Or clothing? Or even toys on their birthdays?"

"I do everything I can—"

Granddaddy spoke next. "You do everything you can for you and you alone. How can you come over here and tell Brian 'happy birthday', three days late, and not have him a present or, at the very least, a card? Anything besides an excuse? If you really wanted to buy him something you could have taken the money you spent on a brand new computer and bought him a present."

"I got it on sale—"

"It doesn't matter how cheap you got it, the point is ... You know what, it doesn't matter what the point is. Why don't you just go next door and play on your little computer and leave Brian alone. While you're at it, why don't you leave us all alone?"

The words ceased. A moment later the front door opened, then slammed shut. Brian ran to the edge of the deck and up onto one of the benches. He peeked around the corner at Daddy as he sulked across the driveway and back into his yard. A moment later, his front door slammed shut.

Brian eased off the bench and went inside, head down, his hands in his pockets.

"Brian," Granddaddy said, "I'm sorry about your dad."

Brian shrugged, tears in his eyes. Without looking from the blue and red rug on the floor he whispered, "It's okay. Daddy's just a sloth. He's lazy."

In his room, he scooted back on the bed. The image in the mirror stared at him with red-rimmed eyes and rosy cheeks. "I'm nothing like Daddy."

Brian kicked off his shoes and crawled beneath the blankets, tucking his head under the blue sheet and gray cover Grandmomma and Granddaddy bought, his head on the pillow Grandmomma and Granddaddy bought, lying in the clothes Grandmomma and Granddaddy bought. He poked his head out, his eyes seeking, finding, focusing on small things in the room, before moving onto something else: the Hot Wheels cars in a small box on the shelf, a scuffed black bike helmet, the television that played Spongebob and Chowder and Fanboy and Chum Chum, a broken model, a wooden box car, the video game system beside the television. Grandmomma and Granddaddy had purchased everything for him, Mary, and David.

Daddy purchased nothing. Not one item in the room, not one piece of clothing or broken toy or birthday card. He thought of Grandmomma and Granddaddy, how angry they had sounded while Daddy was there, and how sad Granddaddy had looked, his shoulders sagging, eyes soft behind his bifocals, when he apologized to Brian because of Daddy.

"Daddy's just a lazy person." What had Pastor Michaels said about lazy people as he waved his Bible over his head, his hair jutting up on one side and his suit coat unbuttoned? *"There is evil in those who do nothing."*

Brian's eyes widened. He sat up and stared at his image in the mirror. "Daddy's evil," he whispered, the words solidifying the thoughts, making it more real.

Brian crawled out from under the blankets, sat on the floor and put his shoes on—shoes Grandmomma and Granddaddy had purchased. He left the bedroom and walked through the house, passing his grandparents sitting in the living room, their hushed whispers growing silent when he appeared.

"Where are you heading?" Granddaddy asked.

"Outside," Brian shrugged.

"Okay," Granddaddy said. "You have fun."

"Okay." Another shrug followed. He walked through the kitchen and out the back door. Mary road her purple bike around the left side of the yard, the part separated from the rest of the yard with a fence—the play area where the toys and bikes Grandmomma and Granddaddy had purchased went.

"You gonna ride your bike?" Mary asked as she sped by.

"No."

Brian went down the five steps and crossed the yard, stepping over broken toys: cars and a wagon, a deflated soccer ball and other odd things they played with. To his right was an above ground pool, emptied for the winter and not yet filled back up, but still it held a foot or more of water and black and brown leaves. Directly in front of him was Grandmomma's plant house, a cinder block structure where she kept all the plastic flowers she used for the arrangements she made. Beside it sat Granddaddy's tool shed, half the size of the block building and packed with tools from front to back with a not so clear walkway running its length.

To Brian's far right sat Daddy's yard, a jungle of dead weeds and one fallen tree. Three old cars sat in various stages of repair, none of them having been touched in well over a year. Rusty tools sat near the cars. Beyond them stood a clothesline, the green wire stretched from one tree to a fence post. Several articles of Momma's clothing hung on the line, having been there almost as long as the cars had gone untouched, their colors faded from dark blues and red and greens to pinks and light blues and yellows.

Brian glanced at Mary. She raced her bike around the side yard, oblivious to him. Brian backtracked toward the house, looked over his shoulder to make sure no one was watching. If Granddaddy saw, he would be in more trouble than he had ever been in, but Brian wanted—needed—to go to Daddy, to warn Daddy he was evil and bound for a hell Pastor Michaels said is hotter than anything the human mind could imagine, whatever that meant.

At the back gate, he flipped the latch and unsnapped two bungee chords holding it in place. He slid out the gate, closing it behind him. Brian hurried through Daddy's backyard and up the three wooden steps to the back door. Turning the handle, the door eased open, and Brian stepped inside.

The stench took his breath away. He inhaled sharply and his throat and lungs began to burn. Brian held his breath as best he could, but the odor was strong. He pulled his shirt over his nose, alleviating some of the acrid smell. The room he stood in at one time used to be the den and washroom. The walls were covered in splotches of black fuzz. Clothes littered the burgundy carpet. A bed sheet hung over the doorway, one that may have been white at one time but had turned a yellowish brown. The washer's lid sat open, water that smelled like sewage inside.

Brian hurried through the sheet. Touching it made his skin crawl. After six years of a neat and tidy home, the filth of the place made his stomach churn and his eyes burn.

The kitchen opened up in front of him. Bugs crawled along the dirty white linoleum. The stove was nothing more than an oven on blocks, the yellow top stained black. Pots holding molded food sat on the stovetop. The brown kitchen table and the floor were littered with fast food wrappers. Roaches raced from one item to the next, getting their fill of what remained before darting off to hide between the walls or under the counter. The kitchen sink had turned brown and was stacked high with dirty dishes. The faucet was missing, leaving only hot and cold handles.

Brian poked his head through the kitchen doorway and into the front room. Daddy sat at the computer, his back to Brian, his shirt unbuttoned, a cigarette in one hand. He blew out a long puff of smoke, sniffled, and clicked the mouse. He punched the table and let out a litany of curse words. Across the dirty monitor, barely visible through the haze of smoke in the air and the dots on the screen, a woman appeared, her breasts concealed by one arm. She held up a finger, shook it back and forth. GAME OVER scrolled across the screen.

"Crap. You won't beat me again, woman," Daddy said and took a long drag of the cigarette.

Brian stepped through the doorway. The front room was like the rest of the house. It stank; trash littered the floor, roaches, big and small, scurried about. A rat scampered into the hallway, its long tail trailing behind it.

"Daddy," Brian said.

Daddy turned fast in his seat. The springs groaned. He blew out a stream of gray smoke. "What are you doing here?"

142

he yelled, his brow furrowed in a crease just above his nose, his lips turned down into a frown.

Brian shrugged. "I don't know."

"Go home," Daddy snapped. "You've gotten me in enough trouble today." He turned back to the computer, clicked the mouse several times.

Brian cocked his head to one side, then looked down at his feet, at the shoes Grandmomma and Granddaddy bought for him before school started. "What did I do?"

Daddy said nothing, only played his game as if Brian wasn't there.

"What did I do?" Brian asked again, this time louder.

Daddy cursed again. The woman flashed back across the screen, the same GAME OVER popped up in brilliant green letters. He spun around in his chair, took a long toke on the cigarette, held it, and then blew the smoke in Brian's face.

Brian coughed, but didn't move, didn't try to brush the smoke away. His eyes stung and watered, but he held firm to his stare on Daddy.

"What did you do?" Daddy asked through clenched teeth. "I'll tell you what you did. You had to ask for a present, didn't you? Well, guess what? I have you a present, I just didn't want to give it to you over there. I didn't want your grandparents to claim they got it for you."

"You got me a present?" Brian asked, his gaze not wavering, heart lifting along with his eyebrows.

"Of course, I did."

"Where is it?" Excitement bubbled in his voice.

"I took it back," Daddy snapped. "You don't deserve a present. You want to get me in trouble? Just for that I'm not buying you another present ever again."

Brian's bottom lip quivered. He clamped his teeth together, holding the lip as still as possible. Tears blurred his eyes. He held them back as long as he could.

"I'm sorry," he whispered.

"Sure you are," Daddy snapped. "Just go home to your new mom and dad and leave me alone, okay?"

143

"But …"

"No buts. Go home. I don't want you around me right now."

With that said, the tears fell, traced down his face and dripped off his prominent chin. His heart ached worse than it ever did before. Brian turned, shuffled back through the kitchen and the den, to the back door.

"And close the door when you leave," Daddy yelled.

Outside, Brian sat on the rickety steps, the door closed, but not locked. Elbows on his knees, he put his chin in his hands and cried. After several minutes, he composed himself.

"I'm nothing like Daddy," Brian said and went down the steps. He kicked garbage around the back yard, picked up several tools and threw them as hard as he could. A wrench hit one of the cars with a loud metallic thump. "I hate you, Daddy," he yelled and kicked at a pile of leaves.

His foot struck a hammer at the base of the pile. It flipped over once, came to a stop a couple of feet from him. Brian stared at the rusty steel head, its claw a deep orange, the hammerhead brown and worn. The wooden handle was a dark brown, months of being wet and on the ground and covered with leaves having taken its toll on its appearance. He squatted to get a better look.

"What are you doing over there, Brian?" Mary called from the fence.

He glanced up. She stood next to her bike. "I don't know," Brian said with a shrug.

"You better get back over here before Granddaddy sees you."

Brian glanced at Mary, and then picked up the hammer. It wasn't too heavy, even with the wet handle. He turned back to the house, went up the steps, and opened the door.

"Brian, don't you go in there," Mary yelled. "I'm going to tell."

He ignored her, went inside and pushed the door gently until it clicked into place. Through the den and the horrible yellowish-brown sheet and into the kitchen he went, stopping in the doorway between the kitchen and the front room.

Daddy's back was still to him, his hand resting on the mouse, its *clickclickclick* the only real sound in the room.

"Daddy," Brian said and stepped up behind him.

"I thought I told you …" he turned in his protesting seat. His eyes snapped all the way open, and he tried to raise an arm to his face.

Brian swung the hammer like a baseball bat, the head striking Daddy's elbow. There was a loud pop, followed by Daddy's scream. He fell out of the chair and onto his knees, clutching his swelling elbow.

"What is wrong with you?" Daddy yelled. His face was red, and there were tears in his eyes and a grimace on his face.

Brian, the kid who had always been big for his age—mountainous—stepped forward, the hammer held by both hands over his head. Anger made him swift. He brought it down on the side of Daddy's head, cracking the cheekbone. Daddy fell over, another scream tearing from him as he held his face. Beads of blood trickled through grease stained fingers.

"I'm nothing like you," Brian yelled, and brought the hammer down on Daddy's left knee with enough force to break the kneecap. Daddy flopped on the floor. "I'm not lazy like you are. I'm not evil like you are." Brian struck again, this time on one of Daddy's bare feet. The big toenail shot off and blood exploded from the new wound.

"Brian, stop," Daddy said between sobs. "Stop, boy."

Brian didn't stop. He swung the hammer again and again, connecting with legs and arms and ribs and head, and blood splashed against the walls and on the floor, on the computer screen where the woman had her breasts covered and wagged a finger. It was all over Brian as well, slick and hot and sticky.

He swung the hammer even as Grandmomma and Granddaddy beat on the front door, even as they yelled for Daddy to open up; they knew Brian was in there. He beat Daddy's lifeless body until Granddaddy ran around the back of the house and up the rickety steps and through the back door, the dirty yellowish-brown sheet, and the kitchen, where the

145

rat scurried beneath the stove. He smashed Daddy's bones, crying, and screaming as he did so about the devil and sin and how he was nothing like his daddy. *Nothing like you at all!*

"Brian," Granddaddy said from the kitchen doorway. His voice muffled in Brian's ears, but somehow smooth at the same time. Granddaddy repeated his name. His voice was no longer muffled. It was Granddaddy's normally calm and understanding voice.

Brian stopped, his arms and legs suddenly weak. His stomach flipped with nausea. He looked at Granddaddy through tear-blurred eyes.

"Give me the hammer, Brian," Granddaddy said and stuck out his hand, palm up.

"Yes, sir," Brian said and set it in his hand.

Granddaddy took Brian, hugged him to his chest, and rubbed his head. Brian liked when Granddaddy hugged him close, liked the way it felt, Granddaddy's warmth and arms to protect him, to love him.

"Brian," Granddaddy said.

"Yes?" He saw the concern on Granddaddy's face, the fear in his eyes.

"Why did you do this?"

Brian shrugged, always shrugging. "He was evil," Brian said. "And Pastor Michaels said we have to cleanse the evil from this world."

With that said, Granddaddy led Brian out of the house, a blood soaked little boy, much too big for his age.

Brian stopped at the bottom of the steps, pulled his hand free. "Granddaddy?"

"Yes, Brian?" His voice was shaky.

"I'm not like Daddy, am I?"

Granddaddy shook his head. "No, Brian. You're nothing like your daddy."

146

The Sad Woes of the Trash Man

Most stories begin the way they end. Most folk don't know that.

I have me a little story to tell, but ain't had nobody to tell it to. Sometimes it eats a man up, right down to his gut and causes him to bleed on the inside. That ain't no good, and it ain't no way to be. Keeping secrets, especially big ones like the one I have, will ruin a person.

So I need to tell someone. I ain't got no wife. Well, I had one, but it just didn't work out. I ain't got no kids, not a one at all; I ain't one of them men who had three or four or five kids, all by different women. I ain't really had but one long term relationship—seven years it lasted, right up until I went to jail. I don't blame her for divorcing me. I was a criminal, a piddly old car thief who got caught on the first try. And she was a nice woman with a nice family, and she ain't needed me no how anyways. I reckon her pappy was all right with that—back in them days it was frowned upon for a white girl to marry herself a man of color, and my skin is just the right shade of mahogany to make her pappy and mammy, and a whole bunch of others, right mad.

I can see the old buzzard now, sitting in his recliner. Mind you, he ain't had no problem sitting in a chair the same color as me, but let me get up next to his little girl and the color sure did matter then. And he probably sat there with Michelle across from him on the couch, her blue eyes full of tear and the skin all puffed up around them, probably rimmed red from crying and rubbing, crying and rubbing. Her hair was probably pulled back in a loose ponytail—ahh how I loved her ponytails, but that be another story for another time.

Her pappy probably had a rich man's pipe in his mouth, a

huffing and a puffing on it. Back then there wasn't any of that flavored smoke, so it was just some regular pipe tobacco. He might have even had one of them newspapers folded neatly in his lap, and his spectacles perched up on his nose like he's some type of professor at the local college.

I bet he went and pulled them glasses right off his face and started to wiping at them with a white hanky while she told him I was in jail, and I was nothing more than a common thief, finishing it up with a 'Daddy, can I please come on home?'

'I tried to warn you.' is what he would have said. I'm willing to bet my next check from the five and dime on it. He done gone and shook his head and sucked his teeth a little, and then he let himself out a big old breath, cause that's what he would do, you know. Just let out a breath, long and loud, so she would know he was mighty disappointed in her.

Then the old buzzard probably went and said something like, "It'll be okay, Sweetheart. You just come on home and we'll forget about the negro you done went and sullied yourself with."

I reckon I done got off topic here, but you know, it's been a long time since I done went and talked to anyone about anything much, and sometimes I get off on a tangent and have to finish up a thought before returning to my original one.

So, now you know why I ain't got no wife, and why I ain't got no kids and why I ain't got nobody to talk to. And you also know why I ain't been to no confessional, pretty much ever in my life. Back in them days, though the world was changing for the black folk, it took a mighty long time to get there. Though the segregation done happened by then, some places still ain't much accepted us as equals. And in this day and age, well, I don't reckon things done got much better.

That's why I'm here, to do me a bit of confessing. I don't need no forgiving or anything, nor do I want it. I get my forgiveness from the Lord up above, not from no man. But, still, I need me someone to talk to.

So, here I am.

I reckon I should get on to my story, eh? I ain't getting no younger, and you probably have more important things to do other than listen to some old black man talk about what's ailing him.

There ain't much light in this here booth, just a little bit of candle left flicking its flame like a tongue. You ever notice how the shadows from them flames look like dancers on the wall? No, I reckon you probably ain't noticed. But the seat sure is comfortable. I can lean back against the wall here and not feel like I'm falling, and the cushion makes it easy on my old back. I appreciate that a mighty bunch, sir.

There's so much to talk about, so much on my mind. I'm of the thought you probably want the story any way you can get it. From the beginning probably helps, so I'll just tell you what you need to know about the beginning and the middle and then get onto the end, if that suits you, okay?

Really, the beginning of this whole mess started when I was 27—that'd be back in '72—you can turn them numbers around and get my age or the year, just depending on how you look at it. I think it's awful interestin', like the year and my age lined up like the stars or planets, and them events was destiny and all. By '72 the whole racial equality thing had been in full swing for a little while, but things still weren't where they should have been. I'm sure you ain't one to want to hear about all that equality mess, cause that's just what it was and has been for a long time.

I was a punk back then; thought I was something special. I had me a cute little white girl with a cute little white girl figure and a cute little white girl family. I reckon she liked me enough to marry me, but you see, her pappy went and cut her off. No money for his negro-marrying daughter. Them are his words, not mine. 'Negro-marrying daughter.' That's what a grown man went and called his little girl. It's a shame now, and it was, all the same back then, though those who thought the way he did, saw nothing wrong with it.

When her pappy cut her off, she and I started having arguments. I didn't make enough money for her, and she ain't never held no job. Why would she have? Pappy had money, and Pappy took good care of her. Now that I think of it, I'm almost certain the problems started when Pappy refused to help pay for the wedding, and we had to run off and find us a preacher man to do the ceremony for us, all justice of the peace style. That man—the preacher man, not Pappy—was just liquored up enough to pronounce us man and wife, but I had to grease his palm with a fifty-dollar spot. Back in '72, that was a week's wages for me.

We made it six years—all but the first four months of it after Pappy done cut her off—before I went and got in trouble and ruined everything for myself.

I didn't know how good I had it. My job paid decent enough, but not as well as it would have if I had been a different color. I had a nice looking wife, and we had us an apartment in an okay section of the city—not great, but not bad either. We didn't have no kids, but we had been talking about it. I knew it wasn't going to happen if she wasn't happy, and I was *never* really sure if she was happy. She stayed home most of the time, watching the stories on television and occasionally talking to her mammy. Pappy, he ain't never called once. Sure, we had a good time together, but things just never felt right, as if maybe she regretted her decision to marry me.

But I loved her, and I wanted to make her happy, so I thought I would steal a car and sell it. You know, make a couple hundred bucks and buy her something nice, maybe even take her on a trip or something. I didn't know. I might have been approaching thirty, but I wasn't all too smart.

The car I stole—it was a nice one all right, a brand new Maverick, but it wasn't like it was when it come off the show room floor. No, I reckon the guy who owned it wanted it to be like a Camaro or a Corvette or maybe even one of them Novas. You know someone once told me Nova in Spanish means No Go. I don't know if it's true, but it sure made me laugh the first time I heard it.

That Maverick was sitting on the corner, all by its lonesome. It was dark—I reckon it was around two in the morning. I had been walking around, looking for the right car, and that

Maverick just spoke to me. It says, "Lewis, you wants to be taking me now. I'll make you quite a bit of money." It didn't really say that, but in my head, well, it was speaking to me, begging me to drive it away from the corner.

So, I did.

Back then, a lot of folk—especially white folk—left their doors unlocked and the keys in the ignition. The fella who owned the Maverick was one of them people. I just opened the door and hopped on in, cranked it up, and drove off. Simple as that. You can't be doing that these days. Folks done learned—especially white folks—leaving a car unlocked and the keys in the ignition is like an invitation to have it stolen.

I got all the way to the next town over and was peddling the car by the next morning. "Three hundred, that's what I'll take."

Ain't none of them white folk wanted to buy from no negro-man. No sir. But one of them sure didn't have no problem letting the police know I was selling it. There's an old joke used to go 'round these parts. It goes like this: "What do you call a black man on a bicycle? Thief."

That's a real knee slapper, now ain't it? Yeah, I ain't think so, either.

I reckon that's what they thought of me when they saw me selling the Maverick. Certainly no colored man could own a car as nice as that one. And they was right, though I reckon if I had tried really hard, I could've owned one of them cars in a couple to three years.

The policeman pulled right alongside the Maverick, and he and his partner got on out. They was both white, and their hair was cut all high and tight. They ain't wasted no time looking me up and down and thinking I done did something wrong, like it was wrote on my face or something.

"How do?" One of them asked, like he was making friendly conversation.

I gave him, a "how do" back, but I was watching them real close-like. The big one had a crooked nose, like it been broke a couple times. He did the talking, while the little guy did the watching. I'll be honest with you; that little guy scared me more than the big one. He was a wired one all right, with his hands all clenched into fists like he was ready to bust some skulls. Truth be told, I reckon he was. His lips were all turned down, and his eyes were like thick lines. Yeah, he was a rabid wolf in a Chihuahua's body.

"What do you have here?" Mr. Big Cop asked, like he couldn't see with his own two eyes.

"A car," I said, all careful and leery—we all knew I was in trouble. It was just a matter of how much they wanted to play with me before they got to the real fun.

"It's a nice car. What are you doing with it?"

"Gonna sell it. I needs some money."

The two cops gave each other a look, and Mr. Big Cop got this smirk on his face.

"How much are you selling it for?"

I shrug my shoulders like I was thinking.

"You know, on second thought, I reckon I'll just hold onto my car."

Then things went all wrong mighty fast. I tried to get by Mr. Big Cop, and I got the door open, but he put one of them meaty hands on it and slammed it shut before I could get in.

"Are you in a hurry?" he asked.

"'No sir," I said all respectful. "I can see you all don't much like me here trying to sell my car and—"

"'Your car?"

Preacher Man, you ever have you an "uhoh" moment. Some of my friends call it somethin' else, but for me, it's just "uhoh." You know what I'm talkin' 'bout, right? It's one of them moments where you know you done made a mistake or you know somethin' bad is 'bout to happen and all you can say is "uhoh."

...

Right. I reckon not.

Well, I had me one of them moments right then. My mind was yellin' "uhoh" real loud and telling me to just run on away. But my feet just wouldn't listen none.

"Yes sir. That's what I said, sir."

He looked at me with the stink eye—that's where you narrow your eyes and kind of cock your head to the side a little. It's the look you give folks when you think they be lyin'. He was quiet for the longest time. When he finally spoke, it was like he was just another white man with a white sheet over his head.

"You know, boy, I don't think this car belongs to you."

Now, he went and called me boy. That just ain't right. I wasn't no boy. I was a grown man, and I didn't like much that he referenced me otherwise.

"I'm not a boy," I said, and he ain't liked me givin' him much lip.

"You look like a boy to me." He reached up like he was going to pat my face. Back then, being a colored man and defendin' yourself against a man of the law didn't go over too well. I swatted his hand away, and that's all they needed to set in on me, but they didn't. Not right away.

Mr. Big Cop gave me the stink eye again, this time his lips were pulled in a massive frown, and his eyebrows came to thick points above his crooked nose.

"Boy, are you going to tell me whose car this is, or am I going to have to beat it out of you?"

I ain't gonna lie none—not here in your booth. I'm supposed to be tellin' the truth in here and the truth is I was scared. I ain't never had no run-in with the cops on the right side of bein' an adult. Sure, I had a bunch of run-ins with white folk growin' up. I experienced the segregation first hand, the anger aimed at my kind, the insults, the bein' cornered on the school yard with a teacher ten feet away with her head turned, actin' like she ain't noticed the three or four guys layin' a whoopin' on me. But all that was different. Gettin' in trouble with the police was bad.

"I told you, it's mine."

He nodded. Chihuahua Cop stood there, his hands all in fists, and his face one big sneer.

"Prove it."

"Excuse me, sir?"

"Prove the car is yours. Show me some paperwork."

I was stuck. As my momma used to say, "Son, you done got yourself into a pickle." I ain't had no paperwork or anythin'. I didn't even have a license.

"Do you have a bill of sale?"

I shook my head. "No sir—it's back at the house."

"You own a house?"

"No sir—I live in an apartment."

"Then why'd you say it was at the house?"

"Just what we call it—it's where I live."

"It's where you live?"

"Yes sir."

"Show me."

That pickle was gettin' bigger. My mind was still screamin' at me to run, and my stomach was a bunch of jitterbugs flippin' and a floppin'. I could get away. Ain't no doubt in my mind, I could get away. I was fast. Years of chasin' rabbits in the fields when I was little made me quick. Bein' fast enough to get away wasn't a question. I was scared what would happen if I didn't succeed.

"My house ain't near here. I drove out here."

"Yeah. In your car, right?"

"Yes sir."

Then I learned my first real lesson about dealin' with the law, and mean folk in general. It was a lesson I should have learned growin' up. Always keep an eye on everyone around you. You never know when they're apt to do somethin'.

"You're lyin', you know that?" He said a little more, but I don't like to use the word he used toward me. Just so's you know, it started with an "N."

Mr. Big Cop's face was right in mine, but I didn't back away. I stood my ground, not inchin' my face from his. I could smell the stench of his breath, and it curdled my already sourin' stomach. A couple of people had gathered around by then, and I knew they wanted a show. Arrest the colored man and kick the tar right out of the tar boy in the process.

"If you don't mind, I need to be goin'," I said.

"I mind," Mr. Big Cop said and shoved me backward with both his hands.

I stumbled right into Chihuahua Cop, and the first punch landed on the left side of my jaw. I took another one in the back of the head as I was spinnin' away, stunned by the first one. I swung, blindly. I reckon I hit the little guy because he looked at me with stunned eyes.

Then I ran as fast as I could, but you know, it didn't do me no good at all. You see, there was all sorts of folks watchin' by then—I just hadn't seen them cause they were standin' by shop fronts or beside their own cars. Only a few of them had approached us to get a good hear of what was happenin'.

And my thoughts of escape ended right quickly. Several of them young white men tracked me down. One of them tripped me up and I fell to the hard road and skinned up both my hands. You ever see a pack of wolves on a wounded deer? They rip and tear away at the meat, sometimes bitin' each other, sometimes fightin' for some of the meat. Them white folk were like a pack of hungry wolves, and I was the deer.

I don't know how many kicks and punches I took, but it was a bunch. Mr. Big Cop didn't bother breakin' it up for a while. By the time it was all said and done, they had to pick me up and carry me to the patrol car. They tossed me in the back like I was a sack of potatoes and slammed the door on me. I was bleedin' and my lips were all busted. I lost two teeth somewhere out there—I think I might have swallowed them. My eyes were swollen shut, and yeah, the bump on my nose came from that beatin' as well. They spared no part of my body, and I could tell by the way my arms and legs and ribs and back and the jewels between my legs all hurt. I could hardly breathe, and I just lay there in the car as they took me down to the station.

They tossed me in a lock up cell while they tried to figure out what to do with me. I was there four days with no medical attention and little food. They didn't kill me when they beat me, but they was gonna starve me if they could. When they finally come and got me out of there, they had found the owner of the Maverick.

A couple of days later I was in front of a judge, and he was sentencin' me to twelve years in prison. There really wasn't much due process they talk about in the justice system. It was the white man sayin' guilty, and the white man sentencin' me to prison.

But they was right, you know? I had committed a crime. I had run from the law on top of that. They asked if I had anythin' to say for myself. I just said "No sir." It wouldn't have done no good anyway.

A week after I stole the Maverick I was headin' to the penitentiary up in Columbia. It was a dusty, dirty place with gray walls and floors and ceilin's and a draft run right through the block I was on.

I could go on and bore you with life in the pen, but that ain't important. What is important is what happened in there. It's what led me to the life I live today.

You see, they had these things called work details. Back then, they weren't as simple as cleanin' the roads and streets of trash. Back then, it was more like cuttin' limbs from trees overhanging rural roads and routes and clearin' the sewage lines of debris that floated in durin' heavy storms. There wasn't a white man on those work details, which was nothin' more than a clean-up crew, and we didn't get paid for our labors.

There sure was a bunch of cops on those details—just about one of them for each one of us. We used to joke they was placin' bets on which one of the inmates would need a crack in the head first. If that was the truth, then the lucky screw would have been Bobby Boggs when some dumb old sack of idiot, Marvin Jackson, tried to run off the detail. Never mind his ankles were shackled together, he thought he was a free man when he hit the field off 385 near Spartanburg. There was a house off in the distance, and right beyond it was some trees. Them trees meant safety if Marvin could have made it. He was 'bout halfway across the field when Boggs caught up to him and whipped him in the back of his head with his pistol. Now, the pistolwhip wasn't so bad, but when

Jackson went and fell down, he was in the tall grass where ain't none of us could see him, but we could see Boggs kickin' and stompin' on him.

We was told to get on back to work, to mind our own business or we might end up like Jackson. So we minded our own business, and when we left, Jackson, well, he was left behind. I reckon he was a freed man after all.

After that day, ain't none of us tried and run away, and for any of the new grunts on the line, we would warn them when they spoke of makin' a break for it.

"There be daylight right down there," I heard one newbie named White say. He was one of them guys some of the others made fun of. The most popular of the jokes was, "Hey, boy, your middle name Ain't?" Even though them jokes weren't directed at me, they got right old after 'while.

White had only been on our crew 'bout three weeks when he decided to be one of them idiots and try to escape. He kept on lookin' up from where we was sawin' on a big old pine that had fallen across Route 31. Ain't nobody ever use Route 31, but I guess the legal system wanted to keep us busy. I ain't never minded it, myself—it got me out the yard and away from them gray walls for about ten hours a day, four days a week durin' the spring and summer months and two days a week durin' the fall and winter months. A man can go plum crazy lookin' at the same walls, the same yard, and eatin' the same foods day after day. Don't let no ex-con tell you no different. If they served any time in jail—and not no county lock-up—then they'll tell you the same.

I've done went and strayed again. Sorry, Mr. Preacher Man.

Like I said a moment ago, White wanted to make a run for daylight on the other side of the woods. The problem with his idea is if there be daylight, then the fool would have been all out in the open, and if he was out in the open, then all it would take is one shot, and he would be dead and left where he fell, just like Jackson.

"Come on, Lewis, we can get to the trees before they can get off their fat butts, and by the time—"

"Shut-up, Carl. We ain't makin' no run for it."

"Why not, man? We can do this."

"You go on 'head and give it a shot. I'm sure ain't none of us will be at your funeral."

He looked at me with them big eyes with the yellow whites like he had him some jaundice or hepatitis or something.

"You gonna let these honkies control you, man? They ain't got no right to do this to us."

"Carl, what you in for?" I asked him straight away. Normally, it ain't none of my affair, what someone else went and did. We let's those who want to talk do the talkin' and those who don't want to, well, we don't make them. It was their right— one of the few rights a man had in prison at the time.

"What's that matter?"

"I want to know. What you in for?" I kept to my end of the sawin'. I pulled, he pushed, then he pulled and I pushed.

He didn't answer for the longest while. Just when I thought he wasn't goin' to say nothin' at all, he spoke quietly, like he ain't want no one else to hear us.

"I killed a man."

"Was he a white man?"

He gave me a nod as simple as an up and a down.

"So then you got, what, forty years? Life?"

"Life."

This time it was my turn to nod. I saw his problem. He ain't never had a chance to get out. He would die one day within them gray walls, and it wasn't appealin' to him. I don't blame him much.

"It was self-defense," he finally said.

"I'm sure it was."

"You don't believe me, do you?" He was gettin' loud now. He was barely pushin' and pullin', and I was doin' my best to keep the saw goin' back and forth, back and forth, makin' sure some sawdust fell to the ground with each stroke.

"It don't matter much what I believe," I said. "If the courts done said you're guilty, then you're guilty—no matter what no other man says, least of all another guilty man."

"You tryin' to say you did the crime you're in here for?"

I shoved the saw forward. "I stole a car, and I tried to sell it. I ran from the law when they caught up to me—I would say I did the crime, now I'm gonna do my time. I'm halfway through with my sentence, and I aim to finish it out. You understand me?"

He shook his head, his teeth all clenched and his lips tucked in like he was about to suck his teeth like my Michelle's pappy went and did.

"You just a negro slave like the rest of them." He was yellin', and his hands was completely off the saw. He was wavin' them all mad-like.

"Quiet down, Carl," I said and kept to sawin', though it's a might more difficult when the other man ain't doin' his part.

"Don't you be tellin' me what to do. I ain't no one's slave."

"You shut on up, boy, before one of 'em guards comes over and shuts you up."

"Let 'em," he yelled. "I could die runnin'—at least I wouldn't be like my ancestors, a slave to the white man, under their thumb and barely gettin' by."

Old Davey Hobbes went and stood up from where he was sittin' in the shade. He unsnapped his gun, and I was scared things were 'bout to get really bad.

"You 'bout to die right where you stand. Now shut up, and grab that saw."

"Enough jabber-jawin'," Hobbes said. "If you aren't sawin', then you aren't workin'."

"It's okay, sir," I said. "He's new and you know how they can be sometimes."

Hobbes looked at me much like Mr. Big Cop six years before, his eyes all a squinted and his mouth pursed into a line.

"We'll get onto workin', sir," I said, then to Carl, "You grab that saw, and you get to cuttin', you hear me?"

Even in all his righteous anger, he did what I said. He took his end of the saw and pulled, then pushed as I did the same. He mumbled under his breath, and the scowl on his face told me he wasn't done talkin' 'bout tryin' to escape. I tried to ease his anger the best I could, though I don't believe I succeeded at all.

"Carl, if you make a run for it, they will kill you, and no one, other than us, will know."

"So?"

"So," I countered, "I done seen them do it to one man. I don't want to see it happen to another. They just look at you as another colored man who is takin' up space and breathin' their air. They gonna treat you like a rabid dog and put you down. Simple as that."

He pushed the saw hard, then pulled it all the same, but he ain't said a word after that. We finished up the day's work and hopped on the bus and headed on back to the prison. There was a guard seated next to each inmate—their way of keepin' us separate and quiet.

Come the next time we went out, Carl White wasn't on the detail team. Ain't none of us ever saw him again. I reckon he either escaped or died tryin' within the three days between details. None of us asked, and no one ever told us what happened to him.

So, you understand, Mr. Preacher Man, those details could be brutal if we weren't careful. The summers were the roughest because we only got two water breaks and a ten-minute lunch that was mostly just a couple slices of bread, and most of the time it was moldy.

For those of us who knew to keep our mouths shut, we managed to stay on for years. For criminals, we were dependable, even if we weren't the right color for them security guards.

About two years before I got out of prison, they had us cleanin' highways. We were a modern day chain gang, complete with the shackles on our ankles and chained together at the waist. But we ain't had no pick axes or hammers, and we ain't had to lay no rail road tracks. Nope, all we had to do was clean up the roadside of trash and debris and stuff left behind when folks got in accidents. After several years of the harder labor—cuttin' down trees with a double saw, then cuttin'

160

those down to size and cleanin' rural routes of thick bushes and overgrown grass, just so it could grow back up later—we was given a much easier job. I still ain't figure out why. Maybe they thought it was a lower job, somethin' only the colored men and women would do, kind of like the clean-up lady at the hotels. I reckon it's always been that way. You don't want to do a job, give it to someone lesser than you. Give them all the crap work.

...

...

You know, though it was work no white man wanted to do, and really we didn't want to either, after a couple months, I found it relaxin'. My muscles rarely ached after spendin' the day with a handful of trash bags and walkin' along the side of a road pickin' up garbage. It was slow work, though—men in chains don't move all too fast. Still, there was somethin' 'bout cleanin' up the mess left behind in good old Mother Nature. I reckon it's like cleanin' up the mess of your life when you done went and fouled things up right nicely.

The messes we cleaned included dead animals that got splattered by passing cars. Most of the time, them animals stank all the way up to Heaven, but sometimes they was still fresh, killed sometime durin' the day we found them.

There was this one time we was strollin' along, bendin' and pickin' up garbage, mindin' our own business along this stretch of road we called County Line Road Number 3. It was one of my favorite roads, not traveled much by folks who ain't lived in the area, and the houses were spread apart, like maybe half a mile or so. There wasn't much to clean up, maybe a bag or two between both our groups—you see one group of six men was on one side of the road and another group of six was on the other side, and we could usually come up with ten or so bags in a trip. Not that day. No sir, we only had us two bags filled up, and I really don't think either one of them were full all the way before they was tied closed.

Pa Jones was in my group and leadin' us along. He was older, like I am now, but maybe a few years younger than me—sixty-five I'm thinkin' He had been in for a long time, somethin' about robbin' a bank and killin' someone when he was tryin' to get away in a stolen car. He had the triple whammy of thieving: he stole money, he stole a car, and he stole a life. You don't get no short time for them three things all mixed up together. Still, he was a good fellow, never talked bad to anyone, always 'yes sir,' and 'no sir,' even to those of us forty years younger than he was. But he moved slow and not a whole lot of trash was missed on the days he went out. He had an eye for it, a slow, sweepin' gaze, from side to side, then back again, like he was readin' the ground, lookin' for hidden treasure. Honestly, if I was to really give it some thought, that's what he was doin'. That's what we all was doin'. We just didn't know it.

Well, Pa Jones was movin' right along, his head goin' from side to side all slow-like. Then he stopped, raised his hand in the air to get the rest of us to do the same. He snap at me with his fingers and pointed.

"Lewis, give a look see over here."

I took a couple steps toward him, then I stopped too. At the edge of the woods about twenty feet away was a deer—and not no little fellow either. He was a big old buck with a fine rack on his head. A hunter would have loved to see him standin' there all still, his black eyes on us just like ours was on him.

It was a nice quiet moment where ain't no one said nothin', not even the guards with their angry heads and hard fists. We all stood there in somethin' like awe, starin' … just starin'.

Then it happened. Down County Line Road Number 3 some idiot in a pick-up truck come flyin' down the road like his hair was on fire. It scared us all enough to back away from the road. It scared the buck as well. It darted out into the road right about the time the truck flew by us. I reckon you can figure out what happened next, can't you?

The truck and the deer collided, head on, like they was playin' a game of Chicken and neither of them was the chicken. It was fast, too—seconds, not minutes.

The grill of the truck hit the deer and flipped it right on over.

162

Its body struck the windshield hard enough to shatter it. We didn't know that right away, though. The deer went over the top of the truck and landed in the middle of the road. The guy drivin' the truck hit the breaks awfully hard and them tires made an awful racket. One of them front tires blew out, and the truck went sideways before tippin' over on its side, then its top, then its other side and so on. It flipped a few times with glass flyin' from it and metal bendin' every which way. The truck finally came to a stop off the road and down in one of them ditches by the trees.

Mr. Preacher Man, if you was to ask me, "Lewis, what did you do?" I would tell you we just stood there for a few seconds. None of us said nothin'. We just looked at the road where everythin' had just happened in one of them stunned silences. There was a little smoke comin' up from the truck, but it was probably mostly just water from the radiator sizzlin' on the hot motor. Then you might ask, "Well, didn't you guys check on the driver of the truck?" To that, I would say no, and that would be the truth. And you might ask me, "Why didn't you check on the driver?" We was cons, remember? If we were to move in one direction or the other, those guards would have thought we was tryin' to escape—all of us chained at the waist—and they would have beaten us somethin' good for our efforts.

The first thing out anyone's mouth was from one of the guards named Paul Levine. He wasn't from 'round here—he was certain to let us know every chance he got. He was from some backwoods town in Alabama, where they ain't had "no problems killin' a colored just 'cause we want to." But Paul Levine with his head full of fluffy hair all matted down at the sides from sweatin' in the summer heat, walks up to the deer and nudges it. The poor animal wasn't quite dead. It tried to stand, but its legs—all four of them—were broken. It tried, though. It tried hard. Levine unsnapped his gun and shot the deer right in the side, I reckon where its heart was. The deer stopped its tryin' to stand up pretty quickly.

Levine went on back to the bus, and you know what he pulls out? One of them double saws we used to cut down them trees.

"Cooper," he yells to the guy behind me, then he says my name as well. "You two get over here and cut the head off this thing."

Cooper and me, we look at each other like Levine was crazy or somethin'.

"Get over here, now, and do what I told you to do."

He had dropped the saw on the ground and had his gun in his hand, and I think he wanted to use it again, but not on no deer.

Me and Cooper and the whole rest of our gang shuffled over to where Levine stood over the deer, the big saw at his feet. We picked it up, exchanged looks again, and then set to cuttin' the deer's head off.

It was bloody work, and we got plenty of it on us. The meat wasn't so bad, but the bone—cuttin' through that was a little more difficult. The saw blade was dull, and it kept catchin'. Finally, the head come off, but not until after it pulled to the side a couple times when we neared the end of the job.

Pa Jones held open a big old bag, and we picked the head up by its antlers—thirteen points, Levine would say on the bus ride back to the prison—and set it in. Pa Jones cinched it closed with a piece of rope, and then Levine picked it up and took it to the bus, where he put it all the way to the back where the tools were kept.

We went back to cleanin', and there was a lot more to do thanks to the guy in the truck.

"Shouldn't someone check on him?" Cooper went and asked.

Old Hobbes was there, and his face was all sunburned, and he looked madder than a hatter. We reckoned he was angry he didn't call dibs on the buck's head. It didn't matter none to us. But he says to Cooper, to all us really, "Mind your business, and don't bother with it."

So we didn't.

We set to cleanin' the glass from the roads with our bare hands. By the time night came, all of us had bloodied fingers, and there was still plenty of glass along the roadside we missed. Not even Pa Jones could get all of it with his sweepin' eyes.

Cooper and I had to pull the deer out the road and down into the ditch.

"Make sure and put him in the woods a good ways," Levine said. It was the one time I thought if we ain't all been shackled together, I might have made a run for it once we set that deer down. Cooper gave me a look like he was thinkin' the same thing.

Before we left, one of the guards—I reckon it was Daniels, an older guy with silver hair and a gut that hung over his belt—ambled on down the embankment and looked in on the driver. He come up a couple minutes later, a brown wallet in his hand. He stopped on the side of the road and flipped through it. There was a few bills in the fold. He pulled them out, shoved them into his pocket and tossed the wallet back into the ditch.

None of us asked about the driver—we already knew he was dead, and someone would eventually find him—but it wouldn't be us tellin' the story of what happened.

Nothin' else happened like that while I was on detail, but that was enough to remind me to keep my mouth shut and do my job. That's what I did for the next year or so until I came up for parole. Do my job. Clean the roads. I watched Pa Jones when he was sent out with us, watched how his head moved carefully and slowly, from side to side. He rarely missed a thing. I started doin' the same thing when he wasn't on detail. It was the beginnin' of my love for cleanin' the roadsides of this fine state we live in.

I got paroled in the summer of 1980, eight years into my twelve-year sentence. I wasn't expectin' to get out until '84, but there was somethin' 'bout a technicality and the courts wantin' to right a wrong. I reckon they didn't believe I got my due process, so I was freed.

Ain't no lyin' here—I was more scared goin' back to the outside world, than I ever was behind them bars. Sure, the guards were mean and every once in a while, I got myself roughed up, but those eight years I spent there were constant. They were routine, if you understand what I mean. Let me see if I can explain it another way. I was familiar with the ways of bein' a prisoner. There was stability there. I had a roof over my head and food in my stomach; I had made a couple friends, and I had me a job workin' on the roadside.

Leavin' that familiarity behind was terrifyin'. I ain't had many skills when I went in. I certainly didn't have many when I got out.

I reckon someone like yourself might say I got fortunate. My parole officer got me a job that started the day after I walked out them gates and got on the bus to the city. It wasn't even the town I grew up in, but it was enough to get me started. He even got me a little place to stay—a halfway house on Bend Avenue. Some of the patrons there liked to call it Bend Over Avenue, 'cause they seemed to think if you were there, then you got yourself screwed righteously while doin' your time. Me, I thought it was a quaint little place.

My room was much like a jail cell, small and cramped with walls the color of concrete. Even the windows were small squares, only these had glass in them and no bars to keep me inside. The only rule was to be home by a certain hour, and I ain't had no problem with that.

The job I had was a simple one: I was a garbage collector, ridin' 'round on the back of one of them big old trucks, hoppin' down in front of houses and pickin' up trash off from the side of the roads. It was much like bein' back in jail. To be all honest with you, I was glad I had the job. Sure, some of my co-workers grumbled 'bout it, 'bout the stench of the nastiness in the back of the truck, 'bout some of the junk people throw out, and even 'bout how some folks weren't even neat about it, just strewin' their stuff all over the front of their yard and into the road. But me, I was happy to have a job; to have somethin' familiar.

I did the job for the allotted year. Then I moved on to a grocery store, baggin' stuff for the shoppers. I worked on a construction crew for a while, made some good money, though most of it was under the table, and I probably shouldn't have gotten my hands greased in that manner. I saved up enough to rent my own place, though it took a lot of searchin' and the refusal to have an ex-con livin' in the establishments of eleven apartment complexes before I found it. There ain't nothin' like bein' turned down time and time again, then findin' that someone who would take a chance on you.

That was one fine day, when I got the keys to my apartment and a handshake from a white fellow. That's right. I said a handshake. I didn't rightly know what to do when he stuck his hand out to me. He had a goofy smile on his face, and it made me a little leery, but, in the end, I took his hand, gave it a hearty shake and let it go.

I slept like a king that night, in a bed with a soft mattress and a pillow and white sheets I bought down at the Woolworth's. I woke up at three in the mornin' just to take a hot shower.

I was a free man, Mr. Preacher Man.

A free man.

...

...

You ain't never been behind bars, have you, Sir? No, I reckon not. You probably wouldn't be in the position you is in now if you were an ex-con like me.

When you in jail, you dream about bein' out one day, gettin' a job and turnin' your life 'round and maybe findin' you a woman to spend some time with, make a family with. That dreamin' is the worse part about bein' locked up. You know why? Because you never know when, or if you gonna get out and get you a job and have an opportunity to turn your life 'round and get you a woman and have them kids. In prison, the American Dream is just a myth.

Outside of prison, it's pretty much the same.

I had me a place, and I had me a job, and I had put back enough money so I could get me a hooker or two for several months if I wanted. But I didn't want no hooker or two. I wanted my Michelle back. You see, she may have left me, but I never left her. She was still my wife in my heart, in my head. But she wasn't now, was she? Nope. She had moved herself on, gotten her a white man and had herself a couple kids. Pretty little things, they were.

How do I know?

Ahh, that's simple. I tried to find her. Spent the better part of a year doin' so. When I finally found her, she was pretty much right where I left her, at her pappy's house. Only Pappy was dead and Mammy was too.

I had taken a big enough risk to go to her parents' old home. I didn't know her pappy was dead. I just hoped to find her, to talk to her, to tell her I was sorry for how things turned out.

I gave the door a solid three raps with my knuckles. Then I gave it three more just for good measure, you know, just in case someone was home and didn't hear the first knocks. I waited for minutes—I ain't sure how many—and when she ain't come to the door, I started down them steps and back up the sidewalk. The bus stop was three blocks away, and it would be a long wait.

I reached the bottom step, and I heard the door open and a soft, 'Can I help you?' followed.

It had been a long time since I had seen her or even heard her voice. After she divorced me, I never once heard from her. She never checked on me at all to see how prison life was treatin' me. I got no letters with sweet smellin' perfumes sayin' she missed me a whole bunch, or she can't wait to see me again or my bein' gone was killin' her. I got nothin' at all. As far as I knew, I was a distant memory for her, a stretch of bad years she would rather forget than to remember. So when I turned around and saw her in the doorway, it was like goin' back in time, only she hadn't aged a day, and I had gained ten years.

She was still a pretty little woman, and her hair was pulled back in a ponytail and it looked like she might have been doin' some cleanin' or cookin' or somethin' since she was wearin' an apron.

168

Ain't neither one of us said nothin' at first. We just looked at each other all dumb, like we was strangers and we didn't know if we should speak to one another.

"Lewis?" she went and said.

"Michelle?"

She looked 'round like she thought someone might be watchin', just like when we met and them white folk thought it was all wrong for a colored man to be talkin' to one of their girls. There was somethin' wrong, for certain. When she turned to look to her left I saw a bruise on the side of her jaw I didn't see when she looked directly at me. There was another one on her upper arm, a nasty green and brown, like it was an old bruise, but one that lingered.

"What are you doin' here?"

It wasn't the question I wanted to hear, but I reckon it was the right one for the moment.

"Lookin' for you."

I took me a step or two forward, then she put her hands out. "Lewis, you need to leave."

"Why? I just got here."

She hesitated, and she sucked on the bottom of her lip. She used to do that when she was nervous or worried, like when we decided to up and run off together. She 'bout gnawed her own lip off that time.

"Your pappy?"

She gave a quick shake of her head. "No. He died."

I ain't said nothin' right away. I wasn't sure what to say, and then it came to me.

"When?"

"About a year after you went away."

Part of me wanted to laugh, just some big old belly laughs like I ain't had in years, but the other part, he said to keep the laugh inside. All it would do is hurt Michelle.

"I'm sorry to hear that."

Understand somethin', Mr. Preacher Man, I *was* sorry to hear it. If it caused my Michelle any pain, it hurt me, and my heart ached for her.

She nodded. "Lewis, you need to leave."

"Can't we just talk?"

"Lewis ..."

Before she could finish what she was 'bout to say, a man appeared by the door. He was shorter than me, but he looked like an angry dog with his pug nose and thick lips and the way his eyes were only half open. He wore a white tank top and held a beer in his hand.

"I believe the woman said you need to be movin' on."

I was stunned a little, not sure what to say or do, but I knew the tone well. I had heard it my whole life, especially while in prison. He was doin' the intimidation thing, tryin' to scare me off. Well, he didn't succeed in scarin' me, but I reckon I did leave, mostly 'cause I was afraid of what he might do to Michelle. I didn't rightly know if he had put any of them bruises on her, but I had a good idea 'bout it. So, I reckon that means he did scare me off, in a way.

He didn't come off the steps, and I reckon that's a good thing. A fiery man like him can cause a lot of trouble, but I had been in my fair share of scrapes—probably more than he had—and I wasn't afraid of fightin'. I was more afraid of what might happen after the fight was done.

"Okay, mister, I'm a leavin' now."

"You're damn right you are." Sorry 'bout the language, but that's what he says to me and he said it with a hatred I thought should have died years ago. I reckon not.

"I'm sorry to bother you, Ma'am," I said to Michelle and backed on up the sidewalk. I reached the end of the yard and hurried down the road, but before I got too far, I heard him fussin' and cussin' at Michelle. Then I heard the slap as plain as I'm sittin' here now, and I can hear my own voice and your breathin'. I looked back and saw him strike her, hard. She fell down, but inside the doorway. He stepped inside with her and the door slammed.

Mr. Preacher Man, I know you can't answer this question, but you ever feel a rage so strong it overrides every sane thought you have? That's how I felt right then. Rage. Anger.

170

My face got all hot and my stomach twisted itself up in knots.

I looked 'round, much like Michelle did a few minutes earlier. I ain't seen no one outside or in their windows starin' out at me. All I saw was a quiet neighborhood, one that had gone downhill a little in the years since I had last been there. I eased myself on back into Michelle's pappy's yard and back along the sidewalk. The front door was locked tight, and I put my ear up to the door and listened.

Michelle was screamin', beggin' that white man to stop hittin' her. And he was yellin' at her about some black man comin' to call on her, and was she doin' things with him, and he ought to just kill her for sneakin' around with a black man, only he never used the words "black man." He used that N word, just like the big old cop who arrested me.

She ain't been sneakin' 'round, that was for certain. And she ain't had nothin' to do with me since I got arrested in '72.

I took another look 'round the neighborhood. There wasn't nobody out there and nobody in the houses close by that I could see lookin' out their windows. I took to walkin' 'round the side yard and through the metal gate. There wasn't no dogs back there, and I was thankful.

The back porch was a few feet away from the gate, and I hurried on up it, hopin' I could get in from 'round the back. What do you know, Mr. Preacher Man? I was able to. The door was unlocked and opened just as quiet as you could hope for.

I had only been in Michelle's pappy's house once, on the day we packed up some of her stuff and got out of town right before we got married. It had been nice back then, all neat and orderly, everythin' in its place. When I crept inside, it wasn't like that. There were things on the floor, not just thrown around, mind you, but not in its place, or at least not how Michelle's pappy would have cared to see his home.

Down the hall a bit, I could still hear him yellin' and slappin' Michelle around. My anger just got worse, and I let it get the best of me. I ain't proud to say it, but I remembered where the kitchen was and I hurried to it, knowin' they was at the front of the house and, unless she come runnin' my way, I could get to a knife easy enough. And they was there, them knives, in one of them butcher blocks. Seven of them, all black handled and sharp. I didn't take the biggest one, but the next size down—it had a long blade, but it wasn't as wide. It felt right in my hand.

It ain't easy tip-toein' your way through a house when you got heavy boots on, so I slipped them off and left them in the kitchen. I got down the hall and looked through the doorway.

Michelle was on the floor, all curled up, her hands tryin' to cover her head and stomach. He would punch her, and when she moved a hand to cover one area, he would hit her in the exposed part. He was a tricky one.

I don't reckon he heard me until I was right on top of him. And I reckon I probably should have just stabbed him in the back, but that would have been the cowardly thing to do.

"Hey Mister," I says.

He stopped his fist in mid-swing and turned on me. If I needed, I guess I could have played the self-defense card like some of them other folks had done over the years. But I ain't had to, but I reckon I would be gettin' ahead of myself, now wouldn't it.

That man was surprised to see me standin' there in his front room. His face was all red, and sweat was spillin' off of it like he had been workin' hard, though all he was doin' was beatin' up my Michelle. There was blood on his knuckles, and when he yelled and swung at me, I drove that knife right into his throat. The blade hit bone and kept goin'. It reminded me of the deer's head we cut off.

His hand went to his throat, and blood spilled from 'round his fingers. There wasn't no gushin' or anythin', probably 'cause I ain't pulled the knife out. He teetered on his heels for a second or two and then tipped right on over and onto the floor, his hands fallin' away. I reckon he was already dead, since he ain't tried to catch himself and keep his head from smackin' the hardwood.

I just stood there, all stunned and not believin' what I did.

Michelle was much the same, but she wasn't doin' no standin'. She was sittin' on her bottom where she had been layin' as he was beatin' her.

We both watched as the blood pooled around his head and soaked into the floor.

"Lewis," she said to me, and I reckon she must have said it a few times because when I heard my name again, she was yellin'. I looked to her and saw one eye was all swollen shut and her lip was like a big fat red slug, and there was blood drippin' off her chin. I think she might have been missin' a tooth, but I ain't sure. I know she had them all when I saw her outside, but when I went to leave a little later, it looked like she was missin' one right up front.

"Michelle," I finally said, and I had a chill runnin' up my spine like I was in more trouble than I ever had been. I should have been.

"You gotta get out of here," she said and stood. She stuck a hand out like she was off balance and stumbled over to a chair. When she did, I saw she was bleeding from behind her ear.

I went over to her, no longer scared for myself, but for her. She was hurt pretty bad. The bruises were formin' on her arms, and I could see where she was bleedin' from beneath her shirt. "Michelle, you're hurt, girl. Let's get you to the hospital."

She shook her head, and it looked like it hurt her all over again. She let out a cry of pain. It broke me up inside. "You can't take me to the hospital, Lewis. They'll know you killed my husband."

And it was out. She had married a white man who used her like a boxin' bag. Now, understand somethin', I never laid a violent hand on Michelle. Up to that point in my life, I had never attacked a person—it was always the other way 'round; me gettin' attacked and havin' to defend myself. But I had been the one to go after him. I had been the one who struck first, and my blow had been fatal.

Let me tell you another truth, Mr. Preacher Man: I would

do it again if it meant saving Michelle all over again. She was alive, and I don't expect you to understand unless you've loved someone so deeply it made you ache when it was over—and that ache ain't never gone away. If you ain't loved someone like that, then you'll never know what I'm talkin' 'bout.

I asked her, "Your husband?"

It was hard hearing her refer to him like he was me. I was her husband. Though I wasn't no more, I still felt like I should have been.

She gave one of them shameful nods, like she had done somethin' awful, like she was ashamed she had divorced me. At least that's what I tell myself from time to time. It makes me feel a little better, even if it probably ain't the truth.

"What we gonna do?" I asked.

"You're goin' to get out of here."

"I can't leave you like this. You're hurt and—"

"Lewis, you are not goin' back to jail for protectin' me."

"I'll do what I got to do."

Then she went and messed my whole world up. Michelle grabbed me by the back of my head and planted a bloody kiss on my mouth.

"I should have never left," she said. "But I did and things are over now and—"

I interrupted, my heart skippin' like it was jumpin' rope. "It ain't got to be over, Michelle. We can begin again; we can pick up where we left off."

She shook her head all sad-like with her head down and her one non-swollen eye spillin' tears. "We can't start over, Lewis. What's done is done, and I know I was wrong, but you need to go so I can take care of this."

"Why can't we start over, like nothin' ever happened?"

"Because I don't love you anymore."

Them were sharp words. I never thought she stopped lovin' me, but I reckon she told me what she had to to get me to leave.

I stood there, more shocked at what she had said, than at me killin' her husband. I had held out hope, you know? I al-

174

ways believed she divorced me because of her pappy. Turns out I was wrong.

"You don't love me no more?'"

"No, I don't."

…

…

…

I ain't said nothin' else. I think I nodded and maybe waved with one hand, like I was sayin' goodbye. I might have looked 'round the room—I ain't all too sure. It's all kind of fuzzy, seein' how it come out of nowhere and just socked me in the face. I went on back through her pappy's house and out the back door. I don't reckon nobody saw me, 'cause I went on 'round to the side yard and then back onto the street where I walked away, not lookin' back. But there was tears all in my eyes, and they was fallin' down my face like a leaky old faucet.

…

…

The next day I was walkin' to my job, and I passed the newsstand on the corner—it's long gone. There's a little diner there now. I walked in and looked 'round. I ain't had no intention of goin' in or buyin' nothin', but I did both. There was a paper right at the front counter where some old white guy sat watchin' *The Price Is Right* with Bob Barker. You remember that show? Bob's Beauties is what they called them girls who showed off the prizes. Yeah, they was some pretty girls.

Anyway, the headline in black block letters that were smaller than the major news of the day, but big enough to catch the eye, got my attention.

WOMAN KILLS HUSBAND IN SELF DEFENSE.

It was somethin' you didn't hear a whole lot 'bout back then. Women killin' husbands 'cause the husbands tryin' to kill them. Mostly you just heard 'bout when the woman was killed, and even then it was a small headline, usually near the back pages somewhere. But there it was, at the bottom of the front page, and it was reportin' at its best.

The story was a doozy, but it was effective and it served its purpose. She escaped her drunken angry husband who beat her 'cause she wasn't in the mood for a roll in the hay. She got her a knife from the kitchen and tried to get away from him. He chased her into the front room where she stabbed him in the throat. The house was supposedly a holy wreck, with a chair broken and part of one of its legs lying on the floor near the abusive husband. That leg was used to hit her in the ribs, which is why she had two of them broke and one of them poked out through skin.

Yeah, it was a good one, for certain.

I've had a long time to think 'bout this. It ain't never added up to makin' any sense to me. How did she get away from him and into the kitchen if he was hittin' her with a broken chair leg? Why would a man as big as he was need a broken chair leg, anyway? And how did she get from the front room to the kitchen and back to the front room without him catchin' her? But, you know what? Them police took her word for gold, and she ain't spent no time in jail.

...

I followed all the goin's on through the papers. I still got them all in a box in my bedroom. She never saw the inside of a courtroom at all, which I reckon is a might different than if it would have been me comin' out and sayin' I killed her husband.

...

She said she didn't love me no more. I don't believe it at all. If she didn't love me, she wouldn't have taken the chance of goin' to jail. She would have let me go down for killin' her husband, 'cause that's what people do. They protect themselves even if it means someone else gettin' in trouble or killed. But she didn't do that. No, she went to the police with a story that made no sense, and they believed her.

...

...

...

...

That's when I took back to cleanin' the streets.

I needed somethin' to help clear my head, to help make sense of my life, and cleaning streets was the thing I thought could do the trick. Then one day I found myself on the side of a road with a trash bag in my hands. Highway 378 it was, back before it expanded into four lanes and before Lexington went and showed progress. I don't reckon the street matters none, but I spent a good chunk of the first Saturday walkin' along that road pickin' up trash. Back then there wasn't as much as there is now, but there was still enough to fill a couple bags.

When I got back to my little apartment I was tired, and my head was no clearer than it was before I went out, but I was a little more at peace with my thoughts and my heart. The next day was a Sunday and there was no work, so I went back out, but this time I mostly stuck 'round close to home, mainly walkin' through the neighborhoods, pickin' up whatever lay about in ditches or along roadsides. I got a few queer looks from some of the white folks and a couple of kids—teenagers who ain't got the sense God gave sheep—made mean comments and probably meant to be hurtful, but I ain't paid them no never mind.

I learned somethin' those first few weeks of cleanin' the roads by myself; you can't haul off much trash if you ain't got no truck. On those work details, we cleared a lot of limbs and trash from the grounds and threw it all in the back of one of those security trucks. For me, I could only haul one or two bags at a time on foot, and city transportation frowns on you when you try to bring four garbage bags on the bus.

I got me a bicycle down at the flea market on Number 1 in Columbia. I had been walking that road for a couple months by then and droppin' by there on Saturday mornin's. It's the only time I ever bought anythin' out there. It wasn't the best bike, but it got me from one place to another a little quicker than walkin', and it had a rack on the back. Still, I couldn't carry more than three bags at a time all strapped down to the rack, and even then that was pushin' it.

I saved up my money, and by the spring of '84 I had me

a pickup truck. Like the bike, it wasn't the best thing in the world, but it ran and ran good. The body was a little beat up, and the seats had a couple cuts in it, but I ain't paid but four hundred and fifty dollars for it, so it was pretty much exactly what I was lookin' for. It didn't need to be all nice lookin' anyhow—it was going to be used for haulin' trash around, not goin' out on dates.

Understand somethin'. I only drove the truck when I was out cleanin' the roads. Any other time, I road the bus to work, even when I switched jobs in '91 and started workin' for the little five and dime I've been at ever since.

You know what the first thing I did was when I got the truck? I got up early on a Sunday, and I drove out 385 toward Spartanburg. The fields were a little different back then, and I reckon I went too far the first time and had to back track. Then I saw somethin' that looked familiar. I remembered the old house with the trees just behind it. It looked different, and maybe that's why I missed it the first time 'round. It was brown, like the paint had worn off, and the roof looked like it could have been saggin'. The grass was still as tall as ever, but I reckon since it looked like ain't nobody lived in it for twenty years, ain't nobody goin' to tend to no field either.

There was no fence, so I pulled off the road and got out. There weren't many cars on the road, but just enough if I was out to do somethin' wrong, someone would see me and be able to point me out as the guy who done it. I stepped off the road and looked 'round. The road looked much the same as it did back then. There weren't no other landmarks that could give me some clue I was in the right spot. But I was almost certain I was. I tried to recall where Marvin Jackson ran, how far in he got before Bobby Boggs got to him and stomped him to death.

After several minutes of just staring at the field and remembering Marvin Jackson's path to his death, I stepped into the tall grass. I didn't run, but walked all slow, my eyes down, scannin' the field the way Pa Jones used to, back and forth, left to right, then back to the left. I saw grass and ground and a jackrabbit run off to my right.

I reckon I was 'bout halfway across the field to the house and I still ain't seen no sign of a body or anythin'. I looked up at the house and saw it was close to fallin' down. Starin' at it, I realized I wasn't in the right spot. I should have come more from my right. I made my way back toward the road, but this time more at an angle and away from the house and my truck.

It didn't take me long to find what I was lookin' for. Fifteen feet from where I had originally stopped, I saw somethin' that looked like a light gray cloth. Back then, our prison wardrobe had been a dark blue pant and shirt deal, nothin' nice, and they was heavy, too. We ain't got but three pairs of them uniforms, so I reckon they were made to last a long while, even against the cold of winter, the heat of summer, rain and snow and everythin' else, 'cause there was no doubt what I was lookin' at was the cuff of one of Marvin Jackson's pant legs.

There weren't no shoes—at least not right there with the clothes, but there was bones, and they was all white, like they had been bleached. I stood looking at them bones, part of which were still inside the worn out pants. Bendin' down, I got me a closer look and some of Marvin's bones were missin', probably dragged off by some hungry wild animal, but there was still enough for me to know they was Jackson's remains. There was a rib cage and his skull was still together, the spine somehow still attached, but there wasn't no arms and legs, just bits and pieces of them.

I reckon if I would have looked a little harder, I might have found the rest of them bones, but I wasn't interested in that. My curiosity had been satisfied—Marvin Jackson had been murdered and left to rot and be eaten.

I left the field, leaving his remains in the same place Bobby Boggs had all them years before. To tell you the whole truth, I was scared to be seen out there, and the longer I was in that field, the better chance someone would see me. But I didn't get in no hurry—remember what I said, back a few years ago a white person would call a runnin' colored man a thief, and again, I ain't wanted to bring no attention to myself.

As I made my way back to the truck I imagined all sorts of bad things, most of which centered around some cop pullin' up behind my pickup and waitin' for me as I came out from the field. There was probably a no trespassin' sign somewhere out there, and you can bet your bottom dollar I was goin' to be busted for bein' on someone's property without permission. Then they would go out to the field, draggin' me along with a 'come on, boy, let's go have a look-see at what you was doin'.' They would find what was left of Marvin, and I would join him, as dead as dead can get.

My skin was all swimmin', and I was scared. It was everythin' I could do to keep from runnin', but the thief thought stayed in my mind, and I just kind of hurried in a fast walk that wasn't too fast. You know what I mean?

I reached my truck and got in as calm as I could. Then I drove off like nothin' ever happened. I ain't been back to that stretch of road since.

From then on I would go down 302 or 321 or all the way down 378 or 221 and park off the road and clean the trash off the highways. Most of the time I managed three or four bags. Occasionally I would get six or seven or eight, and most of it was just trash, stuff people tossed out their cars as they drove along on their way to wherever they was goin'. Plastic cups and soda cans and newspapers and a lot of broken glass and cassette tapes before they became those cd disks. Occasionally there would be clothes or whole bags of stuff that fell out of the backs of trucks without being noticed. Once there was a small mattress, probably once part of a baby crib. There was a brown stain on one side that looked like it could have been where a baby laid its head. It made my mind wonder.

Those were all just things along the road. Most of them I discarded at the junk yard out on Edmond Highway out toward Number 6. There were a few things I kept, though. Money. I always kept the money. It was usually just a buck or a five, but I've found a few Ben Franklins over the years. Sometimes there are tools and toys—I never can throw out them toys. I always picture some kid who probably loved the toy when I find it, and they was probably sad when they lost it out the window.

It was just stuff.

All that time I was out on the road, I was thinkin' about my Michelle. I missed her somethin' mighty and my heart, it ached all the time. I was a lonely man with a broken heart. I should have just stayed away, but if I had, there might have been a different headline in the papers one day, this time sayin' she was dead and not him. And I probably would have never known …

…

…

I reckon I'm almost done. You probably thought me killing Michelle's husband was my confession, but it's not. No, there is another incident … another man killed by my hands, though I think it was self-defense again, this time for my life and not someone else's.

It happened just a few days ago. It was cold outside and the wind was blowin' along, but I had gotten some bad news and, well, I just didn't want to stay at home. The walls felt like they was breathin', and I could hear my heart beatin' hard in my ears. I had to get out, so I grabbed my stick—it's something I made; a shovel handle with a sheetrock screw driven in to one end and the screw head cut off. It made it easy to pick things up off the ground without me bendin' over so much. With my back and legs feelin' older than my years, well, I had to make things easier on them. That stick and I have seen many good years together.

I was out on 378 toward Newberry—a good hour's drive from my apartment. When I left there was clouds all in the sky, but none of it felt like rain. My bones would have told me if it was going to rain. Well, they normally tell me. They didn't this time. I got on out and tucked my bags into my belt loop and started stakin' the papers and Styrofoam cups and beer cans and whatever else I could find. I was a couple hundred yards from the truck when the first raindrops pattered the back of my neck. My legs began to tell me it wasn't just goin' to rain, but it was goin' to pour, and I was goin' to be in all sorts of pain if the cold and the wet got to me before I reached my truck.

A half bag of trash went over my shoulder, and I hurried back the way I came. Back in the '70s and '80s, 378 wasn't traveled like it is now. Now … now it is completely different. There were cars goin' by on the four-lane road, most of them close enough to the curb I could feel the wind sheer as they passed by. There was one wise guy who thought it would be funny to get close enough to the edge of the road to splash a mighty big spray on the colored guy with the trash bag over his shoulder. I reckon he got himself a right good laugh.

The rain began to come down harder, and I was still a good ways from the truck. I lowered my head and stared down at the grass as I walked a little faster. I could see the truck in the distance, but runnin' at my age—especially in the rain—ain't always a good idea. Besides, I was already soaked through and cold, and it ain't mattered none whether I made it to the truck quick or slow; wet and cold is still wet and cold.

I got to the truck and slung the bag into the bed and crawled in the driver's seat. The key went in the ignition, and I turned it. There was a problem; the motor just sputtered like it was asleep and didn't want nobody bothering it none. I kept turnin' the key and listenin' to the motor cough, but it just wouldn't crank up. I sat behind the wheel starin' at the fogged up wind-shield, water drippin' off me and the cold all up beside me. Then I did what any other man would do. I popped the hood and got out the truck, using my stick like a cane as I went 'round to the front.

The truck's motor was pretty basic, with a couple hoses, a battery, starter, block … you know them things that make a truck get up and go. I tinkered with it for a few minutes, checkin' the plug wires and plugs, the gas line, the battery cable. Simple things. I took the air filter off and looked down in the carburetor. Lo and behold, one of the valve flaps had gotten stuck and ain't no gas was gettin' in. I went to go to the back of the truck to grab me a screwdriver, then stopped before I got 'round the front of it.

I couldn't tell you when the guy appeared there beside the road, but I could tell he wasn't a good thing to be seein' right then. He was 'bout my height, but a little bigger than me with muscles on his arms that stretched his work clothes. A ball cap sat on his head all backwards, keepin' the hair out his face. He wore jeans and a flannel shirt that was just as wet as I was.

"Can I help you?" he says, his voice a thick southern drawl. Just hearin' the way he spoke made my skin crawl. This boy meant trouble, and I was the one he was aimin' it at.

"I reckon I got it. Thank you, though," I said and tried to shuffle my way by him.

"Are you sure you don't need any help, mister?"

For one moment I thought maybe he was all right, maybe he ain't mean me no harm, but that moment passed before I could think to trust him.

Though things had changed an awful bunch since '72, he had the look old Mr. Big Cop had, a little smirk on his face, those eyes all squinted like he was tryin' to see somethin' off far away, but the sun was all in his eyes. He also had the walk, the shamble 'bout him that said I was goin' to pay for bein' a colored man, an old one to boot.

You might think I was bein' a little over cautious, and I may have been showin' some racism that had been shown me my whole life. To be honest, you might be right. But havin' lived as long as I have and seen some of the things I done seen, well, you get to where you know the warnin' signs of a dangerous person, and he had several of them.

"I'm fairly certain I ain't need no help, but thank you, anyhow."

He kind of cocked his head to the side, and them eyes seemed to get all narrower than what they already was. "Hey, ain't you the trash man who walks around cleanin' the roads?"

Up to then, I kind of always thought ain't nobody paid me no never mind, I was just another person walkin' the streets, but I happened to be cleanin' 'em, not litterin' 'em. But him seein' me, recognizin' me, well, that bothered me. Sure, there were others who had noticed me over the years, and some of them approached me, but this guy was different. I got all uneasy, like there was electricity in the air or somethin'.

"I reckon," I said and tried to push by him and get to the back of the truck where my screwdrivers were in an old wooden box I built some years ago. He stepped in my way. I could smell alcohol on his breath, and even over all the rain, I could hear the slur of his words, especially all up close to him.

"You ever find anythin' interestin'?"

I gave a nod. "Oh, I don't know. I reckon every once in a while somethin' turns up."

"Like what?"

I took a step back, careful to use my stick to brace myself. There had been a couple times in my days where the curious passer-by would take his curiousness to task and go about askin' questions like that boy did. Them times were the most dangerous, and most of them I ended up on the wrong end of a beatin'. I knew what was comin', I just don't think he knew.

"I found myself a bloody baby mattress once."

He laughed, like he was surprised to hear that. He slapped his hands together and had him a right good guffaw. Me, I just took another step back, the bad feelin' growin' stronger and stronger.

"Did you keep it for yourself, Trash man?"

I ain't never been called Trash Man, and I ain't much liked it none.

"I left it at the dump with all the other trash."

"I bet you did," he said. Then he started gettin' all dangerous, the way I thought he would. His voice was all calm like he done made his mind up to do somethin' … somethin' bad. "I bet you kept that mattress, didn't you?"

I took another step back, shakin' my head.

"I bet you have fantasies about what you could do to a little baby on that mattress, don't you?"

I ain't said a word—I learned a long time ago respondin' to those types of questions meant more trouble than they was worth. I just steadily backed up, and the rain it just steadily

184

poured down on us, and he kept on walkin' forward. I could see his hands were clinched into fists, and his face was mostly dark, but I could still see there was hate in him. It came off him like a stench hangin' in the air.

"I bet you've kidnapped a couple of little girls and put it to them right on that stained mattress, didn't you?"

We was at the front of the truck by then, and I was scared things were goin' to end bad for me. Bein' an older man, healin' wouldn't be as easy as it used to be. With the way he kept on lookin' at me and the way he kept on talkin' and the way he kept on comin' at me, I think bein' old and healin' later on were the least of my worries. He had come up out of nowhere to do one thing to me, to kill me. I ain't got no doubt about that.

He kept on jabberin' about me rapin' little girls and addin' to the stains on the baby mattress and how black folk like me ain't fit to live in his world. His world. That's what he said, his world. Like I ain't never had no right to be here?

Then everythin' happened so fast. He reached into his coat pocket, and I ain't wait to see what it was he was reachin' for. I lifted my stick and swung it at his head. It hit him in the ear, and he did a little spin, like he was some fancy ballerina. He dropped what he had been grabbin' for and I swung again, this time catchin' his elbow. That boy, he howled like a mad wolf and clutched at his arm with the opposite hand. Then he looked at me, and I caught just enough of his face to think he might have been the devil himself come to pay me a visit. Ain't nothin' scarier than the devil payin' a visit.

I took a shot at one of his legs and struck his knee hard, like I was swingin' a bat at him. It made a loud thunk sound, and he fell to the ground, lettin' out another one of those dreaded howls. He grabbed at his knee, and I swung at him again, hitting one hand then his elbow then his leg again when he pulled his hands away. I was angry and scared, and it was all his fault. I had done nothin' wrong since gettin' out of prison, and this man done went and ruined everythin' for me. Just so we're clear, I ain't considered savin' my Michelle from a man beatin' her a crime—I saved her life, no matter which way she saw it. And no matter which way you see it, Preacher Man.

This man … this young punk had decided I wasn't worth livin'. He had meant to kill me, and if I just got up in my truck and drove away, he would have been at the police station in a matter of no time, or maybe he'd have called them on some fancy cell phone. I didn't rightly know either way. I tell you what I did know; this man wasn't goin' to tell nobody nothin'.

I smacked him a couple more times, hittin' him as hard as I could, with all the strength I could muster. Then, when the fight had been taken out of him, just like it had been taken out of me so many times in the past, I drove that cut off screw right into one of his eyes. It made a pop sound and then the entire tip of the stick was in his eye socket, and he was as still as a dead man could be.

I ain't wanted to touch him, but I had to get him off the road and the rain was pickin' up, and somehow ain't no cars went by durin' the whole affair. I pulled him into the high grass. A few weeks from now it's going to be as gray as the rest of the world as winter approaches. When I got him far enough from the road I dumped him, then I hurried on to my truck and searched the ground a bit. I found what he had in his coat pocket, and I think, rightly so, I had defended myself the best I could. On the ground, by the tire, was a gun. I ain't wanted to touch it none so I hooked it with the bloodied screw and lifted it, and then walked it out to the man in the field where I dropped it next to him.

I went on back to the truck and grabbed my screwdriver. I stuck the flathead in the carburetor and shoved the valve flap open. Then I cleaned out what I could and made sure the flap would open and close the way it ought to.

After cleanin' out the carburetor, the car chugged on its first and second attempts, but it cranked up on the third, the motor rumblin' to life as if it had been a bear and had woken from one of them hibernations and was hungry. I drove away just as plain as the rain fallin'. I left that young man in the middle of a grassy field, much like old Boggs had done to Marvin Jackson so many years ago. It wasn't lost on me what I had done. No, it wasn't lost on me at all.

I drove on home and dried off. I ain't bothered with a shower. The only thing missin' from being in the rain was some soap and a towel, so I ain't had no desire to be wet any more.

For the next couple to four months I watched the news, picked me up a newspaper and read it from front to back, lookin' for anythin' on the young man who I left in a field on 378. I still ain't seen nothin' on him to this day.

...

...

But something else I read bothered me more than killin' that fellow. It was in today's paper, right on the front of the Metro News section. **WOMAN WHO MURDERED HUSBAND PASSES AWAY IN SLEEP**. There was a picture of Michelle as she was back in 1982, her face a little battered from the beatin' her second husband gave her. There was another photo of her house and the ambulance people wheelin' his body down the sidewalk all covered in a white sheet.

I read the article and just kind of sat at the kitchen table, head folded up in my hands and tears spottin' the paper in front of me. She died peacefully in the middle of the night two nights previous. I read the piece again and again, not believin' the woman I loved for near fifty years was gone.

...

...

...

Now you know my story, how I had my woman, lost her, saved her life and never got her back, and how I killed two men over the course of my life.

I know you might be wonderin', Mr. Preacher Man, how can you keep this to yourself? You're probably sayin' in that head of yours you got to go see the police, tell them my story, but maybe not the long version of it, you know? I ain't all too smart—if I was I probably would have had a better life than the one I've led—but you ain't got to worry none 'bout tellin' the police. You see, Michelle's funeral is this afternoon, and I got to be goin' and puttin' on my Sunday best so I can go pay her one last visit, you know, tell her goodbye and I love her one last time. Then from there, I reckon I'll be makin' a stop along to the police station.

I appreciate your time, kind sir, but I reckon I need to be gettin' on now. It ain't too long before the service, and I got to get ready. You know, it's kind of funny in a way. Them eight years I was in prison I just wanted to be out, wanted to be free again, but I ain't been free since the day I was arrested. Sure, they let me out from inside them prison walls, but I still be a prisoner all stuck in isolation.

...

I spent all these years alone.

...

...

All these years missin' my Michelle like I was still behind them bars.

...

I ain't never really been free, not since she left me. I reckon I ain't never goin' to be now.

The White

It wasn't quite dark when Danny arrived at the ballpark, the stomping grounds from his childhood that remained as much in his adult years. His kids, almost grown and out of the house, were out and about, no longer hanging out at the field where they first learned the game, their dad as the coach for a few of those years. No, the boys, Danny Jr.—or Danny the Younger, as his ex-wife was inclined to say—and David Allan, were out with their girlfriends, probably at the movies or down by the Old State Road dock where the kids were known to make out.

The boys moved on to high school ball when their time was done in the Under Fourteens, but their dad stayed put at the ballpark where he grew up and then coached as he had since his boys were in Tee Ball.

Not this season. No, this season, Danny the Elder took off to enjoy Danny the Younger's senior year. It had been a good one, and the playoffs were just around the corner. He reckoned he would also miss the next season for David Allen's final year of high school ball. But with no games for his boys that Friday night he went back, like a moth to the light, always returning, always drawn to the diamond.

He parked on the far right, furthest from the fields—something he had done since the first game he coached when Danny Jr. was only four years old. A moment of nostalgia swept over him as he thought about it. He suddenly realized it had been thirteen years.

"Long time ago, old boy," he said and got out of the car. "A lot's changed since then."

He made his way across the parking lot. Gravel and rocks crunched under foot. He stopped to let a car go by. The driver honked, gave a wave.

"What's up, Coach?" James Hardison yelled out the window. He was a year older than Danny Jr. but had started a year late. They had played together right up through the Under Fourteens and separated only because they were zoned for different high schools. James was bound for the majors in a couple years. With a big arm and steely blue eyes, a rock-like jaw, he had intimidation down to an art form when he stood on the mound.

Danny the Elder waved back, smiled.

Still "Coach" to these boys. *Always will be,* he reckoned. He chuckled, though he didn't find it funny. There weren't too many coaches out there who weren't all about winning and who couldn't care less about the kids. Maybe that's why he was just "Coach" and not "Coach Danny." The other coaches went by their names. Coach Paul, Coach Ron, Coach Omar, Coach Davis, (The one coach who refused to allow the kids to call him by his first name. "It's all about respect," Davis bragged. "My kids will never call me by my first name." And few of them would ever like him either), Coach Don, Coach Keith. Most of them were good guys, but none of them was just "Coach." That title belonged to Danny.

The sidewalk split between the first two fields. On the left was Dolan's Field, dedicated to Bobby Dolan, who had autism and was the reason the field was built. Yes, Bobby Dolan played baseball, but no, he would never get beyond Tee Ball with the other kids. The attention span wasn't there, neither were the physical attributes or skills, or the social aptitude, even if there was a unique desire to play.

To his right sat the A Field. The two teams on it were in the Coaches Pitch league. He saw Coach Davis wagging a finger at one of the six or seven-year-olds in his charge. Danny knew the kid—he was the younger brother of one of his former players. He couldn't recall the boy's name, but Danny thought if he were anything like his older brother, yelling at him would do no good.

"You know better than to swing at bad pitches—you wait for a good pitch, one you think you can hit."

Bad pitches?

Danny wondered if Davis realized he was the one throwing

the "bad pitches?" He started to say something, then stopped. Davis's finger wagged, but it was white, like a light. A comet tail trailed behind it, like a New Year's Eve sparkler. Danny frowned, rubbed his right eye and looked back. Davis's finger was back, the light gone.

After Coach Davis finished yelling at the kid, he sent him to the dugout and gave a disgusted shake of the head. Davis saw Danny standing there, probably getting a good eyeful of the downturned lips, the slightly squinting eyes. Davis turned away, and as he did so, the white light came back, this time blocking out the left side of his body.

"No," Danny said, and blinked several times. A migraine was coming—or so he hoped. If it weren't a migraine, then before the night was up, Peter Davis would be dead.

"Hey, Coach," a woman called.

Danny turned away from the field. The woman was whole— no white lights danced along her body or blocked out part of her face or caused a yellow aura to illuminate from her. He recognized her easy enough—Margaret Brown—Maggie to her friends and Maggie-mom to the ball players on most of Danny the Elder's teams over the years.

"Hey, Maggie," he said. They extended arms, hugged tight. If he were still married, he might not have held on as long as he did. But his wife had left him years earlier, back when the boys were still little and impressionable. Maggie was an attractive dark-haired woman who had aged well, the team mom, and once upon a time, the wife of his best friend, Wallace, who passed away three years earlier. "The White" had shone on the day Wallace died. It wasn't Danny's fault, but he still felt guilty he had seen the White—a death sentence if there ever was—and did nothing about it.

And maybe that was the problem for Danny. He didn't try to save him. He often wondered if he could have, if there was any chance he could have done something—anything—to change the outcome the night Wallace died. *Not really*, he concluded. Even if he had intervened, Wallace was as good as dead the moment half his body was awash in white. This had happened before—many times—and the first few times, he didn't realize what was going on. After figuring it out, he tried to save a few people, but they all looked at him like he was a mad man. Many of them did their best to get away from him as quickly as possible.

As for Wallace, he had been drinking the night he died, and when he drank, he was a bear to everyone, including those he loved. How was Danny to know he would hit Maggie several times then jump into his car? How was he to know Wallace would wrap the car around a utility pole?

"How are you, Danny?" she asked, pulling free of his hug and placing her hands on his shoulders.

"I'm doing well. The boys had a night off before the play-offs, so I thought I would come by and catch a game or two."

"You just can't get away from the game, can you?"

He smiled and didn't give it much thought. "It's in my blood, Maggie. So, how have you been?"

"Oh, I'm doing good—taking care of the boys. You know how it is."

"Is Dale playing tonight?"

"Oh yeah," she said, thumbing to Field C, behind the concession building. "They're about to start. Maybe ten minutes from now."

"Okay, I'll come by and watch some of it."

"You do that—we can catch up after the game."

She walked off, and he watched her go, a touch of guilt creeping up his chest for looking at her with such longing, a longing he never acted on, though he supposed if he did, she would reciprocate. Danny turned away, chastising himself for those raw emotions some call love, while others simply called it lust. He walked by the dugout of the team Peter Davis coached, glancing inside the gate and looking at the boys. Most of them were six or seven. There may have been one or two who could have been eight, or maybe a 'big for their age' seven.

The inning ended, and Coach Davis came into the dugout. He yanked his hat off and slapped the edge of the closed

192

gate. There were words said and not the encouraging type. The entire left side of his face was missing.

An ache was forming in the back of Danny's head.

A moment later Davis's team headed onto the field. The kid who had swung at the bad pitch sat in the dugout, his head down. From where Danny stood, he could see the tears in his eyes.

"What are you looking at?" Davis snapped.

Danny gave a glance in his direction. "Umm … Peter, you feeling okay?"

"What?"

It was a reasonable question. Davis's face was red and a vein bulged along the right side of his forehead and temple. Danny couldn't see the left side. That portion of his face was blocked out by the White radiating off him.

"Are you feeling all right?"

"What type of question is that? Of course I feel all right." Davis rolled his eyes, turned from Danny, and focused his attention on the kid on the bench. "Cameron, you keep swinging at bad pitches, and you won't play again this season. Do you understand me?"

The boy—yes, Cameron was his name, Danny remembered now—didn't bother looking up, but shook his head, and said nothing.

"Look at me when I'm talking to you," Davis yelled, and bent down and put his face right in Cameron's. "Are you crying? Are you really crying?"

"Coach Davis," another man said from behind Danny. He knew the voice, and he knew things were about to go from bad to a lot worse real quick. The man—Mike to Danny—was a hothead, and there was no way Davis would be able to take him on in a one on one fight. Danny thought of Wallace, how he hadn't even attempted to save him. He didn't think he would try to save Peter Davis now, but he didn't truly know.

"What?" Davis yelled.

"You don't need to talk to my son that way."

"Your son?"

The vein along the side of Davis's head seemed to bulge, and the left side of his face glowed a brighter white.

He's going to blow a gasket, Danny thought.

"Yeah, *my* son," Mike said. His brows were creased and came to points above his nose. His lips were pulled down into a hard frown that cut grooves along the edges of his mouth. The man put one hand on the fenced-in dugout and pointed at Davis with the other. "Don't yell at him again."

"Excuse me, Mr. Hayes," Davis said. By then most of the parents on the bleachers were no longer interested in the game, but watched the potential confrontation in the home team's dugout. The disgruntled father looked ready to go through the fence. Danny braced himself, just in case he had to stop him. "Cameron belongs to me when he is in my dugout, wearing my uniform and playing for my team. You can have him back and play 'daddy' after the game. Now go sit down and be a spectator, and I'll continue being the coach."

Oh crap.

"What did you say?" It was the typical response, one most dads would come back with in the same situation. Mike started for the dugout gate.

Danny got between him, put his hands on Mike's chest. "You don't want to do this, Mike."

"Coach, just move on out the way. This doesn't involve you."

Coach. Even "Coach" to the parents.

"Mike, listen to me," Danny said, raising his brows, nodding as he did so. "Can you just hold on a minute?"

"If he talks to my kid like that again—"

"He's not going to, okay, Mike? Coach Davis isn't going to say another cross word to your boy. All right?"

"You're right he's not."

With one hand still on Mike Hayes's chest, Danny looked into the dugout. The orb of white light clouded out Davis's entire face. The White shone along his arms and chest and down into one hip, dozens of brilliant dots connected along his body. Danny's headache began to grow.

194

"Cameron," Danny said. "Grab your gear and come on, son."

The boy looked up. He looked more like his mother than his father with those light blue eyes and brown hair, freckles on his cheeks. How did Mike manage to convince him to play baseball in the first place? It wasn't his thing, and Danny knew it. There were tears in those eyes, and Danny could see the delicate innocence flowing down his face. He shrugged, but didn't move.

"It's okay, Cameron. Coach Davis is done yelling at you," Danny said and opened the dugout gate. He stepped inside and motioned for the young boy to come to him.

The umps stood on the other side of the dugout, concern on their faces. The head umpire was tall, his nose like a bird beak, his hair scruffy and his face gaunt. He looked at his watch, jotted something in a small spiral notepad, then placed both pen and pad in his back pocket, but he said nothing at all. Danny had a feeling the incident would get reported right after the game, and then Davis would hear from the league. But only if they had a chance to talk to him. Danny didn't believe Davis would live through the night.

"What are you doing?" Davis barked at Danny.

"Peter, you're out of control," Danny said, then to Cameron, "Come on, son, grab your stuff. It's okay. Trust me."

Cameron didn't bother grabbing his gear. He stood slowly, his eyes on Davis, the fear in them obvious, and then he hurried out of the dugout and behind his dad.

"Mike, you guys head on to your car. I'll get Cameron's equipment. Okay?"

Mike stared at Davis. If the boy's father saw what Danny saw, he might not have been glaring at him. Then again, if Mike knew what Danny knew, he just might have smiled, and stayed to watch.

"Danny, you have no business in there," Davis said at the edge of the dugout, at the gate to the field. By then Mike was walking away with Cameron, his arm wrapped protectively around his boy's shoulder.

"This isn't the time or place," Danny said between clenched teeth, trying to keep things civil. "You're making a fool of yourself and— "

"Coach," the umpire called, "Game's over."

"What?" Davis spun on one heel and pushed open the gate to the field. The umpire danced back quickly, the gate swinging out fast enough to still clip his arm with a loud metal rustle. The other official caught the gate with one beefy hand, but made no movement to restrain Davis. "You can't call the game because of an argument in the dugout."

"Coach Davis," the umpire started, took several steps back, one hand rubbing the spot on his arm where the gate latch had struck. "You're not fit to coach right now, and I think it's best we call the game."

"Not fit to coach?"

Danny followed Davis through the dugout and onto the field. "Brett," he called to one of the other coaches by the first base bag. "Get the kids off the field. Now." He didn't look back to see if Brett listened, but turned his attention to the escalating issue. Davis advanced on the umpire, his finger poking him in the chest to accentuate every word he said.

Not good. Not good.

The pain grew behind his eyes, and Davis became more and more blurred by the White, his body now more of a brilliant silhouette against the newly darkened night. Even the lights on the field were dim in comparison.

He's going to have a stroke, Danny thought, and ran toward the pitcher's mound, where the umpire had retreated.

"Peter. Peter, you need to calm down—you're going to give yourself a heart attack."

But Davis continued yelling, his body a jerking mass of moving lights. Danny could only imagine how red his face was, how huge the veins in his neck were, how crazy his eyes were.

"You need to calm down," the umpire said, his hands still out in front of him, but not touching Davis at all. Danny didn't think the umpire couldn't defend himself. Oh, he thought it

196

was just the opposite. A will of restraint kept him from doing as little as putting his hands on Davis, even just to stop the constant chest poking.

Davis's words began to slur in Danny's ears, and a yellow aura began to form around his body—a sign the end was near. Danny's head thumped, and his skull felt like it was on fire and his brain was in the frying pan. Danny moved as fast as he could, but even then he felt sluggish, as if he had been drinking and invisible walls were closing in on all sides.

"Peter," he said and reached for Davis's arm. Davis jerked away, yelled something about Danny keeping his filthy hands to himself.

The world rushed forward, and though Danny couldn't see Davis's body at all, he knew his head faced him, and there was something very wrong going on.

There was a scream. It was followed by several others. Somewhere in the cacophony of voices the word 'gun' was yelled. A sound, like he had just stuck his ear to a popcorn popper with a microphone placed against it, echoed through the ballpark. Danny didn't hear the screams as they amplified, but he felt the hot sting of pain as it entered his right shoulder, spun him around and sent him to the ground and onto his back. The heat spread up into his neck, down into his lower back and arm. It mingled with the warm fluid beneath him, soaking his clothes and hair. The thought there was mud on the ground crossed his mind, but the reasoning was wrong; it hadn't rained in a couple of weeks, and they didn't make it a habit of hosing fields on game days.

There was crying and more screams, and someone had their hands on him saying, "Coach. Coach. Can you hear me?"

He blinked, but saw very little. Though his shoulder hurt, and he felt like he was drowning, the steady drumbeat in his skull was more unbearable.

The same voice that asked if he was okay, said other words the likes of, "It will be fine," and "Hang tight, Coach, an ambulance is on the way."

His vision, which by then was nothing but White brightness, began to gray along the edges until there was no white left at all. Before fading out, he heard another person screaming for help, but not for Danny.

The hospital room was cold. His skin carried goose pimples along its length. Thankfully, the room wasn't white, and the first face he saw belonged to Danny the Younger, his brown eyes full with concern, but shining, as if he were just as excited as he was scared.

"Dad?"

"Danny? What's going on?"

He was weak and his voice told the story.

"You were shot."

"Shot? By who?"

"Mr. Hayes—he wasn't aiming for you, but you were in the way."

"Not aiming for me?"

"No—he was aiming for—"

Danny's eyes opened wide, and he finished the sentence for his son. "Coach Davis?"

Danny the Younger nodded. "Yeah."

"Is he okay?"

This time his son shook his head. "No, sir. He died."

"Mike killed him?"

Another shake of the head. "No—Coach Davis had a heart attack right after you were shot."

"He'd have died anyway," Danny said, not realizing he had spoken.

"What, Dad?"

"Just thinking, son."

"Are you okay?"

Danny the Elder shook his head slightly. "I don't know."

It was a clear evening when Danny made it back out to the ballpark, one much like the night when he was shot, and Peter Davis died of a heart attack. He parked in his usual spot and sat in the car a while longer than usual. Butterflies fluttered in his stomach, and his hands were sweaty. One arm was in a sling, the bullet having done more damage than the doctors had originally thought. He may never throw another baseball again, but he was alive, and alive was good. He took a deep breath and got out of the car. His skin tingled; his nerves hummed as he made his way across the gravel and dirt lot.

A honk came, and a familiar voice yelled out, "Hey, Coach." Coach. Just Coach.

He smiled, waved back and continued to the sidewalk between Dolan's Field and Field A. Two teams played off to his right, and he recognized the coach of the visiting team. Across the diamond was another one of the coaches he had worked with.

Danny stopped just beyond the dugout. He stared out at the pitcher's mound where he had been shot and where Davis had died minutes later. He scanned the field, then the bleachers. No White shone on anyone.

He made his way past Field A and the concessions building in the center of the complex. A few folks came up, gave their how-to-do's and moved along. He rounded the concession stand and glanced around Field C before heading over to Field B.

There, his eyes fell on who he had been looking for.

"Maggie," he said.

She turned, her face suddenly alight with a broad smile. "Danny," she said, her voice not more than a cracked whisper. She put her arms out, then dropped them.

"It's okay." Danny put out his good arm. They hugged, a gentle, loving gesture between the closest of friends.

She went to let go, but he held her tight.

"Danny, are you okay?" she asked when he released her.

He shrugged. Danny the Elder no longer felt like a man in his forties, but more like a teenager around the girl of his dreams.

"What's wrong?" she coaxed.

Danny looked into her eyes, and a smile traced across his face. There was no White dotting out her face, no yellow aura signifying a coming death. He also knew there was nothing he could do when The White happened, no matter how much he wanted to try. He had been shot, after all, and the bullet had been meant for someone else.

"Maggie, I've wanted to ask you something for years."

"What's that?"

The seriousness showed in her face, but a knowing smile touched the corners of her lips.

"Would you mind going for coffee after the game tonight? Or maybe I can come over, and we could talk."

She nodded. "Coffee's good—Dale is going to a friend's after the game, so I'd love some company."

"Good," Danny said. "We have some catching up to do."

Apartment 306 and Poor Jenny Harris

It's a dirty place, where we live. The walls might have been white once, but now they're a dingy gray color. Down the hall before the elbow that leads you to the elevators, there's an odd brown handprint. It's been there a long time—since before Jake or I were ever thought of, according to Dad. You'd think someone would have washed it off by now, but not here, not in this rat hole at the edge of the city in a neighborhood called Crack Alley.

Crack Alley? That's a welcoming name to give a neighborhood. I guess it fits. You can go to any street corner around here and get a decent supply of drugs on the cheap. The pushers sell it at a discounted rate just so they can make a buck—everyone here is too poor to buy any of the good stuff that makes your head swoon in ecstasy and your body tingle all over as if you just had the best sex of your life. Nope, we get the dollar dosage around here, and that ain't enough for some of these folks. One time, I saw Mrs. Harris from apartment 311 offer up her nine-year-old daughter to one of the dealers—a skinny dark guy by the name of Terd—for a hit of some of the good stuff. The deal went down, and poor Jenny was slung over one of Terd's thugs' shoulder and carried off kicking and screaming and clawing. I'm sure they had a grand time with her. Little Jenny was never the same.

The plumbing only works half the time in our apartment. Dad says there is a clog somewhere in the system. I think there is too much stuff being flushed, and the pipes can't handle most of it. Dad says the landlady is too cheap and lazy to have everything fixed properly. We try to go to the bathroom a little later than normal just so we don't have to pump the toilet. I hate the plunger, and I hate having to clean the floor when the toilet backs up and overflows. I'm sure the folks in 204 below us don't care much for it either.

The heat works when it wants to, and there are no central air units like in some of those fancy apartments in other towns. The window unit we have barely works. It doesn't matter if it runs great; it's in Dad's room, and we're not allowed in there. I guess we have it better than the bums on the streets, with their cardboard houses and newspaper blankets. At least in this apartment we're safe from the thugs outside. Unless they bring guns to the party, and then it's a crapshoot on who lives and who dies.

We moved here years ago, back when I was four and Jake was still an infant, barely out of Momma's crotch. Dad says we didn't have much choice. He lost his job, and Momma was a stay at home kind of gal. She had to look out for us. Momma's been gone a while—I think I was five and Jake might have been one when she died.

I take care of Jake since Dad is always at work or stoned or drunk, more stoned and drunk than at work. Jake follows me everywhere—being eight and having no friends will lead you to sticking around with the only person you know. I don't mind much, though. I don't have any friends around here either. Me and Jake are the only two boys under fifteen in the apartment complex, so not a lot of the older kids will have anything to do with us. And the kids even close to our age live across the street or in other complexes as trashy as ours. That's okay; it's hard enough keeping Jake from the drugs and alcohol with Dad always around, but hanging with some of the other kids could make things worse.

Oh, and Jake, he's dumb, but not like stupid or anything. He just doesn't talk much. He knows how, but he just doesn't. He says 'Momma' more than anything else. I feel sorry for him when he calls out for her—I wonder how much he actually remembers of her.

Sometimes we sit on top of the building and watch the world play out before us. We lean over the edge and watch as drug deals take place, and cops on the take look the other way, the hookers with their skirts around their stomachs and bent over in alleyways, taking it hard from some stranger, or knobbing their tool; it's all the same for them, a bang or a blow for their rent or crack money. Sometimes those shows are better than the ones on the old black and white television with the jumpy screen, especially when the men try to cheat the women of their whore money.

We hung out on the rooftop today, watching the children play in rat infested run offs and the adults do adult things. There was a shooting just half an hour ago—one of the cops didn't seem to like the deal he got from one of the small-time pushers. Put a bullet in his head. People just stepped around the body until someone came and scooped it off the ground. They left a minute or two ago with the body, just picked it up and slung it into the bed of a beat up pick-up truck. That was the most excitement we've had in weeks. I think Jake was more fascinated by it than I was; he barely moved as the whole thing went down. But now we have to leave and head back to the apartment.

Dad usually doesn't like it when we aren't home when he gets there.

"Come on, Jake," I say. He follows me to the stairs and glances back once or twice before we enter the door to the stairwell. I wish I knew what goes on behind his eyes, what he is thinking, if he is thinking at all.

The stairwell is dark except for the weak lighting on the landings. It stinks of vomit and piss. We make our way down the winding steps until we reach the third floor. I open the stairway door and look around. The lights in the hall are dim, like always, and the smell is rank, like always, but far better than the stairwell. We be-bop down the hall, round the elbow and pass the elevators. We round the second elbow, and I see the handprint—the fingers are long, as if the person who made the prints dragged the hand along the wall. Jake looks at the handprint, his mouth open, his eyes somewhat half-lidded. Again, I wonder what is going through his mind, but I know I'll never find out. No one will.

We walk past room 311, and Jenny is sitting there, her skirt tangled around her hips, her legs all open and a vacant look on her face. I can see her dirty yellow panties with the red stains in the crotch. I push her legs together and pull her skirt down over her thighs.

Before we reach our rat hole of an apartment, the door to room 306 opens and out walks the crazy lady. She never seems to know if she is coming or going, but I think she's a little of both. She also never seems to notice us, but Jake always notices her. She stumbles by us, her brown hair a mess of tangles hiding most of her face, her skin dirty and bruised. Her dark dress or skirt or whatever it is, is wet around her chest. I take a second look at her, but I can't figure out what it is on her clothes.

Jake lets go of my hand and takes a few steps toward her. He stops when he reaches Jenny, and her legs are unfolded again. She has taken off her panties in the short time it took us to get from her apartment to the crazy lady's. The woman disappears around the corner, and Jake drops his head. He pushes Jenny's legs back together, pulls her dress over her knees and turns back to me. I see tears in his eyes.

"Momma," he says.

"No, Jake, that's not Momma. Momma's dead."

I open the door, and Dad is sitting on the couch, a bottle of whiskey in one hand and a cigarette in the other. I know this is not good—Dad is never home this early.

"Where ya'll been?" he asks but doesn't look at us.

"Just walking around. We got bored."

"You ain't supposed to leave the apartment."

He takes a big swallow of whiskey and looks at me. His eyes are red, and I can see he is stoned out of his mind.

"What have I told you about leaving the apartment?"

"Not to."

"What else?"

"There are too many bad people out there."

"You're damn right there are, now get to your room. I'll come deal with you later."

I wait for him, but he never comes to deal with me. I hear the front door open and close, and then I hear nothing for a long while. When the door opens again, I hear him, but he

204

isn't alone. There is a small voice with him, begging him not to do "it." I recognize the voice as little Jenny from down the hall. A moment passes, then another, and I hear the first of her cries. I don't know how much Dad gave Mrs. Harris, but I feel anger boiling up in me. I think of Jake and wonder if Dad has ever done anything to him.

The cries settle down to soft whimpers. I am awake through the entire thing.

"Get on out of her you little whore," Dad says.

I peek my head out the bedroom door to see Jenny stagger down the hall, blood dripping onto the floor from between her legs. She tries to open the door but her hand slips. Then she gets it open and is gone. In the second or two she stood there, a puddle formed on the carpet. She stepped in it, leaving a footprint behind. I close my door and hope he is too tired to deal with me. When I lay down, I hug my pillow and wish Momma was still alive.

I wake up, and I hear Dad snoring. Tiptoeing out of the apartment will probably get me a beating, but I need to get away for a minute. Jake is sitting on the couch, his hair all mussed up from sleeping. He smiles when he sees me, and my heart almost lifts.

"Where yah going, Cody?" It's the most he has said in a while.

"Out. You wanna come?"

He nods. We grab his shoes and slip out the door. We don't get very far before we see Jenny. But there is something wrong with her. She's not sitting by the door to her mother's apartment. She is lying in front of it. A fly lands on her small nose, and I see her skin has changed from the lily white it used to be to an almost gray color. Beneath her is a dried puddle of blood. I look from where we stand and see bloody footprints leading all the way to where she lies.

"Jenny?" I'm hoping she hears me, but deep down inside, I know better. "Jenny, you okay?"

The woman in 306 opens her door and steps out into the hall. Like always, she is wearing the same clothes. She walks by Jenny as if she isn't there and rounds the corner just down the hall. I see her put her hand on the wall, and a chill runs through my body.

"Momma?" Jake calls and goes after the crazy lady.

"No, Jake. That's not Momma. Momma's de—" The words catch in my throat, and I look back at Jenny. I know she's dead, but I have to find out for myself. I walk over to her and bend down. Her skin is cold and her eyes are open. I put a hand to her mouth and she is not breathing.

I back away, grab Jake's hand and drag him back to our apartment.

"Momma," Jake says, tears in his eyes.

"Jake, that's not Momma. She's dead."

We huddle in my room and wait. Sometime during the day Dad leaves, and we step out of the apartment for a moment. Jenny still lays on her side, her eyes open but not seeing anything, her privates torn open from where Dad had ... the very thought of it tears at me, and I want to hurt him, make him pay for what he did to her. Who am I kidding? I'm twelve and still just a boy. Dad is old and mean.

Jake and I are going to stay inside. We check, every once in a while, to see if someone has found Jenny yet, but no one has, and if they have, they don't care; they don't bother moving her. She still lies there in a dried puddle of her own blood, still dead. I go to head back inside, and I see the crazy lady from 306 leave the room again. She steps over Jenny, not seeing her, I guess, and continues down the hall. She brushes her hand against the wall, and then she is gone around the corner.

It's hard to take in, knowing Dad is, at least, part of the reason Jenny lays dead out there. There is not much I can do, except call the police, but I am really hoping someone else does it. Does that make me just as bad as everyone else? I think so.

As night settles in, Dad comes home high again. I can smell dope on him, and I close off the door to my room. Jake is inside with me.

The crying wakes me. It is a little girl's voice, and I swear I hear a scream or two before the crying really sets in. My skin crawls with chills, and my heart speeds up. My stomach knots and my bladder suddenly feels full. The moments pass slowly, and I wait, my blanket pulled up to my face even though it is hot in the room. After the crying stops, I stand. Jake is still asleep. For that I am relieved. I walk over to my door and open it.

I blink several times, not sure what I am seeing. Jenny walks past me and goes to the front door. She pauses, fumbles with the knob and then opens the door. She goes out, just as she did the night she died. I run to the door and open it. She sits down where her body is and my heart stops.

"She's a ghost."

The apparition tilts over onto her side and blends in with her lifeless body. As I stand here, the woman from room 306 exits her apartment and walks away. She doesn't look at Jenny and her hand touches the wall right where the brown handprint is.

"Momma."

I spin around to see Jake standing in the door of our apartment. He is holding an old teddy bear—one Momma had given him when he was born. His eyes are full of tears, and his bottom lip shakes.

"Momma?"

He nods.

"Do you think the crazy lady is Momma?"

He nods again.

I walk down to apartment 306. I want to try the doorknob but my hand refuses to move. I can taste the fear on my tongue, and it's like salty sweat. I feel time slipping away as if my life is going with it. With a quick jab, my hand finds the doorknob, touches the cold metal. It sends shivers through my arm. I try the knob and it turns. The door clicks open, and I am stunned by the simple fact it hasn't been locked all this time.

"Should I go in?" I ask Jake.

He nods and holds his teddy bear closer to his chest. The

knuckles on his hands are white, and his brown eyes are as big as I have ever seen them.

The door pushes open easy, and a rush of heat spills out from the room. A stench comes with it, and it smells like something old, like the room hasn't been cleaned since it was last rented.

I look in. It takes a few seconds for my eyes to adjust to the intense darkness of the apartment. There are shapes in that darkness. The place still has furniture. There is a couch and a table in front of it, a chair off to the side, and another one tipped over on the floor, one of its legs broken. I step in. Dust stirs around my feet.

"Stay here, Jake," I say.

He nods. It's what he does.

I step further into the darkness, my eyes adjusting a little more and the black becomes shades of grays. I make my way down the dark hall, and my heart hammers hard. A light coating of sweat has formed along my body, and my skin tingles in fear. Something tells me to turn around, and I stop just shy of a closed door to my right. I think it is a bedroom, but I am not too sure. The knob turns, and the door creaks open. More dust stirs around me. I cough as some of it gets in my mouth, tickling my throat. Then I walk into the room. There is nothing in there, not even an old bed. I go back out into the hall.

The door to my left is closed as well, and I open it. It is the bathroom. I know right away something is wrong in here. Laying on the floor is the sink basin, which should have been attached to the wall. The toilet seat is torn off and the bathtub looks a little odd—even in the darkness. There is something in it. I bend down. I don't want to, but I can't help myself. My hand touches the cold porcelain, and I push my fingers forward. They stop on something smooth and trace their way up until I am touching what feels like hard stiff cloth.

I jerk my hand away. I back toward the door, running my hand along the wall until I find the light switch. Though I don't believe the light will turn on, I flip the grungy, cake-dusted switch and look to where I am certain the light bulb is. There is a hum, and then the light flickers. It casts a gray light, and I can see the bulb is covered in dust. I turn my eyes to the bathtub, and a scream freezes in my throat. My breath stops somewhere between my lungs and mouth. I can't move. I can't make a sound. I can only look at the tub and what occupies it.

"Momma."

I spin around to see Jake standing behind me. His eyes are focused on the skeleton in the bathtub. Long matted hair hangs from a skull that has long since lost its flesh and is now nothing but smooth bone. There is a black shirt and skirt on the body—it is the same as the crazy lady.

I step over to the tub and look down. There is a knife sticking out from the woman's chest. My mind reels for a second. I need to throw up. I put a hand on the wall to steady myself. My spinning world slows down, and my vision seems to have restored itself to normal.

I force myself to look back at the tub. Dried blood cakes the once white porcelain. There are several bloody handprints on the tub, and I realize she is the woman who made the handprint on the wall down the hall.

"We gotta get out of here, Jake." I say and turn to leave.

"Momma."

I say nothing and try to turn Jake around. I stop when I see the woman walking down the hall. She goes to the door and acts like she is opening it, even though we never closed it. Her hand clutches tight to her chest, and blood spills from between the fingers. Then it falls to the side as she stumbles from the room and into the hall. I hurry after her and watch as she touches the wall right where the handprint is.

An angry yell comes from behind me. I duck, dropping to the nasty floor. I cough and try to stand. I barely get to my knees before I hear the angry voice again.

"Stupid whore. Get back here!"

A cold rush of air blows by me. Following it is the stench of alcohol, blood, and sweat mixed together. I lean out the door, and I see the woman backing up, one hand is on the back of her head gripping at her hair. The other one is on her chest. Blood is pouring down her arm. She screams and looks as if she is being pulled back to the apartment.

She brushes by me, and I feel the chill of her spirit spill over me. My eyes follow her into the bathroom. She screams again, and I hear a horrible sound like the heavy thud of something striking the floor ... or a sink basin. Her head snaps back and another loud sound, this one a crash, as the basin falls to the floor. Her body tips into the tub where it melds with the bones already there.

"Stupid whore," the angry voice says and slams the bathroom door.

For a few seconds all I hear is silence. Then I hear crying. I turn to see where Jake is. He hasn't moved from the time the woman's ghost appeared until the scene played itself out. The crying isn't coming from him. I follow it down the hall and to one of the bedroom doors. I open it and look inside. The crying is coming from this room, and it grows louder as I stand there. It's as if the crying is coming from ...

"Momma?" I say and turn.

I am the one crying and memories flood my soul, making me dizzy. Vomit rises in my throat, and what little I had eaten the previous two days spills out onto the floor. My knees buckle, and I almost land in the mess. I take a deep breath, let it out, take another one. My ribs and back hurt, my head is swooning.

I try to stand, but my foot finds the vomit and I slip, almost tumbling to the floor. I lean into the wall, my shoulder crashing hard enough for it to cave in a little. I straighten up and push myself along the wall. I stumble past the bathroom, and I am thankful the door is closed.

"Come on, Jake," I say and grab him. He barely moves. I tug on his arm. Now, he is coming, and I lead us out into the hall.

"Momma?" he asks.

"Yeah, Jake," I say, very certain of the truth he had tried to tell me all this time, but I had ignored. "That was Momma."

I walk him to the stairwell, open the door and push him inside.

"Stay here, Jake. Can you do that for me?"

He nods and sits down, clutching his teddy bear tight. More tears are in his eyes, and anger rises in my body. I want to hold him, but I fear I might take my feelings out on him if I am not careful.

"I'll be right back. Okay?"

Another nod. A sniffle follows.

I turn away, but I can feel Jake's eyes on me. I feel horrible for him, but I feel worse for me, for what I had seen when I was smaller and had somehow forgotten. Shame filters in as well. I could have helped Momma, I think. Maybe not. Maybe Dad would have killed me, too. I don't know, but I recall it all now. Momma and Dad arguing, the sound of him hitting her, the flash of the knife as I peek out my door and see him stab my mother in the chest. Her screams. Her attempt at leaving and him attacking her outside the apartment. All of it leading to her death at Dad's hands.

"What are you looking at, boy?" he had asked and slammed the bathroom door in my face.

Somehow, I find myself in the dirty bathroom. The light is on, and Momma's skeleton is lying in the tub. Her bones aren't as white as I thought they were. They are more of a gray color, but that is not what holds my attention. The handle of the knife juts out of her body. I'm guessing it is held in place by her top. I bend down and put my hand around the handle and pull it out. Her shirt tears, and her body moves. A sound like someone letting out a deep breath comes from the body, and I step back. The blade is crusted with dried blood. Now tears fill my eyes.

"I'm sorry, Momma," I say, and it is time for me to leave.

She is standing in front of me. Her eyes are sad, but she smiles. I feel something I haven't felt since her death—loved. I want to hug her, to tell her how much I miss her, how much Jake and I need her. Instead I say, "I gotta go. I have to take care of something."

Momma steps aside, and I hurry pass her. Out in the hall I see Jenny's dead body still on the floor. I can't believe no one has noticed her yet. My anger grows.

Two doors down and I stand in front of my apartment. I open the door and step in. It is dark, and Dad is nowhere to be seen. I know where he is. I stand here, knife in hand and hate burning inside of me. I flip the light on, and the darkness runs away. There is trash on the floor—stuff I guess I'm going to have to clean up soon. The television is tipped over, and I wonder if Dad had come out when I left the apartment. A spear of fear spikes me, and my body becomes cold.

Jenny comes out of Dad's room, the blood trickling down her leg. I watch the ghost as it fumbled for the knob, gets the door open and exits the apartment. Tears are spilling from my eyes now, and I am moving across the room, down the hall. I stop in front of Dad's room, and I take several deep breaths. I put my ear to the door and listen. He is snoring, and I know this is my only chance. I must do this. If not for Momma or Jenny, then for Jake.

The door opens easily, and I look in. It is dark, but I can see Dad lying on his bed. I can also see the clear bag of white powder sitting on the end table. If he were awake he would be stoned out of his mind or drunk. Or both. I don't care. I just want him dead, and I want to get out of here, out of Crack Alley, away from this Hellhole we have lived in our entire lives. I want to find Jake help. I want so much that I'll never have if we stay here.

I try to be quiet as I cross the floor. Dad rolls over, his back to me. I reach his bed, and I want to stab him in the back, but only cowards stab people in the back. I shrug. Most of the people around here are cowards. That's why they shoot each other—they're afraid if they don't kill then they will get killed. I'm not afraid of dying—but I am afraid of Dad, even if he is asleep.

He rolls back over, and I worry his restless sleep will do me in. If he wakes before I can kill him, he will kill me and probably Jake, too.

"For Jake," I whisper.

Dad's eyes open. I am startled, but I bring the blade down, driving it into his stomach. He lets out a scream, and his eyes get as wide as anyone's I have ever seen. I pull the knife out, and my skin crawls with the feel of his skin tearing again. His hands reach for me, but I raise the knife and bring it down again, this time in his chest.

"You killed Momma!"

I pull it out and drive it back down, slicing the arm he is trying to protect himself with. I feel my anger with each thrust, and I know I am killing him. And I don't care.

Blood spills from his mouth, and I stab him one last time—in his crotch. Dad doesn't move as blood soaks into his mattress. His hands fall to his side, and I let go of the knife. "That was for Jenny."

I turn to leave and stop in the hallway. Momma is standing there. Beside her is Jenny. They are both smiling at me.

"I'm sorry, Momma. I had to do it."

She says nothing. As I watch, they both fade away, their bodies going from solid to nothing at all. This time I can't hold back the tears. I lean against the wall and slide down, until my knees are at my chin. I rest my forehead on my arms. I cry, I have to let it all out. I'll compose myself and go get Jake, but for now, I need to scream.

I don't know how long I cried, but I finally wipe my nose with the back of one hand and I stand. I hope Jake is still in the stairwell waiting for me. I walk out the door, and I see Jenny still lying on the floor in front of her mom's apartment. I knock on the door hard and listen for footfalls. When I hear them I run. I round the corner as the door opens. At first, Mrs. Harris fusses at her daughter, probably not too sure what is going on. Then realization kicks in, and her screams fill the hallway.

I enter the stairwell. Jake is sitting quietly on the landing. The teddy bear is in his arms, and one thumb is shoved into his mouth.

"Come on, Jake," I say, and we head up the steps. My face is dry now, and I no longer feel anger at anyone. I have to take care of Jake, and there is no time left for me to be sad or fearful. We reach the roof and walk out into the dark night. The stars and moon are out. We find our favorite spot overlooking Crack Alley and sit down.

In the distance there are sirens, but it's not unusual around here. I wonder if they are coming to see about Jenny's death.

Jake scoots a little closer to me, and I put my arms around him. He looks up at me, his innocent eyes not knowing much except maybe pain and suffering.

"Momma's okay," he says, and my heart leaps.

"Yes, Momma's okay, Jake. And we will be too."

Not so far in the distance now, the sirens grow closer.

A Memory Best Left Alone

The gloom of the cemetery fit her mood. Stephanie walked along the familiar red brick path, tombstones on either side of her. Trees dotted the graveyard, Mother Nature's tall, thick guardians of the dead. The wind rustled leaves, pulled them from their limbs and sent them fluttering along the dying grass.

Stephanie wrapped her arms around her chest, hugged herself tight. Fingernails dug into the skin just above the elbows, leaving in their wake slivers of pain that lingered for a second or two before fading away. She found a spot by the crumbling wall on the west side of the cemetery. Cracks lined a deteriorated head stone leaning a few feet from the wall. Most of the engraving had long since faded, but she could read the first name: Susanna.

She sat on the soft grass, her knees to her chest, arms around her legs. Stephanie cried …

… and she remembered.

"Stephanie, how do you feel today?" Doctor Clayburn asked as he pushed his glasses up on his nose.

"The same," she whispered, not looking at him.

"The same? The same as what?"

"The same as always."

"The same as always?" he asked. He shifted in his chair and crossed one leg over the other. "But, you weren't always like this, right?"

She looked at the white walls. Four lights pointed from the middle of the ceiling toward the corners of the room, leaving the center of it in a gray shadow. She shrugged, shifting her eyes to the red carpet, which was not bright, nor dull.

"Why a red carpet?" she asked and looked up at Clayburn. Their eyes met momentarily.

His brows lifted. "Why not?"

Just like a shrink to answer a question with a question.

"It looks like blood."

"Finally, I found you."

Stephanie opened her eyes to a blurry figure. Her heart sped up, and she swallowed hard. The hairs on her neck stood; her skin became clammy. She bit her bottom lip, letting the pain swim over her. "Please don't hurt me."

"What? Steph?"

She frowned, blinked, and then wiped tears away with the back of one hand. Her eyes focused. "Carlton? What are you doing here?"

"I could ask you the same thing," he said and extended a hand.

Stephanie reached out but drew back before their hands could touch. There was blood on her fingertips. She lifted her elbows and looked at them. Four crescent moons had been etched into both arms. Blood had congealed in the fresh wounds. Her cheeks flushed with heat, and she lowered her arms. Wiping her fingers on her jeans, she hoped he didn't see.

His face told her he had.

"You're bleeding." Carlton's hand was outstretched, still seeking hers.

"I can see." She pushed to her feet, ignoring the offered hand.

"You need help, Stephanie."

"I'm seeing a shrink."

Carlton shifted from one foot to the other. "That's not what I mean. You need to get out more, socialize with your friends and family. They're worried about you."

"I'm out right now."

"You're in a cemetery."

"The dead don't hurt the living, Carlton."

The hotel room was nothing like her house. It was one bedroom and a bathroom with a kitchen area set off to one side. It was small. The heater was loud and reeked of burnt dust. The carpet was brown, and the remote to the television was chained to the end table. The entrance was a steel door, and the windows were sealed. One way in. One way out. It was nothing like her house.

"Come on," Carlton said as he stood outside the hotel room. He tried to enter, but Stephanie shook her head, her eyes thin lines, her jaw clenched tight.

"I don't want to go out." Stephanie stared past him. Her stomach rolled once. Her chest tightened, and she couldn't get enough air in her lungs. Her head grew light and she stumbled backward. The bed broke her fall.

"Steph!" Carlton yelled. He ran to the bed and reached for her.

"I'm okay," she said, pushing his hand away. The thought of being touched made her stomach churn. "I'm okay."

Carlton frowned and stood.

She saw the hurt in his eyes, the way one side of his lip curled up in a fake smile. A moment passed, and she wanted to grab him, hug him tight, and tell him she was sorry for pushing him away. Instead, she stood on shaky legs and hurried to the bathroom. Her stomach heaved, and she vomited.

"Stephanie." Carlton's hand was warm through her shirt.

She stiffened and slapped at his arm. Through deep breaths she yelled, "Don't touch me!"

Carlton pulled his hand away. The air changed as he left the bathroom. He said something she didn't understand and was gone, closing the door on his way out.

Tears trickled from her eyes; heat swept over her, and

her skin tingled. She plopped onto her bottom and scooted against the shower stall. Hands covered her eyes, fingernails dug into her palms ...

Water on her face cooled the heat. Trails of red mixed with the water from the half-moon marks on her palms. Adding soap stung. She inhaled sharply but didn't rinse it away. The pain cleared her mind.

She stepped into the hotel bedroom staring at the door, its two locks slid into place. Stephanie's hands shook as she undid the top bolt, and then she stepped back. She paced from one end of the small room to the other, a hand on her jittery stomach.

"I need to do this."

It had been four days since she ventured outside the hotel room. Composing herself, she unlocked the second bolt, grabbed the door handle, and pulled. One swift motion and the sun was in the room, cool air wrapping around her and the world just beyond it.

The door slammed shut, the locks slid back into place. She put her back to the door. Three fingers went into her mouth to stifle the scream that pushed into her throat. She bit down on them as salty tears spilled down her cheeks ...

... and he was there, in the darkness, ripping at her clothes. He said little, only yelped once when two of his fingers slipped into her mouth when he tried to cover it. She bit down hard, drawing blood ...

Her eyes snapped open. Her fingers throbbed, and a bitter heat spilled into her mouth. She looked at her fingers. Teeth marks and torn skin peered back at her.

"What happened to your hand?"

Doctor Clayburn's green eyes held her gaze. His expression was more of a question than the words he had spoken.

"Car door," she lied.

He gave a nod and jotted something on the yellow pad in front of him. "You've been going out, then?"

She said nothing and stared at the red carpet.

"Stephanie, other than here, have you gone anywhere besides your house?"

"I haven't been back to my house."

"Really?" His brows rose.

"Not since ..."

"I see," Clayburn said. "I thought you were staying at home."

She shook her head. "No."

"Then where are you staying?"

Stephanie looked at him with untrusting eyes. Previously, when men would ask where she lived, she considered them with a flirtatious smile and a bat of the lashes. Now ... "I'm ... just ... staying somewhere."

Clayburn released a deep sigh, placed his pen on the pad, and leaned forward. "Stephanie, you have to trust me if you want my help."

"I *can't* trust you."

"Thanks for coming with me," Stephanie said.

"That's what sisters are for," Betsy responded and brushed a strand of dark hair from in front of one eye.

"You're a good sister." Stephanie fumbled in her purse, searching for the swipe key to her room.

"So are you."

Outside the vehicle the world went on. There were cars in the hotel parking lot, mostly long-termers, just as she thought she would become. The janitor put trash into the dumpster, then walked off whistling a tune she couldn't hear. The dumpster stood out against the backdrop of the gray wall behind it.

She could see a man, hear his heavy breathing, smell the stench of alcohol on his breath and sweat on his skin. She could feel him pushing into her, the pain of dry friction ... In another world, the dumpster would have held her dead body, trash heaped on top of her. She may not have been found until the rats had eaten her flesh and the maggots had nestled in her eye sockets. Instead, she lived, though deep inside she wasn't so sure she wanted to.

"Stephanie. Stop it. Stephanie."

The fog lifted from her mind, and she blinked several times. "What? What's wrong?"

"You zoned out and cut yourself."

Her left arm bled from the ragged gash across her forearm, and the swipe card held traces of red.

"Let's get you inside and ..."

"No," Stephanie interrupted. "I'll take care of it. You've done enough. Really, you have."

"Stephanie, please ..."

"I need to go." Panic settled against her breasts and grew with each breath she took.

"Why don't you just stay with Bart and I for a few ..."

"Bart's a man."

"He's my husband, Stephanie."

The look of hurt on her face was unmistakable. The way her lips curved down, the brows dipped in toward her nose.

"I'm sorry, Betsy. I just can't."

She got out of the car, closed the door and stepped onto the sidewalk. It was ten feet from the car to her room, but for Stephanie, it looked like several miles. Head down, she walked towards the building. The janitor rounded the corner, his wiry frame somehow intimidating. He smiled and nodded.

Stephanie wanted to put her hands over her breasts, to cover up below her waist. Her breath caught in her lungs as the janitor strolled by. He gave her a second glance, and his face screwed up in confusion.

He knows, she thought. *He knows what happened.* Her

220

eyes were wide as she hurried to the door, swiped the card and pushed her way inside. Once the door was closed, she set the double locks and went to the bathroom. A woman she didn't know stared back at her from the mirror above the sink. Her long blond hair, normally shiny and combed straight, was dull and in need of washing. Waxen skin replaced what was once smooth and tanned. Gray and purple bags sagged beneath her eyes. A slight indention sat below one of them, a permanent reminder. She had been pretty in another lifetime.

As she stared in the mirror, her distrust for men began to morph into a hatred for herself. She slid her shirt over her head, and tore her bra off, tossing it aside. She kicked off her shoes. Her pants and undies came next. Naked, her body a curvy road men had once desired, she thought she could see the faint traces of bruises on her ribs and hips and along her neck where he choked her; the still fresh scar beneath her right breast. The scar was there. The bruises were not.

He was there with her, a calloused hand on her throat while the other one gripped tightly to one breast, squeezing as she screamed in pain. Her hands pinned behind her, one shoulder throbbing, she struggled ... until she managed to free one arm. She swung, open handed ...

The mirror shattered, sending several pieces to the floor and into the sink. Stephanie sucked in air through gritted teeth and pulled back lips. Bright blood spilled from the gash on her palm. A sliver of glass peeked from torn skin. Mesmerized, she stared at the wound as crimson drops fell to the floor.

In the mirror, a hundred distorted versions of an ugly woman stared back at her.

"You were such a tease," she said in a low whisper. "You got what you deserved, you stupid slut."

She picked out a long piece of mirror from the sink and stared at its sharp edges. Her breath came in quick bursts, and her eyes lost all focus. The first cut was across her right thigh. She closed her eyes and held her breath as the second one came at her hip; an inch, then two. The feeling of skin slicing apart and pulling away made her shake. The third slice was on the inside of her left thigh. Wet heat spilled down her legs. Stephanie dropped the piece of mirror and staggered to her bed. She wrapped herself in the sheets, red flowers blossoming through them. Rocking from side to side, she cried until sleep held her in its arms.

***

She traced the name on the headstone with a fingertip. The four fingers on that hand were covered in bandages made from torn sheets, as were the wounds on her thighs. The bruises on the fingers of her other hand had become black, and there were purple rings between each first and second knuckle.

"Susanna." Stephanie leaned her head on the marker. A chill ran the length of her spine.

The stone was rough, and little else was legible, either by sight or touch. The pads of her fingers found their way along another portion of the marker. She retraced the etching and realized it was a number.

"Twenty-three." She sat up and stared at the grave marker. "Same as me."

***

The knock on the door was loud, waking her from a fitful sleep on the couch. Three new cuts had been made on her forearm, the bleeding a little more substantial than before. Crusted blood clung to the wounds. Stephanie shook her head, trying to recall the night before.

She sat up when the knock came again. Her head swooned,

and bright white dots danced in her vision. A moment of nausea came and went.

"Steph. Open up. It's Carlton." Another rap on steel came. The hollow sound echoed in the room.

She tried to speak, but her words came out as a raspy bark. Instead of clearing her throat, she rolled off the couch. The blade of a knife sliced into her knee. Stephanie bit hard on her lip to keep from screaming. Carlton would never go away if he heard her.

"Steph, I know you're in there. Open up, please."

"No," she said soft enough he couldn't hear. The knife came free easily, the blade dripping. On hands and knees, she crawled into the bathroom, and gently closed the door.

The knocking continued, though muffled, like Carlton's voice. In the darkness of the small room, she held the knife tight. She slipped her shirt off and ran the blade along the edge of the scar beneath her breasts. Her breath caught and …

Her hand struck the side of his face. He growled in anger and leveled a solid punch to her eye. He wore a ring—she felt its hard surface just before the explosive throbbing began. Then a knife slid beneath her breast. The pain froze her. The immediate sensation of fire and the warmth of blood trailing down her side scared her much more than the man on top of her. When he was done, he would kill her unless …

The side of her head rocked suddenly from the back of his hand. The eye swelled from the other punch. His fingers in her mouth, her teeth clamping down … then darkness …

"What have you been doing to yourself?" Doctor Clayburn asked. There was no notepad, no pen. He took off his glasses and wiped the lenses with the end of his light blue tie.

"Nothing."

"Stephanie, have you been hurting yourself?"

A slow shake of her head was followed with, "No."

"Are you sure?"

A nod. "I've never hurt myself."

"Then why all the bandages?"

She looked at her hands and her arms, then up at the shrink. "It helps me forget."

"Forget?" he asked. "Maybe you need to remember instead."

She wondered what Susanna looked like. A blond like her, maybe? Blue eyes? She wondered if the men loved her or if she shied away from their touch. She wondered how she died at such a young age. Sickness? Heartbreak? Raped and murdered, left for dead by the riverbank by a lover or a stranger?

"I thought I would find you here."

Stephanie looked up at the familiar face of her once very close friend. Carlton stood like a comic book hero, hands on his hips, his body cutting a shadow across Susanna's headstone.

Her heart sped up, her palms grew sweaty, eyes watered. She backed away from the grave on her bottom, pushing with her legs.

It's Carlton, her soul screamed. *He's your best friend for crying out loud.*

"Come on, Stephanie." He rounded the stone and knelt down beside it. "You can't keep coming here."

"Why not?"

"You need help."

"No. I just want to be left alone. Is that too much to ask?"

"Yes."

"You don't understand."

"I'm trying to."

Thick silence filled the distance between them. Carlton

224

turned to the stone then back to Stephanie.

"Why do you keep coming back to this grave?"

"She comforts me."

"She?

"Her name was Susanna." Stephanie paused, letting out a slight chuckle. "She was twenty-three when she died. The same as me."

"You're not going to die."

She swallowed hard, forcing back the tears trying to form. "How do you know?"

He shrugged, inching a little closer. "I don't. But if you don't stop cutting yourself, I may not be able to save you."

"Save me?" Anger flashed in her eyes. Tears followed. "Where were you when I needed you to save me? Where were you when I was being raped and stabbed and beaten and left for dead in a dumpster? You were nowhere, that's where. You couldn't save me then. How do you think you can save me now?"

He stared hard at her, this time with no hurt in his eyes. Instead, anger showed in the scowl masking his normally warm face.

"Steph …"

"No," she interrupted. "I just want to be left alone. That's all. I'm tired of everyone telling me things will be okay. They won't. They never will. It doesn't matter what you or the shrink or Betsy or Mom and Dad or anyone else thinks. You don't know what it's like. You don't know how I feel."

"Help me understand then."

Stephanie stood, wiping snot from her nose. "You want to understand?"

"Yes."

"When you get raped and go through the fear and violation and thinking you're going to die, then come talk to me. Until then, just leave me alone." She gave Carlton a wide birth as she went by. Her body shook, and her heart ached. Her thoughts were a muddle of words and images crashing together.

"You want me to leave you alone?" Carlton called back.

Stephanie stopped near the tiny stone where a baby had been buried. Thick grass grew up along its base. Like Susanna's, the marker had eroded through time and weather. Her mind shut down for a few seconds then slowly started back up. "Yes," she whispered, though deep down she screamed, "no."

"Fine. If you want me to leave you alone I will. But eventually, you're going to have to face your demons, Steph. Until then, no one can help you."

"I'm going to go home," she said from her seat. She stared down at what she now thought of as the Carpet of Blood.

"Really?" Clayburn asked.

"Yes."

"When?"

"Betsy's taking me when I leave here."

No wonder, she thought as they sat in front of her house, the car idling. *My house is secluded from the others. I never noticed it before.*

Trees formed a natural fence to one side, separating her yard from the nearest neighbor. On the opposite side, a street ran by the corner lot and towards town—not one house to be seen along that stretch of black top.

"Are we going in?" Betsy asked.

"No."

"What?"

"We're not going in. I am."

"Steph ..."

"I have to do this. Alone. Just me, Betsy. I have to face this ... this ... demon. Please understand."

The expression was back. Hurt mixed with aggravation.

Stephanie got out of the car, wanting to get away from Betsy, wanting to get it over with. The house loomed in the distance, the lush, overgrown grass before her, the sidewalk leading to the steps—three of them advanced onto the porch and the door *he* had come through that night. Stephanie's chest tightened, her bladder tingled. A moment of pure fear threatened to shove her back into the car and tell Betsy to get them as far away from there as she could.

Her legs shook as she took the first step. Her hands were tight fists. Three more steps and her quivering knees threatened to drop her to the concrete sidewalk.

Don't look back, don't look back, don't look back, she thought to herself, certain if she did the fear would take complete control, and she would run away. At the steps, she could see letters overflowing the mailbox. Some lay on the porch.

Her skin danced as if electricity ran through her veins. Her throat was dry, and butterflies did more than just flutter in her stomach. A hum buzzed in her ears. She glanced back, cursing herself for doing so. Betsy stood outside the car, a worried frown pulling on her face, her eyes wide. Stephanie gave a nod, turned back to the house, and took a deep breath.

Her foot lingered over the first step, the breath caught in her lungs. She exhaled, clamping her teeth together against the anxiety swelling in her chest and made her way up to the porch. She dug the key out of her front pocket and slid it into the lock. The sound of the tumblers and the lock giving way sent shivers along her spine. A sweaty palm turned the knob. The door opened freely.

The couch sat to the right of the door, the television across the room, a recliner off to one side. Her mug still sat on the coffee table in front of the couch next to the newspaper she had read that morning. If she were to look into the cup she would see the dried out remains of the coffee she hadn't finished. The room was stuffy. Dust motes hung in the air, visible in the sun's rays shining through the still open blinds.

Stephanie's muscles tensed, and knots formed in her stomach and shoulders. Her mind whispered warnings: *What if he's still here?* She licked her lips and made her way to the kitchen. In the third drawer from the left of the sink sat the utensils. She pulled out a steak knife, holding it tightly in her right hand.

At the hallway leading to the back of the house she stopped suddenly. Her body shook.

This is where …

… the noise came from behind her, like a soft clink of metal on metal. She turned, and he was in the shadows with her. A scream escaped just before the first punch to the side of her head, just below the ear. She crumpled to the floor, dazed; the world a gray fog from the neck up …

Stephanie leaned against the wall, the shock of the image filling her world. The knife raked across her forearm, peeling skin away and releasing a rush of blood. She shook her head, and pushed further down the hall.

The bedroom was still in shambles, her blankets and pillows on the floor, the bed sheet ruined with brownish-red stains.

Fingers in her mouth. The taste of skin and bitter blood as she bit down. Blinding shot to the face. It all rushed back, flooding her system to the point of almost drowning her. *The pajamas had been cut away, skin sliced in spots as well.*

And he was in her, hard and rough, hand around her throat.

His knife tore into the underside of one breast. Her mind shut down, and the fight left her. Images of how they would find her lingered like snapshots in her soul. How many times would he stab her before she died? How many times would he stab her afterward? The dumpster from another world was there, and she could see her body being tossed in, thrown away like the rest of the garbage.

She could smell his breath, the sweat on his body. His weight was heavy on her. He stiffened, finished, and pulled free. Stephanie opened her eyes, and in the slight light of the moon in the window, she caught a glimpse of the side of his face ...

She trembled as she sat on the floor, eyes blurry from the many tears, heart torn open and disbelieving. She closed her eyes, letting the knife slide under the cup of her bra.

"Stephanie!"

Weightless, she floated, her head in the clouds, the world around her zooming in and out of focus.

"What have you done? What have you done? Oh my God, Stephanie!"

"Do you remember anything?" Clayburn sat in the familiar chair. A thick manila folder sat open on his lap. He flipped through several papers before looking up at her.

Stephanie sat with her hands folded in her lap. She had deep-set eyes, light gray bags beneath them, thinning cheeks, and dirty hair. Her clothes were a baggy, button down shirt and jeans a couple of sizes too big.

"I remember enough."

"Like what?"

"Waking in the hospital."

"Which time?"

She looked up at him. "There was more than one?"

He raised one brow, nodded. "You tried to commit suicide."

"I did? When?"

"You don't remember?"

Stephanie frowned, eyes narrowed. "Doctor, what I remember is being home at night. By myself ... and being attacked. I was raped. I was stabbed. I was beaten and left for dead in a dumpster. And I woke in a hospital. Isn't that enough to remember?" She stared at Clayburn with a strong disdain building inside of her.

Clayburn said nothing.

And she remembered ...

The phone rang six times before the answering machine picked up. After the recording, she left her message:

"Hey, it's Steph. Can we talk? Please? You know where to find me."

The cool air cradled her soft skin. She sat next to Susannah's tombstone and ran her fingers along its faded engraving. The trees rustled with the early fall breeze. Brightly colored leaves fell to the ground.

"Susannah," she said. "It's almost over."

With her other hand she brought the blade of the knife across her palm. She let the blood pool in her hand before pressing it against Susannah's marker.

"So young—too young to die. At least you didn't live through it. You would have been dead anyway ... dead on the inside."

The blade slid across the top of her hand and over her wrist. It made its way toward the crook of her elbow before she heard him.

"Stephanie," he said. "What are you doing?"

She fell back on the soft grass, her hand going limp, the knife lying in her palm.

His hands were on her cheeks, warm and rough.

"Carlton." Her voice was weak, her chest heavy, her head light. "I know."

Something pressed against the long, gaping wound on her arm. She heard the metallic clink of his belt buckle as it unsnapped. Her eyes popped open at the sound, so hollow, but so loud. Carlton was shirtless, and his belt slid free of his pants. This time she wouldn't fight. No, this time …

"I know, Carlton," she repeated, as pressure was applied to her elbow. The belt cinched tight, pressing the shirt into her wound to staunch the flow of blood. "I know …"

Carlton lifted her head off the ground. "You know what?"

"I know, Carlton. I know …"

He shook his head. "You know what?"

"I know who raped me."

Carlton stiffened, his arms grew rigid as he held her.

"You should have killed me."

She gripped the knife tight. It was slick in the palm of her hand. Even in her weakened state, her strength didn't fail her. She drove the knife into Carlton's throat.

Carlton grabbed her wrist, his eyes bulging, mouth hanging open and moving, speaking silent words Stephanie would never know.

As her world dimmed, Carlton's hand released hers, and he slumped backward.

The sun warmed her face. She looked up to the blue sky and let the clouds carry her mind away.

"Do you like it here?" Clayburn asked. He sat in a metal folding chair, an identification badge on his shirt. His hands were on one knee crossed over the other one. He looked different in the sunlight, with his eyes squinting. He looked uncomfortable.

Stephanie shrugged. "It's okay, I guess."

"Better than home?"

Another shrug. "Better than out there." She half-heartedly pointed beyond the brown-bricked walls of the giant recreation yard.

"You could have opted to have this meeting at my office, you know?"

"I know."

"You could have gotten out for a couple of hours, under my direct supervision, of course."

A nod.

"You didn't want that?"

"You're a man ... I don't trust men."

"You can't be afraid of men forever, Stephanie. One day ..."

"I didn't say I was afraid of men. I said I don't trust them." Her jaw flexed. "I faced my demon, and I killed him. And now I'm here."

"By choice," Clayburn added.

Stephanie gave a small smile, something she hadn't done in over a year. Her fingers itched, and she rubbed them along her elbows. "Yes, by choice ... but not for me."

Clayburn frowned, cocked his head to one side. "Then for who?"

Stephanie's smile broadened, and her eyes glistened in the sunlight. "For you. For all of you."

Dear Faithful Reader,

I hope you have a few more minutes to spend with me. I'd like to tell you a couple more stories. Unlike the ones in this collection, these are true pieces of life that shaped people I know. Sit back down and grab your beverage of choice. If it is cold where you are, wrap up in a blanket. If it is warm, have a seat in the sun and prop your feet up, and let me talk with you a little while longer.

The first of these stories is about my dad and I. Growing up, we didn't have a lot of money. Like most kids, I would ask for things hoping my parents could afford them. I knew we didn't have much money, and I really didn't understand how it worked. I just knew I wanted things (again, like most kids).

When I was around ten all of my friends were playing baseball. One day I asked my dad if I could play, but there was a problem; we couldn't afford new gear for me to do so. Disappointed, I walked away and went onto something else (what that was, I don't remember, and honestly, it is not all too important).

A couple of Saturdays later, Dad came to me and asked if I wanted to go to the flea market with him. Of course, I said yes. It was an opportunity to spend time with my dad, and back then Dads were their sons' heroes.

Flea markets are great little outdoor yard sales where most folks try to get rid of their junk and hope it is someone else's treasure. Dad and I went to the Number 1 Metro Flea Market in West Columbia. I didn't really do much looking at stuff, thinking we wouldn't be able to get anything.

Then Dad stopped at this one table. I didn't think much about it, again, not really looking, not really wanting to see something I liked and not be able to get it.

"I'll take that one," I heard Dad say, but I didn't look at what he was buying.

"That'll be two dollars," the man said.

Two dollars was a lot of money for our family back in the

summer of 1980. I looked up in time to see Dad pull two crumpled dollar bills out of his wallet and reach across the table to give to the man.

"Thank you, Sir," he said and picked up the baseball glove from the table. Inside it was a ball. He looked down at me, a half smile on his face, his eyes slightly squinted the way he did when he was trying not to show a lot of excitement on his face. "Here, Son," he said to me.

I don't know if my eyes lit up. I don't know if my face glowed. I do know it was probably the happiest I had ever been in my childhood.

"I'll teach you how to throw when we get home," Dad said. He clapped me on the shoulder (his gesture of a hug).

For the record, I wasn't very good at baseball. I could field and throw, but I couldn't hit my way out of an invisible bag. The point is this; my dad knew my disappointment. He also knew the value of a dollar. He spent two bucks on a ball and a glove (the glove was probably twenty years old in 1980). Two bucks back then was twenty or thirty or fifty dollars today, and when you didn't have much money to begin with, two dollars was like gold. I realized then how valuable that glove and ball were, not just to me, but my dad.

I used the glove for years. When the webbing tore, I created a new pocket for it out of shoelaces. When the rawhide that held the fingers together snapped, I used wire to fix it. Why? Because my dad had spent two precious dollars on it, so I could play a game I never became good at.

I also learned the value of money and the even more important value of putting others before myself.

The ball is long gone, but I still have the glove.

This is one of my fondest memories from my childhood.

A lot of my views on life were shaped by my dad. How I treat people, my work ethic, the lack of sleep I get (yeah, I blame Dad for that one, too). Sportsmanship.

Stick with me a few more minutes. I promise, there is a point to the rambling. When I was fourteen, baseball had taken a backseat to a passion I carried with me well beyond my

234

thirties: basketball. By then, Dad was giving me an allowance for helping him in the yard or around the house. I was able to save up money to buy stuff I wanted (see how the value of money played out?). One of the things I purchased was a basketball.

Dad built us a backboard and got a rim and net and hung it on a tree in the back yard. My friends came over to play ball all the time. One day, my buddy T beat me in four straight games of one on one. Understand something, I had not lost four straight games at any sport, and losing that many at basketball, a game I was good at, was enough to make me crazy.

I cussed. I fussed. I raised a ruckus.

Dad came out of his shop and waved for T to go home.

"Boy, what's the problem?" he asked as he approached me.

I cussed. I fussed. I raised a ruckus at Dad about losing four straight games.

"I see," he said and then added, "Can I see your ball?"

I cussed. I fussed. I raised a ruckus as I handed Dad the ball. He then pulled out his hawk bill knife and cut the ball in two. He handed the two pieces to me. I stared at it in complete disbelief.

"When you learn how to lose with a better attitude, I'll buy you a new ball."

Dad turned, walked off, and left me standing there. My dad's actions were greatly influenced by my own actions. As a result, my actions were greatly influenced by what my dad had done.

This brings me to my point; most everything we do in life is based on something someone else has said or done. If not for our parents having a little fun (wherever they chose to have a little fun), we would not be here. Our very existence is based on others' desires, lusts, wants, or whatever. Our lives are formed by those around us and the circumstances we are in. Life galvanizes us.

We are not born hating others. This is learned. We are not born loving others. This is also learned.

In the grand scheme of things, every life impacts another one. A kind word can go a long way to building someone's confidence, where as an unkind word could be destructive. The right coach can help a kid become great, whereas the wrong coach can end any desire to pursue a sport (more on that in my author notes). By their actions, teachers can mold or tear down students. A homeless man who no one thinks about can receive a note from a five-year-old girl, and it could be the sweetest thing ever to happened to him. A man can sexually assault a woman and ruin her entire life.

Good or bad, everyone has a story. It doesn't matter how short or long it is, everyone has a story. The stories are of stillborn children, gone before their first breath to the hundred-year-old woman who watched a century pass by, along with most, if not all of the friends of her youth. Billions of stories happen between the baby and the woman, and each one of them is important. Each one of those lives, no matter how insignificant they may seem, plays a role in shaping the world around them.

The pieces in *Voices* are slices of those stories, of lives impacted or that impacted others. They are stories of abuse, rape, neglect, death, and sorrow. Some rise above the murk, while others sink below it. In every story, the events of each life in them matter. This is just me giving their stories a voice.

I hope you enjoyed *Voices*, and I thank you for coming along with me on this journey. Until we meet again my friends, be kind to one another.

A.J.
11/30/2016

Voices Notes

The following is a brief look into what inspired the stories in this collection. Enjoy…

In the Shadows They Hide: Sciophobia is the fear of shadows. I think at one time or another, most people deal with a form of sciophobia. For most I would venture to say the fear manifests itself in the middle of the night when you wake from sleep and see something standing just on the outskirts of a night light or a street light casting a glow into the room through a window.

I know this was the case for me when I was a kid. There was a street light directly across from our house. Just enough light shone in my room to cast shadows along the walls. Those shadows always looked like they were moving. There was nothing I could do about it, either. I couldn't move. I could only hope and pray—and pray I did—whatever monster was across the room wouldn't eat me.

When I sat to write this piece I tapped into that very real fear. Instead of a little child, I made Spencer a teenager who was not only afraid of shadows but of girls as well. It was a double whammy he had to face. But there is more to Spencer and the shadows that follow him. This is evident when Sarah and her boyfriend play a cruel prank on Spencer. I found the ending fitting, given the circumstances.

In the Shadows They Hide originally appeared in the anthology Night Terrors II (January, 2012).

Chet and Kay's Not So Marvelous Adventure: Cate and I and the kids took an afternoon trip to the lake one day to see her grandparents. Just before we left our house it began to snow. It wasn't a hard snow but enough to make me a little anxious—we would be heading to a colder part of the state where there would probably be more snow than in our little town of West Columbia.

To understand this a little better, I live in South Carolina where, historically, the drivers suck when the weather is nice. Can you imagine how bad they are when it is raining, or, I don't know, snowing?

So my worries were warranted.

We made the thirty-two mile trip to Saluda with the snow falling down around us, sticking to the ground, but not to the road. Thankfully.

Then came the red Ford Ranger barreling down the road right behind us. It whipped by us in the oncoming traffic lane and ran off the road before pulling back onto it. The truck didn't wreck like in my little tale, but the story formed quickly, and I began writing it that afternoon.

The Scarring: You met the main character of this story as Nothing, the guy with all the scars and pent up hate and anger. I knew him by a different name when I started writing this piece. But a funny thing happened as I wrote this story; the main character didn't want to use the name I had given him. He kept whispering to me, "My name is Nothing." Of course, I didn't listen to him. Then he decided to stop the car and tell me to get out, just get out if I'm not going to listen to him.

I was stubborn, as I'm apt to be. Just ask my wife, or really anyone who knows me. I was determined to use the name I had given him. He was determined to not cooperate until I called him Nothing. In the end, I lost the battle of wills. Here's the funny thing; for the life of me, I can't remember the name I had originally picked out for him. The use of his name wasn't meant to be; he was meant to be Nothing. And so he is.

This is a decidedly different story, one that is more telling than anything else. At least until the end. It also came about because of a scar on the palm of my left hand, put there by a nail over twenty years ago. Nothing like a hammer, a nail, and a rotten piece of wood.

Claire, The Movie: I don't watch award shows. They bore

me. That said, I walked into the living room one evening, and Cate was watching the Oscars. I stood and watched for a couple of minutes before turning and walking out. I had completely forgotten why I had gone in there in the first place. What I did remember was all the women in expensive gowns and all the men in expensive suits and tuxedos and how all of it looked fake.

Let's give credit where credit is due; there are some actors and actresses who are so good you can't tell where the character begins and where it ends. It's like they actually take on the role of the characters they play. As I thought about acting, a young woman named Claire came to me clearly. She was fearful of her father, but also tired of being fearful. She was a great actress because, truthfully, the acting and the life were one and the same. She needed to do something about her situation, and what better place but at the Oscars where she could expose him for what he really was?

Black Storms: How many times have we heard about the end of the world, complete with dates for when it would happen? How many times have we seen certain sects of people go off the deep end, proclaiming everyone would die, some going so far as to commit mass suicides? This is the premise of *Black Storms*, but without the mass suicides.

Many end of the world scenarios claim the rapture is going to occur, something that may just happen, but not on the human clock. No, the rapture will happen only when God says it will and the time is not known to man. Ahhh, but I'm not going to preach. Not here, at least.

But this story is different from how we believe the rapture will happen. It doesn't happen all at once with every saved soul leaving behind their bodies and rising into the air. Instead, it happens one soul at a time, but with somewhat of a terrifying twist that leaves the main character somewhat unnerved and afraid of the storms that bring on the rapture ... or is it a reaping?

Anymore: This story is one of my favorites in this collection because it was inspired by a local band here in Columbia called Prettier Than Matt. It consists of two people. Yes, two people. Jeff Pitts and Jessica Skinner.

Cate and I first learned of PTM at the Crawfish Festival in the spring of 2015. (You know you live in the south when you have a Crawfish Festival.) We went to hear another band play, but it turns out the band wasn't really to our liking. Since we had already paid to get in, and we had a kid sitter for the day, we hung out, perused the booths and ate lunch. Then we went looking for other bands to watch. We came across one of the marquees at the festival's center. There were several bands listed, all playing around the same time.

"Let's go to this one," I said.

"Why that one?" Cate asked.

"I like the name. If we don't like them we can go see one of the others."

The name? *Prettier Than Matt.*

We went to the stage where they were playing. We thought it was a good sign there were a lot of people at the stage—more than we had seen at any of the others. They were already playing by the time we arrived, but the song still sticks in my head: *All I Want is You.* No, not the U2 song, but a song written by Barry Louis Polisar. It had a folksy sound to it. I instantly liked it. Then they did covers of Michael Jackson's *The Way You Make Me Feel* and Cyndi Lauper's *Time After Time.* They did a few others, but one stuck in my head, even after they stopped singing it: *The La La Song*, a PTM original. After the show we bought one of their albums and listened to it on the way home, and then at home, and then when we went out somewhere, and then … you get the picture, right? We listened to it. A lot.

Since then, Cate and I have been to see them probably 3 dozen times. I'm not sure I would call us groupies, but we definitely are fans. Being a writer, I want fans of my work. As a music freak, when I hear something I like, I latch onto it and soak up as much of it as I can. I like PTM. How can you not

like a band who describes themselves as "being cool enough for the edgy and sweet enough for the sensitive."
(From Reverbnation.com)

Like I said earlier, this piece was inspired by the first song on one of PTM's albums, *Better Left Said*. The song is titled *Anymore*. Before you try and figure out how the song inspired the story, let me go ahead and say I doubt when they wrote *Anymore* their thoughts were anywhere near what my thoughts were when I wrote this piece. I'm sure they didn't envision two young adults at the river doing a Viking funeral pyre and facing the memories of the drowning death of a friend.

When I finished writing this story I wasn't sure the title would fit. *Anymore.* I thought on it for a while, going over other possibilities. Then it dawned on me; it fits just fine. There are a lot of things going on here, including not feeling guilt anymore for what happened.

The story, itself, starts out sad and maintains that mood until the end. Then it gets a little sappy and a touch humorous. I like the way the mood changed but kept its tone. To me, it was the important thing about this one. That and life, love and redemption—good themes for a short story.

Now, let me talk about the names of the two main characters: H and B. I sometimes catch grief when I name my characters something out of the ordinary. In this case I chose the letters H and B as names (H being the male and B the female). I didn't wish to name the characters, but as the story progressed I knew the standard pronouns were going to get annoying, redundant, and in some instances, confusing. So I gave them names. Why H and B? Simple: H stands for Honey. B stands for Babe. They are two terms of endearment we hear couples call each other all the time. Sure there are other, less endearing names, but these are the two I call my wife. Just remember H is Honey, which you will hear a lot more women say than men, and B is Babe, which you hear men say all the time.

Crisp Sounds: This story was written in a very short time in

2016. It was for the anthology *The Ladies and Gentlemen of Horror*, put out each year by Jennifer Miller. A few years earlier, I managed to get into an edition of this anthology, but didn't get to work with Jennifer for too long. When the opportunity came to be in LGOH again, I jumped on it.

It was cold on the evening I started this story. I had been out in my front yard looking at the sky. It was cloudy, and it looked as if it could snow. With my breath coming out in vapors in front of me, I heard a sound. I don't know what it was, but I remember thinking how loud it was, so much louder than a noise would be if it had been warm out.

The first line of *Crisp Sounds* came from a thought I had: *When it's cold sounds are crisp.*

I really enjoyed writing this story. The human aspect of it made it quite rewarding.

Numbers: Of all the stories in this collection, this was the most difficult to write. I wanted to do a piece where numbers and words had to match up, and if they didn't there would be dire consequences. This is where Dane came in, a girl with a boy's name, who suffers from the fear of what will happen if she says the wrong combination of words. The math of each word spoken was like finding the right piece in a jigsaw puzzle—it wasn't easy to get those pieces to make sense.

This was also one of the more enjoyable and satisfying stories to write. Creating Dane and her warped mind made the simple difficulties of the math well worth it.

Numbers won one of The Wily Writers Online contests and appeared there in June of 2013.

To Bleed: This was written for a contest many years ago. It was an online contest put on by *TheHouseofHorrors.com*. The contest itself was a duel: two writers faced off, writing about the same topic. The stories were voted on by fans of the site. It was a lot of fun, and several of my stories won. I can't remember if *To Bleed* won or not, but when I looked at this piece, possibly for this collection, I thought it was still

242

pretty good, and cleaned it up, and shaped it into the piece you read here.

Not Like You: This was one of those difficult to write stories because of the subject matter. The kid in the story, Brian, is really a sweet kid, but he is not all together a part of this world. I wanted to paint the picture of how bad he and his siblings had it for so long, and the experience had damaged him.

Even damaged, he still looked up to one of the two people who neglected him, his father. This is natural. But then there is the level of hurt Brian experiences when his father doesn't give him a birthday gift. The aftermath is his father being mad at him for bringing it up in front of his grandparents. When blamed for his dad getting in trouble, Brian experiences yet another bout of pain.

Then the epiphany, Dad is evil. For a damaged child who sees the evil as the preacher said it was, what could he do? Well, he could set his father free.

I have been told this story escalates too fast. I disagree. You have to remember, Brian had been neglected by his parents, and though it is in the past by several years, the memory remained. It didn't help that his father didn't treat him well and blamed Brian for him getting into trouble.

Sadly, a lot of this story is based loosely on some people I know. I've seen the neglect and the way the young boy was treated. I've seen parts of this story play out, and I always wondered what the breaking point would be for someone like Brian. This is my interpretation of that breaking point.

The Sad Woes of the Trash Man: Cate and I were heading somewhere for one of our Daycations. I honestly can't remember where we were off to. The kids were in the back seat. What I *can* remember was seeing a work crew alongside the road cleaning trash from the curbside and the fields beyond it. Every fifteen to thirty feet along that stretch of highway sat orange trash bags. The men doing the cleaning didn't wear prison jumpers, but they didn't look like they were there because they wanted to be.

Just beyond where those men worked sat a beat up pick-up truck. It had definitely seen better days. Off in the distance, an older black man was walking away from the road. He was easily forty or so yards away from his truck and the highway.

I would have loved to stop and talk with him for a while. But as I thought on it, I didn't think that would have been a good idea. What if he were looking for something he wanted no one else to know about? What if he were looking for a body, one he may have put there? My imagination leaned in and whispered into my ear ever so gently, "There's a story. Now write it."

And I did.

The White: I love baseball, but not just any baseball. I love Little League Baseball. I love the innocence of it. I love the atmosphere of a little league ballpark. Those kids want to win. They want to be the hero everyone cheers for. They want to make their parents proud of them. They're not playing for a paycheck, but to have fun and to win.

It is in the little leagues where children either fall in love with or out of love with the game. The coach is one person who can influence a kid's love for the game (or lack thereof). A good coach can cultivate the desire and turn it into a passion. A bad coach can crush the spirit, squashing all desire and potential love for the game.

I witnessed this firsthand with my son, when a coach of an established team ended up with him and didn't want him on his team. It was obvious to me in the first—and only—practice he attended with the team. He never instructed my son what to do, only yelled when he messed up. It was all I could do not to storm onto the field and have words with the coach. Cate made me walk away at one point.

The coach was a jerk, and after an hour or so of watching him "coach" my son, I finally walked into the dugout after my son had taken just ten swings with the bat (after being the last to bat while the other boys on the team received thirty pitches or more). I gathered up my son and his equipment and we left. The coach started to interfere, asking where we were going.

"We're done here," is all I could say and keep my cool.

As we walked away, him holding my hand and me carrying his gear, this conversation took place:

The Boy: Daddy, I'm bad.
Me: No, you're not.
The Boy: I didn't do anything right.
Me: No, son. You did everything you knew to do.
The Boy: The coach didn't like me.
Me: You don't worry about him. You will never play for him.
The Boy: I won't?
Me: No. I'll let you quit before I let him talk to you again.
The Boy: I'm sorry, Daddy.

There is more to the conversation, but you can see how sad he was because of the coach's actions. I wanted to turn around and ring the man's neck.

For the record, I didn't let my son quit, but we had him removed from the team. And, one other note, my son no longer plays baseball, and that's a shame because he was good, and he would have loved it.

I told you this story so I could tell this one; we often go to the ballpark my son played at. I coached for three years there, and I like to see some of the kids I coached play. It was on one of those visits where the onset of an ocular migraine began. At the time I had been looking at the field, at the coach yelling at one of the kids. He grabbed the boy's facemask and pulled on it. He was the same coach who had yelled at my son.

With ocular migraines I often lose vision in one eye. What replaces it is usually a swirling mass of white dots. As I looked at the coach yelling at the kid, all I saw was half of his body. The other half was white.

That evening. with the migraine abated some, I sat and

began writing *The White*.

Apartment 306 and Poor Jenny Harris: This was written way back in 2007. At the time I was experimenting with the first person present tense. I had written a couple stories I was less than pleased with. But this one … this one was fun, and difficult to write. Fun, because I was able to write a long first person, present tense story. Difficult because of the subject matter. This was one of the first stories where I pushed the limits of what I thought I could write. In this piece there is murder and sexual abuse (though none of them actually "seen" by you, Faithful Reader) and a child killing his father.
Earlier in this collection you read *Not Like You*. It was another child kills father story, but on a different level and with the brutality a bit more written in. *Apartment 306 and Poor Jenny Harris* laid the groundwork for several of the pieces in this collection.

A Memory Best Left Alone: I wanted to do a story about a woman who cuts herself as a way of coping with a traumatic event. I had never written this type of story so I was stepping way outside of my normal comfort zone. In order to create the story successfully, I had to create the event that caused her to cut herself. What was the event? She was beaten and raped one night in her home in a break and enter. Her mind does what many minds do in order to protect her. It shoves the events to the darkest areas of her soul—into the shadows.

A peculiar thing about people: they always want to try and unlock what the mind hides away. Head shrinks like to explore the mysteries of damaged psyches. In this case he should have probably left it alone.

I'm going to be honest with you here; my favorite part of this story is the last paragraph, where Stephanie tells the head shrink she chose to meet in the prison and not outside, not for her, but for the shrink's safety. That gave me chills when I wrote it. It still does. I hope it did the same for you.

The Great Big Page of Appreciation

It's true what many people say about the act of writing; it's a solitary endeavor. The very act of taking thoughts from your head and putting them on paper (or computer screen via the fingertips) is completely singular in nature. Even collaborative efforts are still done by one person at a time. However, putting together a good book often takes more than just the author. With that in mind, I would like to thank the following:

Lisa Vasquez. In the couple of years or so I've known Lisa I've seen my work take off. I credit part of that to Lisa's unique way of marketing the authors under the umbrella of her publishing house. Lisa and I communicate several times a week and we bounce ideas off of each other, making each other better in the process. I consider Lisa a very good friend and one heck of a business associate.

Donelle Pardee Whiting edited this collection of stories, just as I have edited some of her work in the past. She hates the way I do my ellipses, so if you've seen them in here, then more than likely, you have seen the correct way to do it. We have a unique relationship in we give each other crap on a regular basis, but we also encourage each other all the time. Like Lisa, I consider Donelle a very good friend, even if she doesn't like the way I do my ellipses …

Though writing is solitary most writers have significant others who support them in one way or another, often encouraging and listening to their doubts and complaints. I am no different. Without my wife Cate I would have quit a long time ago. Her constant encouragement has kept me going all these years. Don't think just because she is my wife she doesn't criticize some of my stories. She does. If she doesn't like a story she tells me. If she thinks the writing is bad she tells me. She doesn't sugar coat things to spare my feelings. She's honest about it, and that is worth its weight in gold.

I can never thank everyone, but there are a few folks who

have challenged and encouraged me over the last year or so and they are, in no particular order: Briana Robertson, Jenna Miller, MF Wahl, James Matthew Byers, David Court, Justin and Robert Dunne, Frank Knox and H. Herbie Himperwheel, my muse.

As always, I thank you, my faithful readers, for coming back for more of my work. Your continued support and feedback lets me know I am doing something right.

A.J.

Author Bio

A.J. Brown is a southern-born writer who tells emotionally charged, character driven stories that often delve into the darker parts of the human psyche. Most of his stories have the southern country feel of his childhood.

A.J. writes in a conversational style that draws the reader in and holds their attention. His characters are average people with average lives who are layered with memories and emotions and are fallible, just like anyone else.

He draws inspiration from every day events and conversations. The characters of his stories are drawn from people he has met or seen during his life.

Though he writes mostly darker stories, he does so without unnecessary gore, coarse language, or sex.

A.J. is also a husband to Cate and a father to two kids, who often inspire him in the most interesting ways.

More than 150 of his stories have been published in various online and print publications. His story *Mother Weeps* was nominated for a Pushcart Award in 2010. Another story, *Picket Fences*, was the editor's choice story for Necrotic Tissue in October of 2010. The story, *Numbers*, won the quarterly contest at WilyWriters.com in June of 2013. John Malone won the Voice Arts Award for audiobook narration in the Science Fiction category for his voiceover of *Dredging Up Memories.*

If you would like to learn more about A.J. you can check out his blog, Type AJ Negative. You can also find him on Facebook at ajbrown36, Twitter at ajbrown36 and Instagram at ajbrownstoryteller.

You can purchase his other works, *A Stitch of Madness*, *Dredging Up Memories* or either of his other short story collections—*Along the Splintered Path*, and *Southern Bones*—on Amazon. You can also find his novel *Cory's Way* and his short story collection *Ball Four* on Amazon. A list of his publications along with links to many of his stories can be found at Type AJ Negative (https://typeajnegative.wordpress.com).

Other Works by A.J. Brown

Along the Splintered Path: Three tales of souls splintered by the events of life. How to overcome those events is the question. The answer could be the difference between sanity and madness.

Southern Bones: Welcome to the South. Recognized for its traditions, beliefs, and hospitality. The people are genuine and a helping hand and a home cooked meal are never too far away.

Welcome to the South. Where some traditions are better off forgotten. Where some beliefs are based, not on the Bible, but on what men want you to believe. Where behind the hospitable smiles are angry snarls trailed by the feral snaps of rabid people.

Welcome to the South. Where a house stands lonely on a hill, its owner a man deformed by life. Where children aren't quite as naïve as they appear. Where the darkest secrets are found within its families, and where dying sometimes isn't the end.

Welcome to *Southern Bones*, a collection of eleven short stories from the mind of A.J. Brown.

Cory's Way: After his father leaves in the middle of the night, Cory Maddox and his mom Gina are forced to start over. Left alone while Gina tries to work her way out of debt, Cory deals with life as the new kid in school with no friends. Fleeing from the school bullies, Cory ends up under an overpass where an old homeless man lives. After being saved from the bullies, Cory and the homeless man, Mr. Washington, become friends.

But things don't get any easier for Cory. Children are disappearing from around the state, and the bullies haven't forgotten his escape the first time they went after him. And there is something wrong with Mr. Washington … something terribly wrong.

Accompanied by his only two friends and the unlikeliest of allies, Cory sets out to keep a promise to the ailing homeless man. Will Cory and his friends find a way to keep the promise, or will the journey prove too difficult for them?

A Stitch of Madness: Madness: extremely foolish behavior. Imprisoned for the murder of his best friend, Johnny Cleary sets out to tell what happened on the day Bobby "Buster" Lennon died, but are the words he writes true or does the deception run deeper.

Madness: the state of being mentally ill, especially severely.

There is something wrong with Irene. Momma's dead, and a ragdoll speaks to her in a voice that is hauntingly familiar. And what about the stitches, the very things that just might hold Irene together?

Madness: a state of frenzied or chaotic activity. After an odd stranger pays Robert Wallenger a visit his world begins to unravel, and the past comes rushing back, along with a sickly sweet scent.

There is madness in everyone. For most, the madness never surfaces. For others, all it takes is one thing, big or small, for them to spiral out of control.

Dredging Up Memories: In the best of times loneliness is difficult. At the end of time it can be deadly.

Hank Walker is alone and struggling not just with the undead but with depression that threatens to swallow him. Searching for the family he sent away at the beginning of the rise of the dead, Hank is left to deal with loneliness, desperation, and his own memories that haunt him.

The dead are everywhere. The few people still alive are scattered, and the ones Hank comes across may be more dangerous than the biters.

With an unlikely traveling companion, Hank's search takes

252

him across the state of South Carolina and to the depths of darkness like nothing he has ever experienced before. Can Hank find his family and survive the biters? Or does he completely unravel in the world of the dead?

Ball Four: There's nothing like the sound of a little league ball park. From the dugout chants to the ping of the bat on ball or the heavy smack of a glove making a catch, nothing quite compares to kids playing America's pastime. It's the true innocence of the game on display; it's the real effort to win as a team. Its kids being kids.

Though America's game is at its best in the Little Leagues, it is also at its most tragic. There's nothing like losing when your heart is all in. There's nothing like failure when the game is on the line. But what if winning and losing didn't matter?

What if it's a bully getting what he deserves? What if it's an old ballpark where dreams were once lived out, but now no one plays on? What if it's a bad pitch or a base not stolen? Or what if it's just a run short of glory? What if it's the memory of a game many years in the past?

What if it's lost innocence?

The Forgetful Man's Disease: Homer Grigsby is in the twilight of his life. His body is frail, and his brain isn't as sharp as it used to be. Having outlived his wife and friends, and even his only son, Homer is left with his thoughts on most days. It's on those days—when he is alone—Homer's mind drifts away, and the ghosts of the past visit him.

"It's time to go," the ghosts say, but Homer resists their calls. Instead, he ventures back in time to a painful memory … and one buried deep in the recesses of his soul.

Afflicted

By A.J. Brown

Pryor jerked awake, a scream tearing from his throat. Darkness surrounded him. He rubbed his eyes. Behind tired lids he saw the remnants of a dream, the images fading until they were nothing.

He pulled the lamp chord. Darkness ran for the corners as light flooded the room. Pryor sat up the best he could, his arms shaking beneath him. Pain raced up his spine and into the back of his skull. His hands quivered as he reached for the pills on the lamp stand. He dry swallowed two of them and laid his head back on the pillow.

After several minutes, and with great effort, he pushed himself up and propped his back against the headboard. He pulled the sheets away. A road map of scars dotted his legs, ran down into his white socks and up into his boxers. An indention sat where his left kneecap used to be, reminded him …

Screeching tires; the sound of metal on metal and screams—his. Smoke and the strong scent of gasoline; heat wrapped itself around him. Then nothing. No feeling, no sounds, or smells. Only weightlessness.

"Stupid drunk," Pryor said and punched the mattress.

The hospital stay lasted two months. Surgeries—a seemingly endless amount—did nothing for the almost unbearable pain in his legs and back. Shattered bone and shredded ligaments made the procedures to repair his knee more difficult than the doctors would have liked. Though they had replaced the knee with a hinge, the indention remained. He could walk, but not without a cane.

Pryor eased his legs over the edge of the bed. Tears soothed his tired eyes and blurred his vision. He reached for his cane, tipped off balance and fell forward. He landed hard on the cold floor, and a bolt of pain streaked from his left ankle up into his hip. It traveled along his spine and into his head where yellow orbs danced in his vision. His scream gave way to crying.

When the pain subsided, Pryor struggled to roll over. He used the bedpost for leverage and pulled himself up and onto the mattress. He picked up the phone, dialed Doctor Milsap.

The door swung open. Pryor hobbled in, gritting his teeth and forcing back fresh tears with each step. A rush of air followed as the door closed behind him. After checking in at the front desk, he sat down as close to the receiving counter as possible. A door to his right opened and a light skinned nurse called out a name, and waited for the patient—a woman with gray hair and Grandmother's Syndrome—before they both disappeared into the maze of halls and examination rooms.

"You be afflicted," the elderly man said and sat down beside Pryor.

"Excuse me?"

The man was darker than anyone Pryor had ever seen. His brown eyes held wrinkles around them and bags beneath them. Yellowed fingernails and bright white teeth contrasted the black skin. "I says, you be afflicted."

"Afflicted?"

"That's a-right, son. Afflicted."

Pryor gave a nervous chuckle. "If you mean I'm in pain, you're absolutely right."

"No, son. I mean you be afflicted. You has a sickness."

Pryor frowned, his brows creased. "No, sir. I'm not sick. Unless you count being sick and tired of hurting all the time, then okay, I guess so."

"Nah. You afflicted up here." The man tapped his temple several times before dropping his hand into his lap.

Pryor laughed, though he didn't find anything the man said funny. "I'm not crazy."

The man smiled. There was knowledge in it. "We all a li'l crazy, Sonny."

"Okay, sure. Whatever you say."

Pryor braced himself on his cane and went to stand. The man placed one hand over Pryor's. Warmth raced up his arm, into his shoulder and down his back, easing some of the hurt. "I knows som'one who can help you."

Pryor stared for a moment, his eyes wide, teeth clenched tight. The warmth of the man's skin on his didn't bother him. The fact the man had touched him did. "No, thank you. I'll take my chance with my doctors."

"This ain't 'bout no body aches. This is 'bout your mind, your soul. When you see what you be afflicted with, you be better."

Pryor pulled his hand free. "That's okay, old man. I just want my medicine and I'll be on my way."

The man shook his head and reached into his shirt pocket. He pulled out a crumpled piece of paper and held it out.

"I don't want that," Pryor said.

"Take it. You call. You be better."

"Really, I don't want it."

"You 'fraid, that's all. Take it."

The man's voice held strength in it, making his command feel as if Pryor had no choice in the matter. He took the paper and shoved it in his pocket. The man nodded, folded his hands one over the other in his lap and looked directly at the wall.

"Pryor Lee," the nurse called as she opened the door.

Without hesitation, Pryor pushed himself to a standing position. Pain ratcheted down into his legs and raced up his spine. He looked back into the waiting room as he passed through the door. All the seats were empty.

Sleepless nights drained him. Unable to get comfortable in bed, he laid on the couch in hopes of dozing, even if only for a few minutes. He moved from the couch and shuffled toward the recliner, a Herculean effort since the accident. A simple action, like standing and moving from seat to seat took seconds before, but now took him long, agonizing minutes.

He made it to the chair, relaxed and let out a deep breath. He set the cane by the recliner and reached for the television remote. His hand brushed the paper the old man had given him the week before. Picking it up, Pryor unfolded it and stared at the scribble of black ink.

"Miss Lillie Mae McCoy. Old State Building 3, Route 19. Cures all known and unknown afflictions. No appointment necessary. Need penny with birth year."

Pryor started to toss the paper aside. One word caught his attention; the same one the old man had used: affliction. The man's words came back to him.

This ain't 'bout no body aches. This is 'bout your mind, your soul. Once you see what you be afflicted with, you be better.

"I'm afflicted with two screwed up legs and a bad spine. That's what I'm afflicted with. No voodoo magic can fix that."

Pryor crumpled the paper, dropped it to the floor. He closed his eyes and hoped for sleep.

He woke with the sun shining through the blinds and a hazy dream vanishing from memory. A dark man had beckoned him, told him a truth and faded. Though he didn't remember the rest of the dream, he recognized the man.

Reaching for his cane, Pryor noticed the note in his hand. It was no longer crumpled into a ball and the black ink stood out against the white backdrop.

"What do you want with me?"

He stood, let out a whimper and hobbled on stiff, aching legs to the bedroom. He took his pills and went back to the recliner. The medication did nothing to alleviate the pain, or even take the edge off even just a little. He sat back in the recliner, dialed the familiar number to the taxi company and requested a ride.

He didn't like cars. Or trucks. Or busses. Or really anything with wheels that zoomed by on roads. Before the accident, he lived in his car, going from place to place without much thought. Now ... now, getting in any vehicle made his stomach quiver with nervousness. Still, they were a necessary evil, and taxies were quite possibly the worst of the bunch. He handed a piece of paper to the cabbie.

"You sure this is where you want to go?" the cabbie asked. He had a Northern accent, and Pryor took him for a New Yorker, maybe even from Jersey. Pryor stared at the guy from next to the door. He looked huge from that angle, like someone Pryor never wanted to meet in a back alley.

Pryor licked his lips. "Yes, sir," he said and got in.

"Okay, but I have to tell you, there isn't much out there."

The cabbie drove out of town and out into the country where long, winding roads were lined by tall trees with knobby, bent branches. The car came to a stop in front of a crumbling concrete wall. The gate that divided its two sides lay on the ground.

"This is it, buddy."

Pryor paid the fare and got out. The door clicked shut and the cab pulled away, doing a U-turn and speeding down the pothole filled road.

A cool breeze ruffled leaves and sent tingling chills through Pryor's body. He checked the address on the paper. "Yeah, I guess this is it."

With his cane out in front, Pryor limped around the fence and entered the large unkempt yard. A dirt path ran through the center of the yard, dead flowers and weeds lining it in brittle grays and browns. A shack sat a couple hundred feet from the gate with tall pines standing guard. Near the edge of the house were several crumbling headstones. It sent a ripple of ice along his skin.

Pryor struggled across the rugged path, stopping near the weathered building. A rocker sat on the sloped porch and the entrance held no door to keep the world outside. Six warped steps led up. Even when he had full use of his legs Pryor wasn't so sure he would have climbed up the worn wooden slats, but hobbled as he was, there was no way he could make it to up.

"Hello? Anyone here?"

He waited, listened to the wind rustle through the trees as leaves sprinted across the ground. Pryor had seen this scene before, dozens of times in cheesy horror movies. A person visiting a creepy place alone because either they wanted to do something exciting or they were prompted to by some crazy looking person who talked weird, but intrigued the unwitting victim. Yeah, that was Pryor, unwitting victim number 317 to the Affliction Yard.

He called again and wished he had asked the cabbie to wait for a short time as Pryor went to investigate. The entire situation was appropriate. In the movies, the cabbie would have left anyway.

"Who be on my property?"

The voice came from the blackness within the house. Pryor licked his lips. Running sounded like a good option, but even the oldest of men could have caught him easy enough. He stood his ground, his stomach dancing with the flutters of a thousand moths. If he needed to, he could get one, maybe two shots in with his cane before whoever called to him took him down.

The woman stepped out of the shack, her onyx skin pulled tight around her face and glistening in the sunlight; her bald head shining. She wore a white blouse, stained with several spots and a brown skirt that reached to her dirty shoes.

"Miss Lillie Mae McCoy?"

Brows raised, McCoy stared at Pryor. "What be your bus'ness here, white man?"

He held out the card with a shaking hand. "I was told you

could help me."

McCoy went down the steps, each one groaning under her slight weight. She took the note. "Mr. Jacobs done talked to you, eh, white man?" she sighed. "I reckon yah done come this far. May as well, see yah through. D'yah have the pe'ny?"

"Yes Ma'am," he said and fished the coin from his pocket. "It was harder to find than I thought. Had to make the cab driver wait for me while I looked through my penny jars."

Lillie Mae took the penny, held it up to the sky. "When was you born?"

"1974."

"No, white man, when was you born? Not the year, the day."

"October eighth."

She nodded and handed the cent piece back.

"Don't you need this?" Pryor asked.

"No. You do." She walked to one corner of the house. Before disappearing around the side, she motioned for him. "Come wit' me."

Pryor limped along, the pain like shards of glass in his knees and spine. His skull pulsed with the extra effort of trying to keep up with a woman that looked old enough to be in the grave for more years than Pryor had been living. He rounded the corner to see a hill. At the top sat a well.

"You're kidding, right?" he said under his breath. The hill was disheartening, but it wasn't what he focused on. "A wishing well?"

"Some things isn't what they seem," Lillie Mae said without looking back. "You want to be healed, you must have faith. If not, you wastin' your time here."

Pryor's face flushed. He started up the hill, his cane digging into the dirt path, legs pushing harder than normal. Ice-like daggers rippled through his body, bringing fresh tears to his eyes. He stopped several times along the way, wanting to turn back, but refusing to. If that old lady can make it up the hill with ease, so can I.

By the time he reached the top, Lillie Mae had found a

seat on a stump, and whittled on a long piece of wood with an old pocket knife. Pryor leaned against a tree for support, his breathing coming in wheezing rasps.

The well was larger than it had appeared from below. Adobe brick covered with years of dirt, and moss extended upwards to his waist and formed a near ten-foot circle. A board, much like a cot, dangled from well-worn ropes hanging from a crossbeam. Two rusty pipes held the board up, their ends jutting from the holes on either side of the well.

"Do I toss the penny in, now?"

"Don' be in all sorts of hurry, white man. You afflicted, and you can't see it 'cause you blind. Nothin' go in the well 'til the well be ready."

Pryor nodded, said nothing else.

"Come and sit," she said and motioned to a tree stump. Pryor did as she said. She pulled out a bottle of clear fluid, opened it. The smell of honey filled the air as she dabbed her fingers into the liquid. Lillie Mae closed her eyes and stood over Pryor. "October chil', wastin' 'way. Blind eyes keep rest a' bay. Body in pain, bones goin' sour. Lift this curse wit'in the hour. Only faith can clean yah soul. Dip down in and be made whole."

Lillie Mae dabbed the honey water behind each of Pryor's ears and onto the back of his neck. Shivers raced along his body.

"Go on down, now. Come back all fixed up."

"Go down?" Pryor asked.

"Yup. In'a the well. Go down."

His mind screamed horror movie moment. This is where the poor lonely victim dies. He wanted to run, but what good would that do him? He wanted to lift his cane and swat at the old lady, but what if he missed? Worse still, what if she was a demon and all that did was anger her? His death could be torturous, but worse if she were mad. He scrambled for an excuse, seizing on the one that seemed less like a lie and closer to the truth.

"I can't get up there. My legs—"

"You can if you believe," she snapped. "Get on up there, white man. Or go home."

Go home? This is your chance, Pryor. Hobble your happy butt out of here, and let's go. You can call a cab from the bottom of the hill. Just go.

Pryor stared at the well. His chest tingled, the moths returned. Sweat formed on his face, hands and armpits. The thought of crawling onto the cot nauseated him, the pain it would cause, and the ache that would linger. But what was it the woman said? He had to believe? Was that what it's all about? Believing in something you have no right believing in? The only thing he had faith in was waking up each morning to unrelenting pain. That was real, not make believe, like the voodoo the lady hack on the tree stump professed. Believe? Seriously? But turning back after going so far …

Again, he was the horror movie victim, pondering his life and what it meant and really, is it living or just going through the motions? There would always be pain, and the quality of living had dropped considerably since the accident.

This isn't living. This is dying a slow and painful death.

"Okay," he said, took a deep breath. "What do I have to lose?"

Pryor pushed himself onto his feet, shuffled over and sat on the edge of the well. The platform moved slightly as he inched onto it. It rocked from side to side after he had slid all the way on. Lillie Mae pulled the two pipes away and gripped the rope in both ancient hands. There was a moment where Pryor's heart and lungs seized, and he knew he was going to plummet to his death.

"Take the pe'ny down, make your wish, toss pe'ny in, and wait."

"I can't just toss it in now?"

Lillie Mae shook her head. "No. The pe'ny be paym'nt, but the body be the sa'rifice."

"Sacrifice? But—"

"'Nough talk."

"No! Wait!"

Pryor tried to scoot off the platform, but it descended quicker than he could move. He grabbed at the wet, moss-covered brick, but found nothing to hold onto. He yelled for her to stop, to pull him back up, he didn't want to do this after all. The cot came to a stop above a pool of black water. The damp smell of moss and rotten wood clung to the walls. Above him, Lillie Mae spoke in soft whispers. He strained to hear, but couldn't make out anything. His heart thumped. A lump formed in his throat.

Pryor peeked over the edge of the cot, and stared into the murky black water. No reflection looked back, winked, or made a silly face to ease the tension. Above him, Lillie Mae continued her soft words, a chant Pryor couldn't make out at all.

As he studied the water, he realized he still held the penny tight. He opened his hand. The penny sat, head side up. It had a shine to it, like it could have been brand new, if not for the date on it.

Pryor kissed it, took a deep breath and whispered. "Show me my affliction. Take the pain away." The penny made a hollow plop and sank into the murky water.

Nothing happened, and after less than a minute, Pryor began to feel stupid, as if he had been snookered. And what if he had been? There was no way he could pull himself from out of the well. He would die in there. This much he became certain of. Then the water began to ripple. Then it began to boil. Bubbles popped, sending hot water onto Pryor's skin. He flinched several times, let out a yelp of pain. The horror movies were real.

"Mrs. Lillie Mae? Something's wrong down here." He tried staying composed, but his nerves inched closer and closer to panicking. The boiling grew intense, bigger bubbles appeared, burst, and cast splatters of steaming liquid onto Pryor, singeing the hairs on his arms and leaving angry blisters in their wake. "Pull me up," he yelled. "Pull me up!"

When she didn't respond, he grabbed one of the ropes and tried to pull himself out. He managed to stand on the wobbly

264

cot. With both hands he reached above him, his legs shaking and pain searing from ankles to skull; heart hammering, skin burning. Pryor pulled himself up a few inches, tried to hook one damaged leg around the rope, but it wouldn't bend.

He looked down and saw a slithering tentacle surface, its pink and black skin edging along the side of the board.

"Help," he yelled, and tried harder to bend his leg around the rope. "Get me out of here. There's something down here."

Gray steam rose from the water's boiling surface, bubbles floating higher, bursting all about him, stinging his bare arms and face. Pryor reached further up with one hand, lifted himself a foot higher.

The tentacle whipped the cot. One rope snapped and Pryor swung to one side, bounced against the well's mildewed wall. The tentacle gripped his ankle and yanked. Pryor screamed. He kicked at the limb, but the efforts were too weak to do any good. With a quick jerk, the tentacle pulled him into the water, one arm and his head striking the plank. An explosion of heat engulfed him.

Tentacles crept up his body, tiny suckers pulling at flesh, burrowing into his legs. He opened his mouth to scream again and a rush of hot water filled it, burning his tongue, gums, and throat. Air left his lungs, replaced by mire. His eyes snapped open, and sludge filled them. His head hummed, as if there were thousands of wasps angrily stabbing at his skull. His ears rang, and pressure built up behind his eyes.

Pryor's body grew heavy, and he sank deeper into the well. The tentacles ravaged his body, one of them tearing into the skin of his lower back, another one creeping along until it reached his mouth, slithered in, and slid down his throat. His feet touched bottom, but by then, Pryor couldn't think straight. His eyes hurt behind clinched shut lids, his head throbbed, and his chest was tight and felt like it was swelling. The only thing he knew was he was going to die, suckered into thinking he could be cured by a voodoo witch who was old enough to have cheated Death many times over.

Affliction. The word popped into his head, and if he could

have laughed, he would have. His thoughts became muddled; his body felt as if someone was squeezing it. Consciousness faded, and he was somehow ...

... traveling along a side road, driving home from Wade Brown's house. His mind hung in a cloud. He rolled the car window down, cool air rushed in, helping him to stay awake. Pryor shook his head several times, trying to force away cobwebs. His eyelids slid closed, and he wavered behind the wheel.

Lights from an oncoming vehicle appeared from the darkness behind closed lids, snapping Pryor awake. Shielding his eyes with one hand, he held the steering wheel tight and flicked his lights several times, hoping the driver would get the hint and turn his bright lamps off. The car swerved/ Pryor grabbed the wheel with both hands, jerked it to the right and slid along the gravel shoulder. Pulling to the left, he over corrected, and his vehicle went into the other lane.

The other car slammed on its breaks, veered off the road, struck one of the few street signs on that stretch of blacktop. The woman driver jerked forward, her head hitting the steering wheel.

The back end of Pryor's car lifted off the ground and flipped. The top crumpled, the hood flew off, sparks danced along the road as metal grooved blacktop, and windows shattered. He was tossed about in the car, his seatbelt flapping around instead of locked in place. The car came to rest on its top. Screams echoed in his ears and then there was heat ...

Hands gripped him beneath the arms, pulled him. Glass scraped across his body, his legs hung limp, bones broken or shattered. Each jostled movement sent lightning bolts throughout his body until he passed out from the pain.

He snapped awake. He lay on the ground next to the well, the grass cool beneath his body. The stars hung overhead, shimmering in the night sky. He put his hands over his face as tears wet his eyes. "It was my fault," he said. "It was my fault. I fell asleep behind the wheel. If I had—"

"Yah be healed, white man," Lillie Mae said from her stump. She held a long stick in her hand, intricately carved into a tentacle, complete with suction cups encircling it. At her feet lay an impossible amount of shavings from the branch she had been carving on before Pryor went into the well.

Pryor sat up. "But it was my fault. I caused the accident. I'm the reason I got hurt. I'm why my legs—"

"Do yah not be listenin'?" Lillie Mae asked and stood from her stump. She braced herself on Pryor's cane, and her face screwed up into an expression of agony. "I say, yah done been healed. Stop yah yammerin' and be leavin' now."

He nodded and pushed himself to his feet. His eyes widened. He pulled his pants legs up—the dimple in his knee was gone, as were the scars from the many surgeries. Pryor put his weight on his right leg, and then switched to his left.

"There's no pain. The wounds, they're gone."

Lillie Mae smacked her lips together several times. "You be no longer afflicted, white man. If ya don't be mindin', I'm gonna head on back to my house. You need to be leavin' soon."

Pryor's heart lifted, and a smiled formed. "Thank you so much," he said. "You don't know how long I've been in this pain. I'm going to tell everyone about you."

Lillie Mae turned on her heel, bracing herself with the cane. One yellow nailed finger poked out at him. "You be tellin' nobody, ya hear? I don' want nobody in here that ain't be needin' to be."

"But there are some really sick people out there. They could use this ... this ... healing well or whatever it is. You could help a lot of people."

"I help many. You can' be choosin' who yah help—and I can' be helpin' ev'rybody. Now, if yah don' mind, you can leave now."

Lillie Mae turned, put the cane out in front of her and hobbled down the hill at a snail's pace. Pryor frowned. She hadn't limped on the way up the hill, and she hadn't been bowlegged and hunched over. He didn't notice it when he came to, but as she walked away she left droplets of water behind her, spilling off her skirt. Dumbfounded, he stood for a minute longer before walking to the edge of the hill. He looked toward the house. Lillie Mae was already down the hill and out of sight— an impossibility with how slow she had been walking.

Pryor headed down, following the trail of wet ground. It didn't go up the steps and in the house. Instead, it went around the porch and to the other side of the shack, stopping in a pool at the foot of the headstones. Pryor knelt, his knees not popping or groaning; no aches flared up and down his legs or along his spine; his head didn't pitch him off center from a surge of blinding pain. He pushed aside a few dried up vines, and read the name: Jacobs McCoy.

A jolt of electricity surged through him, and he felt as if he stood outside of his body for a brief second. Then he was back inside himself, brushing away the vines from the second grave.

"Lillie Mae McCoy. Died September 1856."

Pryor brushed away the rest of the dirt and dead weeds, revealing a single word: AFFLICTED.

A tentacle pushed from beneath the hard soil. Pryor fell backward, scooted on his bottom for a few feet before standing. The appendage slipped back into the ground. The date on the headstone had changed: Died October 8, 1974.

Pryor glanced toward the house and the hill beyond it, but the structure was gone. He frowned, confused. Then he looked back at the stone. The date had reverted to 1856. He looked around and realized he was in an ancient cemetery, one with just two graves and a collapsed steel fence around it. Pryor stumbled backwards, then stood and ran, his new legs pushing as fast as they could. He bolted up the rutted road, his affliction behind him.

www.ingramcontent.com/pod-product-compliance
Lightning Source LLC
Chambersburg PA
CBHW061554170626
46811CB00001B/198